WI... CAN'T BE HIDDEN

A NOVEL

BRANDON ANDRESS

This is a work of fiction. The characters, places and incidents portrayed, and the names used herein are fictitious or used in a fictitious manner. Any resemblance to the name, character, or history of any person, living or dead, is coincidental and unintentional. Product names used herein are not an endorsement of this work by the product name owners.

1st Edition

Cover design and layout by Rafael Polendo (polendo.net)
Cover image by oOhyperblaster (shutterstock.com)

ISBN 978-1-938480-94-2

This volume is printed on acid free paper and meets ANSI Z39.48 standards.

Printed in the United States of America

 QUOIR

Published by Quoir
Oak Glen, California

www.quoir.com

ACKNOWLEDGMENTS

Special thanks to my tribe of helpers who offered their skills and insights in the development of this book—Jenny Andress, Adam and Jackie Garn, Angella Dykstra, Nevie Dewhirst, Seja Brumley, Seth Price, Erica Sahm, and Brent Schebler.

To my mom, for staying home
and reading to me when I was little.

To my dad, for working hard
so mom could stay home with me.

To Dr. Kathy Barbour
For opening my eyes
to the creative possibility
of the written word.

For she is fairer than the sun
and surpasses every constellation of stars.
Compared to the light, she is found more radiant;
Though night supplants light,
Wickedness does not prevail over Wisdom.

Wisdom, Chapter 7: 29-30

PROLOGUE

The forest canopy covered everything below it in darkness. All that was visible were contours and edges, grays and black. From underneath, it was midnight. From above, the sun had reached its highest point of the day.

With eyes for anything unusual, Pali and Machi regularly scouted the woods on the west side of the island beyond the edge of Patrida. The brothers walked in faint shadows as they surveyed the diverse terrain populated with dense black pine. Like every other day for Pali and Machi, this day was a lesson in going through motions and following the same familiar paths.

The young men had been loosely following a creek originating from a freshwater spring in the Patridian village. With each step in the forest, the pair drew closer to where this single flow diverged into two separate, smaller streams. At this juncture, the brothers knew they were getting closer to their midday destination.

This divergence marked the location where the pair would soon make a short descent down a rolling, moss-covered embankment. At the bottom stood a towering megalith jutting out of the soft, rock-littered ground. The impressive monument stood nearly twenty feet skyward and appeared to challenge the height of the smaller oaks around it. It had an unusually sacred appearance for a structure not made by human hands, like an obelisk, tapering toward the top. As far as the brothers knew from their intimate knowledge of the terrain, there were no other rocks like it on the island.

It was in this magnificent place, in the spongy moss surrounding the natural obelisk, where each young man would take a turn relieving himself. While one enjoyed the privacy of his side of the rock, the other kept watch on the opposite side. The bald, muscular, and tattooed brothers were not barbarians in any sense of the word, but when they were together and by themselves, they always found great pleasure in the senseless and inane.

The strict and rigid culture of Patrida, coupled with their growing responsibilities in the Patridian guard, necessitated an occasional outlet from the tension and division within their increasingly dysfunctional community. For a few short moments each week, Pali and Machi would devolve into the mindset of prepubescent boys. They would laugh in hilarity at each other's grunts as they leaned up against the towering, noble rock and squatted over their hand-dug holes.

This was the kind of tragic irony running deeply through Patrida. A darkness evading the light. An aimless ambling in shadows without direction. A divergence in the life-giving flow. An oblivious soiling of the sacred. Symbols and metaphors, such as these, pointed to another story below the surface needing to be discovered about the loss and rediscovery of wisdom.

～

Machi picked up his pace and ran ahead of his brother. He crossed the divided stream in less than a dozen, longish strides. Hurriedly, the younger brother barreled down the gentle slope toward his side of the rock, into which his initials "MP" had been scrawled at eye level. As he began to mark his territory, a tremendous crash and subsequent groan, which was just as thunderous, startled Machi.

In Pali's haste to keep up with his younger brother, he made a foolish mistake any experienced guardsman who understood the terrain's nuances would have known. He planted his foot squarely on a smooth, wet, algae-covered rock in an attempt to quickly cross the stream. Catastrophically, the frictionless, leather-colored stone upended Patrida's head guardsman. In his uncalculating urgency, Pali lay lifeless a few feet from land's edge in the flow, his arms out to each side, blood mixing with the crystal water.

This kind of carelessness was typical of Pali and his approach to everything. Although he was older than Machi, he was less discerning and significantly more reactionary. While those particular attributes usually do not make for a good leader, when combined with his gruff and brutish personality, and penchant for communicating through force, they were precisely what Patrida's leaders desired in their head guard.

As the waters rushed vigorously around him, Pali sat up in foolish oblivion. While he could hear his younger brother laughing hysterically at his mishap as he approached, the elder brother could hardly see anything for the blinding sunlight in his eyes. A single ray pierced through the seemingly impenetrable forest cover like a spotlight highlighting his comedic fall.

Placing his left hand over his menacing brown eyes in frustration to shield the unwelcome light, Pali cursed out loud and attempted to stand up on the unstable rocks. Bellowing in laughter at water's edge, Machi clapped his hands in appreciation of his brother's fine performance.

"A perfect ten, brother! But maybe the old man needs to replace this with a cane," Machi said, as he picked up Pali's wooden staff that was as rough around the edges as he was.

Indignant and still seething in his short-fused anger, Pali stood up and bum-rushed his brother, knocking him back on his sandaled heels. As the younger brother stumbled and attempted to keep his balance, Pali ripped away his weapon with force and assumed an offensive posture with the staff at Machi's neck. The two brothers stared at each other, waiting to see who would make the next move. With water still dripping from his bare, dark-skinned chest and down his skirt of leather and multi-layered fabric, Pali subtly smiled as if gesturing his dominance. He stood ready to attack if his brother moved.

"I'm not too old to take you down," the elder brother boasted without breaking eye contact. "There's a reason why I'm the head guard, and you're not. Don't forget that, brother."

Pali dropped his staff and turned to make his way down the embankment when he heard a growing rumble from behind. Machi full-fist punched his brother's back shoulder and howled like a wolf as he ran past, making his way back down the hill again to his side of the rock.

"I'm first, grandpa. You keep watch," Machi shouted as he ducked behind the far side of the megalith once again.

Shaking his head at his brother's idiocy and insubordination, but also his own carelessness at the stream, Pali leaned his wet back up against the cool rock. The older brother rested his head on a slight indentation that appeared as if someone made it for that purpose. Closing his eyes but still burning with anger, Pali stood in silence and cursed under his breath. He cursed his careless mistake. He cursed his wet clothes. He cursed his brother.

As seemingly disagreeable as Pali's relationship with Machi appeared at times, the relationships in Patrida were not remarkably different. In this relatively small community of nearly seven hundred, antipathy and animosity had been slowly breaking through their religious veneer, turning small fissures among the people into gaping divisions. One never knew when a minor incident or misunderstanding would explode into full-blown chaos.

This deterioration was not only true for the townspeople, however. Rumors of discord clouded Patrida's leadership, as well. Over the years, the town's Leadership Council, and those like Pali and Machi who protected the town, had become manifestations and caricatures of the very ugliness the townspeople projected. But while it would be easy to place the blame squarely on the dysfunction of the towns-people, there had been forces at work in the Leadership Council from the beginning that initiated and then perpetuated this sad trajectory.

In Patrida, conflicts were always closed doors eliciting the worst possible reaction by all, whether as verbal altercations or physical aggressions. This way of life on the island had been the norm for so long no one ever contemplated opening a door to other possibilities. Self-awareness and individual reflection had been buried in Patrida long ago. The Leadership Council enacted strict rules and exacting laws to keep people in line or face the swift and unforgiving hand of judgment and the heavy weight of punishment. For all of Patrida's intentions to control its people's behavior and enforce morality, their lives remained as dark as the city itself.

The people of Patrida were shallow and becoming even more shallow, superficial and becoming even more superficial. They lived on the circumference of life, having abandoned wisdom without under-standing their great need for substance or depth. They believed they were free but remained imprisoned. Peace was on their lips but far from their hearts. And without any sort of guidance or voice to challenge their status quo, they continued their downward spiral as a community.

Pali stood impatiently on the mossy ground, waiting as he listened to his brother's beastly grunts, fully expressing himself. Raising his head off the rock, the older brother wiped his sweaty forehead from the early summer humidity. He wished he was already back in Patrida, if for no other reason than to get out of his wet clothes. As he lowered his dirt-stained hand from his face, he noticed an anthill a couple of feet away from his left sandaled foot. The head guardsman began to momentarily watch the ants move about freely and do their work. But his restlessness was soon accompanied by boredom and irritation. Pali stepped to the side, lifted his staff, and drove it down into the anthill without giving it a second thought.

"Let's get going! I'm wet and rea…" the older brother shouted out in irritation before being interrupted by a shadow moving across the embankment they had descended.

Pali froze, his eyes trained on the few oak trees where he had seen the transient movement. With his heart beating more rapidly, each breath closely following the next, Pali was frozen in place as he scanned the area, looking for the slightest movement. A subtle breeze began to gently move over the area. The rock on Pali's back did not feel as cool as it had earlier, but his wet clothes sent a chill throughout his body. Slowly and methodically, the head guardsman placed his strong hand on the wooden staff and awaited any eventuality or threat.

Pali knew from experience in the woods that the shadow was likely an animal reacting to his staff hitting the anthill. While only a few guards had ever scouted the entire island, the people of Patrida typically never ventured out this far into the forest. Most of them would walk for a few miles along the creek, but hardly anyone had ever made it as far as the megalith. Pali also knew that no other community resided on their isolated island or any other landmass near them. The movement he saw was certainly not another human being.

But in moments that seemed like an hour of silence to Pali, the only thing disrupting the stillness was Machi, utterly oblivious to what was transpiring on the other side. The older brother trained his focus on two of the mature oaks he suspected. But as he began to look away, there was another slight movement and shadow beside one of the trees on the embankment's north side. Trained in on the exact location, Pali saw the face of a man peering around the base of the tree. The man looked directly at him. Neither moved. No matter how hardened and impenetrable Pali's exterior may have been, the man's eyes locked on him and stared directly through him. But as soon as the face appeared, it was gone.

Without hesitation, reacting on instinct and adrenaline, Pali charged up stone and moss, tearing earth with the force of each step.

Forgetting his brother was with him, Pali's only thought was to eliminate the threat. Within seconds, he was already within line of sight
of his target- a tall, slender but muscular young man with shoulder-
length brown hair blowing feverishly behind him.

Though Pali got a quick glimpse of the man's face in the shadows, there was something unusual about his dark, penetrating eyes.
They communicated curiosity, not hostility. Invitation, not ill-intent.
But they were unfamiliar. This man was not from Patrida. That fact
alone was all Pali needed to classify him as an enemy and continue
the pursuit.

Back at the rock, slow to realize something was not right, Machi
looked around for his brother and then immediately took off up the
hill. He could not quite see his brother once he reached the ridge, but
he was close enough to still faintly hear the shouting. Being strategic
in combat, Machi fell back rather than follow behind in pursuit. He
determined he would circle through the woods and head off Pali and
whatever he was tracking if there were indeed a threat.

The pursuit had initially taken Pali past the fork in the creek and
then further upstream before cutting back into the woods through a
mix of black pine and checker trees to a narrow, nearly indiscernible
game trail. He had not entirely lost sight of the young man at this
point, but he was also not gaining much ground on him either. As the
head guardsman knew very well, game trails could be aggravatingly
deceptive. At some points, these rarely linear routes appeared to offer
an efficient path cutting through the brush. However, at other points,
they came to abrupt dead ends that were difficult to navigate because
of the dense forest undergrowth.

Pali once again found that these game trails offered little more
than false hope in expediting his passage. The maddening labyrinth,
along with Pali's still wet battle gear and sandals, significantly slowed
him down. But for whatever variables appeared to disadvantage him,
his unrelenting determination and training in hunting and tracking

was his advantage. The guard would never stop until he neutralized the threat.

As Pali cut through the forest, the dense partition above appeared as if thousands of pins pierced through its veil all at once, scattering beams of sunlight across the forest floor in picturesque brilliance. With every breath matching his resolute stride, he could see his target more clearly. Pinpricks became widening apertures enabling Pali to see the young man standing in an opening a hundred feet ahead. Pali's incessant pursuit became a cautious approach as he edged closer to the opening. The almond-skinned young man, wearing a stained, white linen shirt and shorts that looked as if they had been cut off above the knees, stood in the center of a near-circular clearing. He stared intently at Pali. It was evident to the head guardsman that there was no longer any urgency in his enemy's disposition.

After a moment of checking his surroundings to ensure he had not been lured into a trap by the young man, Pali shouted out.

"You're surrounded, boy! There are two of us here, and we're armed. There's another guard directly behind you."

This statement was not entirely true, as Machi was not yet behind the young man. However, Pali knew his brother's tactical instincts well enough to know he would soon be approaching from the flank. So he continued his bluff.

"Go ahead and get down on your knees and put your hands behind your head where I can see them," Pali shouted out.

Unfazed by Pali's command and imposing posture, the young man stood peacefully, neither breathing heavily nor sweating. He was cool without the appearance of being intimidated. Not even the threat of being surrounded seemed to concern him. His posture continued to communicate a surprising non-defensiveness as he stared below Pali's furrowed brow and directly into his dark eyes.

From Pali's perspective, neither the young man's submissive stance nor the appearance of being unarmed negated the risk posed to Patrida by an outsider. The young man was most definitely not alone. For all Pali knew, the enemy represented one of many hostiles that could be on their way at any moment. The quick and effective way to prevent being caught off guard by a surprise attack would be to get answers from the man.

Like clockwork, Pali could see his strategically calculating brother stealthily moving between trees and brush behind the intruder. Machi put himself, as quietly as possible, in the most unobstructed position so he could come in directly from behind without being seen. Without communicating, each knew what the other was thinking. They would knock out the threat with overwhelming force and then beat the answers out of him.

"Why don't you tell me who you are and where you came from?" Pali shouted out with a hollow request. The head guardsman was not interested in answers. He was distracting the young man as Machi got into the perfect position to take him out from behind.

"What's your name, boy?" Pali called out again, continuing the questions in rapid succession. "What's your story? Where's your people? They on their way here too? You know you got yourself in quite a predicament here."

Rather than answer Pali, the young man slowly turned around and directly faced Machi, who had been ready to launch. For a second, Machi's aggressive posture slightly subsided, as he was surprised the young man knew he was there. From the center of the opening, blades of grass hugging his legs above the ankle, the young man slowly turned back toward Pali and methodically raised both arms with his dirty palms upward beneath the overcast skies. The brothers watched intently. They were not quite sure what was going on or what his next move would be. The young man lowered himself to the ground, placing one knee in the grass. Still holding his palms up, as if to signify his submission, the young man put his other knee beneath him.

The brute and unforgiving force that came from behind was so swift and overwhelming that when the young man hit the ground, he folded like a blanket. He could barely catch his breath. With Machi on top, pinning him to the ground, Pali rushed in with a violent kick to his side.

"When I speak to you, you answer. Do you hear me, son? Do you understand what I'm telling you!" Pali screamed.

The young man's mouth opened and closed as if there was no oxygen available in the atmosphere around him. He could not answer for gasping. Pali kicked him repeatedly, each time with more unrestrained brutality. Realizing there was no longer any threat from the young man, Machi slowly released the armbar from behind his neck and pushed his head into the unyielding ground as he stood over him in dominance. Pali and Machi looked at each other and smiled in accomplishment. But they quickly looked back to the ground, as there were many questions their enemy needed to answer.

"You have a lot of explaining to do, boy," Pali barked. "So whether it's here with us, or in front of the council, you're gonna start talking. You're gonna tell us exactly how many of you there are on this island and what you people want."

The brothers understood the nuances of personal and social interaction, but they always operated at the lowest common denominator when faced with conflict. They only understood the Patridian way of peace through strength at any cost. This mantra was on full display as the brothers took turns conducting their physical interrogation with more violence. As more dark clouds ominously moved into the area and blanketed the clearing, the young man grabbed handfuls of the long grass and struggled to breathe amidst the pummeling. Pali and Machi wanted answers, but without air to breathe, no words materialized from their prisoner's mouth.

Bloodied and tattered, the young man turned his head haltingly to one side and looked up at Pali as if he was attempting to say something to him. With blades of broken and dried grass pressed into his face, a single drop of blood crept slowly from the crease of his mouth into the hair on his chin. The brothers mistook the young man's gaze as something in between resentment and contempt. Realizing no answers would be forthcoming, Pali raised his rugged, wooden staff in the air and struck their enemy in the head, knocking him out.

CHAPTER 1

Thura stood alone, quietly cutting fresh bread and aged cheese, as she had each afternoon for nearly ten years. The long, narrow room in which the young woman made preparations for the evening's council meeting welcomed a soft, gentle light through its northern window. This room contrasted the adjacent council room, which was dark and windowless. Thura's increased awareness of this light and dark dichotomy and how the latter appeared to be eclipsing the former in Patrida weighed heavily on the bondservant.

"Do you need anything else before I go?" A teenage voice called out from the shadows of the council room. "I finished pushing in all the chairs and straightening up the room, as you asked."

"Thank you for your help, my young friend. And thank you for delivering this bread," Thura said with a delicate smile. "Would you mind lighting the lamp on the table on your way out? And please, take this extra loaf of bread with you for your family. There is always so much left over after these meetings."

"Thank you, Thura," the young servant girl said, taking the hand-woven basket with the extra loaf of bread. "Are you counting down the days yet? The other girls have been enviously talking about you."

Thura turned abruptly back to her work and continued cutting an already cut piece of bread into even smaller pieces without responding.

"I'm sorry," the young girl said, realizing her question was not met with the excitement she expected. "I didn't mean to say anything wrong. I will light the lamp on my way out and see you again tomorrow at the same time."

"Thank you. I look forward to it," Thura responded, as she listened to the young girl light the oil lamp and then run down the wooden stairs back to the Monon.

Thura was different from others in Patrida in many ways. Her waist-long, fiery red hair, which she braided to one side while she worked, stood out in a community with either dark or graying hair. But it was more than her red hair. She did not share the same sense of duty and honor as the other young women who anxiously awaited their arranged marriages at the end of their forced service. While the others counted down the days anticipating their emancipation, Thura counted them as days remaining until her final death sentence. This deviation in her thinking was not an accident. An old, imprisoned woman named Sophia, to whom Thura had delivered a nightly meal since her service began as a thirteen-year-old, secretly seeded this divergence in perspective.

Thura had been born on the island a couple of years after her family's arrival. She spent most of her early years like everyone else, reverentially and faithfully following every stringent rule and strict expectation handed down by the Patridian Council. But she always did it gladly and without question, desperately wanting to please her parents and anyone else in authority. As a young girl, Thura was always the first person to arrive at each evening's mandatory community gathering in Sanctuary. She always sat in the front row waiting for the rest of the town to arrive. But as she grew older and began taking the nightly scraps and leftovers to Sophia in prison, Thura's perspective and understanding began to slowly change along with her eagerness to be at each evening's gathering.

During her first year delivering food, Thura would drop the scraps in a small, rickety wooden bucket and hang it below the prison door's window. But introverted eye contact turned into simple pleasantries.

Simple pleasantries became small talk. Small talk evolved into deeper conversations. And deeper conversations led to Thura taking her meal with her and sharing it with Sophia as they talked.

Through this decade-long gradual transformation, Thura learned that sharing a meal with another person humanizes them, even a person the community has locked away for nearly two decades. She also learned that the beliefs one has about another can change over time, especially when you look them in the eyes as a human being and listen to their story.

For these reasons, Thura's previously distorted image of the old woman began to change from prisoner to person. It was also how she ultimately discovered that Sophia was not quite the monster everyone painted her to be. Thura found her to be a sage woman who could speak to the depths and essence of another person's soul with the most profound kindness. Developing this intimate relationship with Sophia first opened Thura's eyes to her town's harsh realities. It also kindled a spark within her to begin asking wise and insightful questions about who she was and what she wanted in her life.

Staring blankly out the northern window, Thura watched despondently as men, women, and children moved about the Monon. She saw her fellow servants in their obsidian black dresses circling from place to place in vain attempts to finish their unending work. She watched as married men sauntered along in their gaudy, handmade suits, walking with their subservient wives in their homely, servant-sewn, white frocks. Even the children appeared monochrome, running aimlessly in their own circles. But for the children, Thura's heart ached. She watched them move amongst the people. They were oblivious to the imprisoning structures surrounding them and the subconscious messages their malleable, impressionable, young minds absorbed.

The Monon was a meticulously constructed cobblestone road cutting directly through the heart of town. But it was more than a way of getting from place to place. Patrida's leaders designed this thoroughfare as a symbol of orderly civic and religious life. It was a showcase of Patrida's most prominent and influential.

Their houses and businesses, systematically lining each side of the central passageway, were constructed with sourced stone and wood. They were uniformly painted flat white with no visible color or contrast. There were no flowers, no plants, no decorations. Everything along the Monon was whitewashed and perfect. And it continually reminded the people of Patrida's supposed virtue.

Branching off the Monon were narrow and gravelly side streets and alleyways that formed a grid-like configuration with smaller houses lining each side. These side streets told a story about Patrida's hierarchy. The closer one lived to the Monon, the greater their notability and influence and the whiter their house.

Each step away from this main thoroughfare in any direction was a step down Patrida's social ladder, with the bottom rung being Patrida's uneducated, poor, and imprisoned. Their houses were on the margins and edges of this small town in their deliberately gray and black houses. As one might imagine, this kind of intentional stratification and ingrained division led to significant friction and conflict among the people over time. For as virtuous and upright as the people of Patrida may have appeared from the center of town, another fractured reality surrounded it. While movements throughout the segregated grid of Patrida told one story, movements east and west along the Monon told quite another.

On the far western end of the Monon, the imposing criminal's gallows were hauntingly and intimidatingly displayed. At the center of this large, wooden structure were thirteen steps leading up to a modest, rectangular platform. A rugged and sizable support beam adorned two nooses directly above two drop floors. This dark and sinister visual, constructed purposefully to impede a view of the ocean from the Monon, reminded the citizens to follow the rule of law or meet a swift death. For those in the Patridian Council, their small community's moral fabric was held together by adherence to religious law backed by swift, decisive justice.

Facing the gallows on the eastern end of Patrida, hugging the forest's edge, was an area called Sanctuary. At the center of this communal gathering place was a venerated freshwater spring. Beautifully ornate rocks, which almost entirely encircled the spring, created a small pool around it that opened on the backside for water to flow freely as a creek into the woods. Enshrining the spring stood four limestone arcs placed equidistantly from one another. Each arc's base was set outside the decorative rocks, with each one rising to meet the others triumphantly over the center of the spring. Planted firmly at the conjoined arcs' apex, the Patridian flag flew high to ensure everyone could see it. This magnificent shrine, their holy sacrarium, elicited the awe, reverence, and allegiance of all who gathered there for worship each evening.

~

A slow-moving ceiling of slate gradually moved inland over the choppy, westward waters, joining both the humidity of late afternoon and the people of Patrida pouring out onto the Monon. Thura pushed aside her wooden tray of freshly sliced bread and aged cheeses and mindlessly reached for a bottle of sweet, red table wine to open. The young woman continued to watch the Monon from above, taking inventory of every preoccupied person under the darkening sky.

Thura imagined the men quietly discussing the latest chatter and political fodder surfacing from sources close to the town council. She thought about how their wives must be searching for any reason at all to smile. She pretended she could hear the conversations of others standing in front of their homes and businesses, gossiping about those in other homes and other businesses. Thura passively rolled her eyes at the dedicated few rushing along the cobblestone and down the center aisle of Sanctuary, as she once did, to territorially secure their seats before the evening service. Lining the outer perimeter on each side of the holy sacrarium, the Patridian guards stood stoically at attention.

As Thura's eyes wandered, she began to follow her white-dressed servant girl who had just delivered the basket of freshly baked bread to her. She watched as she weaved in and out of the masses, attempting to make her next delivery. But as she tracked her young friend, Thura began to notice the maze of movement and the general hustle and bustle along the Monon had suddenly stopped. Every head began to turn eastward. Although her window was closed, Thura could hear urgent and resounding male voices cutting through the concerned people's chatter.

Nervously taking off her apron and opening the crosshatch window, Thura placed her hands on the sill and stuck her head out to see what was causing the commotion. The faithful who had already assembled at Sanctuary sat in deathly silence without a move. The Patridian guards moved from strict attention to a defensive posture with their staffs held in front of them at the ready. The calls continued to grow louder and began to overtake everyone on the Monon until they hushed to whispers and then to complete silence.

Everyone nervously stared at a narrow opening close to where the spring flowed from the sacrarium. This particular opening into the woods led down a series of manmade and natural steps following the creek before fading into an endless array of game trails choked off by dense black pines. The people knew if someone approached Patrida, they would likely exit the woods through this opening near Sanctuary.

The men's intense shouts accompanied decisive movements from the brush, which finally convulsed a dirty and unrecognizable man. Emerging with a length of rope tightly secured around his abraded neck and dried blood smeared across his swollen face, the man took a few staggered steps forward to the edge of the scrub and then summarily paused and looked at the people.

While the first few humble steps toward Sanctuary were those of the captive, Pali and Machi moved ahead and pulled him aggressively by the neck toward the Monon. The prisoner clutched the rough rope with his hands but was too weak to offer any resistance to the brothers' brute strength. The face of each person who watched the embattled prisoner stagger along behind the men conveyed utter disbelief. But disbelief soon became uncertainty, and uncertainty devolved into fear, as the unthinkable became an undeniable reality.

A foreigner was walking among them.

Patrida's paralysis and paranoia grew with the disheveled prisoner's every labored step. Fearful citizens began to consider what eyes might be watching them from beyond the tree line. Their collective panic birthed out of what they did not know. It then manifested into speculation about the enemy's intentions and fear for their lives and freedom.

One by one, every man, woman, and child began to nervously follow the enemy's procession in silence along the cobblestone road. But nervous silence was soon broken by a lone voice belonging to a tall, lanky mustached man with a black, receding hairline who began to scream at the top of his lungs while lunging threateningly at the prisoner.

"Who are you, boy!" the man shouted. "You're not from around here! Speak up! Where'd you come from! Where's all your people! Hidin' in the woods! What do you want from us!"

With the prisoner doing his best to look at his feet as he walked and not engage, one man's screams became a chorus of screams and shouts throughout the crowd erupting into a more riotous roar.

"There has to be more coming for us!" one suited man shouted, pushing others out of the way to get to the brothers at the front of the line.

"I heard there are hundreds, even thousands, coming for us right now!" another white-suited man shouted as his terrified wife buried her face in her hands and cried.

"You are not going to destroy this town and take everything we have!" screamed a mother holding her baby as she smacked at the prisoner with her free hand before grabbing a handful of his shirt and ripping his left sleeve.

Patrida had been a tinder box for quite some time. But all it took for anger to blaze into a raging wildfire was igniting it with fear. The vicious mob suddenly became more frenzied and hysterical as the more bold and aggressive ran toward the prisoner and continued to rip at his clothing, venomously spewing their threats and hateful epithets.

Unfazed and without any show of emotion, Pali and Machi continued to march forward, unflinchingly dragging the object of scorn behind them along the Monon toward the jail. As Machi unlocked the door and Pali threw the man into the cell, rioters continued to incessantly grab and rip at his soiled shirt and hit him with their closed fists. The people of Patrida demanded answers the young man was unwilling to give them.

Thura watched the unholy procession and unquenched blood-thirst of her fellow townspeople the entire length of the Monon. Not a single person tried to stop the madness, she thought. No one thought twice about this man or what they were doing to him. Staring in sadness at her prematurely calloused hands placed on the wooden countertop in front of her, Thura closed her eyes and considered the words Sophia shared with her a few days prior.

Living daily in shadows keeps us from seeing ourselves and others as we truly are. In darkness, we obscure our fundamental humanity, which keeps us from discovering greater depths of relationship and experience.

While Thura did not always understand Sophia's words, she could see that shadows had become real life in Patrida. It was the only life anyone knew. It was how they saw themselves as individuals, how they related to one another, and now how they treated an outsider they knew nothing about. Thura's heart ached as she looked out the window one last time and surveyed the crowd. Not a single person standing on the Monon could ever imagine another way of dealing with conflict, or relating to others.

A loud shuffle in the stairway caused Thura to quickly open her eyes in a panic and hastily grab the platter of food. She should have already been out of the council room long ago instead of watching the madness along the Monon. But as she placed her hand on the door to open it into the main council room, two men entered and sat at the long, dark hardwood table. Thura's heart began to race. The young woman leaned against the door and heard Father Prodido's voice.

Father Prodido was the key religious leader of Patrida and the sole visionary behind the town's construction. While he was not the prominent leader, the tall, gaunt, intimidating man was the council's central guiding figure with his strict, nearly unrealistic idealism. The religious leader believed a community's righteousness was predicated by following clear rules of morality. In that way, each citizen would experience freedom and avoid God's judgment.

Each servant of Patrida, which was every non-married girl from thirteen to twenty-three years of age, was regularly instructed to stay clear of Father Prodido and not be caught in the same room with him under any circumstance. No one knew the reason for this strict provision, but some speculated that he wanted to avoid the appearance of impropriety. Others were convinced he must have been hurt by someone close to him long ago, like his mother or a lost love.

Either way, Thura understood the consequences of disobeying this particular demand. Father Prodido caught the last young woman who served with Thura loitering in the council room several times when he arrived for a council meeting. At first, he reprimanded her publicly at Sanctuary for insubordination. The second time, he had her whipped at the gallows. The third and final time, he had her hung as the entire town watched, including the children.

Thura could have attempted to humbly and apologetically walk through the council room and pray Father Prodido would disregard her first indiscretion. But the truth was that she did not want to leave the room. While fear was a factor keeping her behind the slightly cracked door, Thura's curiosity of the prisoner produced an even stronger feeling within her.

Thura knew there was a chance the prisoner could very well pose a threat to Patrida. But there was also an equal chance he represented something else entirely for her. Freedom. Having only known the heavy-handed rule of Patrida her entire life, the thought of running away, even though Thura did not know what that meant, produced an indescribable feeling within her. All she knew was that she longed for something else, for something more, and it was worth the risk of leaning forward and opening the door a little more.

CHAPTER 2

The flickering flame of the oil lamp, centered on the council room table, projected Father Prodido and Tyran's shadowy silhouettes upon the unadorned, chestnut brown, wood plank walls. The otherwise austere room held a single, old painting with a frame the same color as the walls. The painting depicted a man and child sitting in a rowboat on a shoreline with other boats leaving far on the horizon. This singular decoration had been hung by Patrida's leader to the mild protests of both men already sitting at one end of the rectangular table.

When Ochi entered the council room, both men immediately stopped talking and stood out of respect. As the founding leader of Patrida positioned himself at the head of the table, he leaned forward with both hefty forearms on the table and ordered the men to take their seats.

"Tell me what I need to know," Ochi said, folding his rough, calloused hands while studying Father Prodido and Tyran with his tired, brown eyes.

Neither man immediately responded. Tyran shuffled uneasily in his seat and glanced at Father Prodido. The religious leader did not make eye contact with either man for his preoccupation with a dusting of dirt on the left sleeve of his pure, white vestment.

At last, noticing the silence and his protégé's fidgeting across the table, Father Prodido turned his head slowly toward Ochi and responded.

"Ah yes, your Excellency," he began. "I am afraid we know about as much as you do. We watched the parade from my house as Pali and Machi entered town with the foreigner."

"Well, whoever this foreigner is," Tyran interjected with a nervous laugh, "he got a real Patridian welcome."

Unamused with his son's poor attempt at humor at such a grave and uncertain moment, Ochi stared blankly at him before turning back toward the sober-minded religious leader.

"We'll get a full report from Pali when he arrives momentarily," said Ochi. "But in the meantime, what's the current sentiment among the people, Father?"

"Well, your Excellency, it depends on how you look at it," the religious leader said. "There is no question the people are afraid. Even now, we hear their fearful chants outside. But with knowing so little about the prisoner or the potential threat he brings, it is safe to say there is an air of uncertainty that borders on bedlam. However, I would be remiss not to mention that I have not seen this kind of enthusiasm and zeal among the people since, dare I say it, the Great Liberation."

Ochi adjusted his chair but was careful to keep eye contact with Father Prodido and not appear bothered by his comment.

"As you know best, your Excellency, a common enemy certainly has a way of bringing together strange bedfellows," Father Prodido continued. "The enemy of my enemy is my friend if you will. At least for now, it appears many of our internal conflicts may have subsided. Our various factions may have ceased being at each other's throats. Of course, this is likely temporary while their sights are set on this shared threat."

Father Prodido straightened the gold medallion hanging over his religious vestment's lower chest, which he never failed to wear for the status and position it conveyed to the people. The religious leader then looked across the table at Tyran as if permitting him to finish his thought.

"Uh yes," Tyran stumbled, "this is a real opportunity for us to show our strength and bring the people together against a common enemy. Whether there is a real threat beyond the tree line or not doesn't matter. The people will rally around the flag if they believe someone is threatening their freedom."

Father Prodido nodded in agreement and attempted a half-smile at his protégé's comments.

"But honestly," Tyran continued, "if we don't control this narrative quickly, or if we give the appearance of being indecisive, this whole thing will come back to bite us."

Ochi leaned back in his chair, crossed his muscular, olive arms, and stared at the men in a long silence, contemplating the merits of their strategy. As Patrida's singular leader since arriving on the island in his mid-thirties, Ochi's no-nonsense, binary approach in dealing with people had traditionally served him well. He had always been stern in his decision-making, never leaving any room for guessing where he stood on any issue. While he was certainly not a visionary, Ochi was precise and meticulous, knowing how to implement Father Prodido's vision for Patrida. It was for these reasons Ochi always had the respect and obedience of those around him.

But while his heavy-handed, black and white way of governing had earned him the town's favor in the past, he could sense their support for him was slowly eroding. This shift often kept him up at night, as he could not quite put his finger on what was changing in his relationship with the people. Ochi was not sure whether their opinion of him was changing, or his view of them was changing. But as he sat around the table and considered what to do with the prisoner, Ochi knew he needed to do something to instill confidence in his leadership to mitigate a complete disaster.

Two firm knocks at the door interrupted the extended silence of the room. Greatly anticipating information about the prisoner, the table of leaders stood for Pali. Machi remained in the corridor to ensure the chaos of the Monon did not make its way up the stairwell and into the council room. Closing the door and placing his bloodied staff against the wall, the calm and collected head guard stood at the opposite end of the table and detailed their pursuit and capture of Patrida's prisoner.

〜

Thura leaned even closer to the solid wooden door, which was still slightly opened, to hear every detail of Pali's account. She pressed her face gently against a rugged seam between two of the door's planks, taking slow and deliberate breaths so as not to be heard. Misjudging exactly how close she was to the door, Thura's face slightly bumped it forward, producing an inevitable creaking sound that magnified and echoed in her tiny room. The young woman froze in terror, as all talking immediately ceased in the council room.

Did they hear me? Thura wondered. Do they know someone is listening behind this open door? Do they know it is me? Thura waited without breathing. Can they hear my heart beating out of my chest?

The sound of a heavy, wooden chair scooting away from the table sent panic throughout Thura's body. Slow and deliberate footsteps moved across the room toward the door, convincing Thura someone had discovered her. The young woman backed away hastily so as not to appear as if she had been intentionally listening. But in her uncalculated urgency, Thura's left elbow hit a single metal chalice of red wine with a force that caused it to crash into the others in an unfortunate succession.

Believing she could still somehow catch all three and avoid complete disaster before they crashed to the floor, Thura lunged forward with both hands outstretched. Appearing as a court jester comically juggling the chalices, the young woman watched in slow motion as each hit the stone floor with a bombastic crash. Helplessly dripping, her white apron soaked with red wine, Thura turned to face Father Prodido, who stood hauntingly over her at the entrance.

"It appears you have blood on your hands, young lady," the religious leader said in a low baritone.

Thura put her head down and pushed past the religious leader. The young woman darted through the silent council room, naively hoping her lack of eye contact meant no one was looking at her. However, had she looked up, Thura would have seen a subtle, hairline smile appear on her father's face. But with her eyes transfixed on each sandaled foot passing beneath her, Thura marched forward nervously. The young woman opened the heavy, wooden door and left it wide open behind her, rushing out into the dimly lit hallway past Machi. As Thura ran down the corridor, she prayed no one would come after her.

With each stride alternating between profound fear and unrestrained excitement, Thura turned toward her room and stopped, breathlessly listening for a single footstep, which never came. Confident the council's more immediate concerns were of greater import than the offense of her loitering and eavesdropping, the young woman leaned against the cool, stone wall outside her bedroom door and closed her eyes.

The soft, hazy light of the sunset shone through the open windows lining the opposite wall. Its warmth enveloped Thura. She meditated on the pink of her eyelids, attempting to let go of the fear accompanying her. Thura replayed the moment she pushed Father Prodido and ran down the corridor, imagining what it would be like to escape the imprisoning confines of Patrida. But before her thoughts could entertain the possibilities of what that meant, a shuffling around the corner immediately sent fear back by her side.

At once, one of Thura's fellow bondservants charged up the stairway from the madness of the Monon and began shouting out to Machi, who immediately interrupted the council meeting.

"The people have lined the alleyway in front of the jail," Machi shouted. "It's too much for the guards to handle on their own. The people are overtaking them and trying to get to the prisoner."

Frustrated by the growing chaos and his town's impatience, in addition to the continued interruptions in the council room, Ochi stood up and slammed his chair against the table. Despite the noise along the Monon, the council room grew uncomfortably silent as Ochi began to shout.

"Pali, you can stop talking! We've got it! We have an enemy combatant on the island," Ochi barked. "I want you and Machi to go down there and get the situation under control. If you have to use force, then use it! Tell people to go home. We'll make a formal statement about the prisoner at Sanctuary later tonight."

As the brothers rushed from the room, Father Prodido attempted to dampen the hysteria that had flooded the council room. The religious leader stood up from the table next to Ochi and paced back and forth.

"Your Excellency, excuse me for being so bold," he began. "I know you are frustrated at the moment, but let me offer some additional perspective on our unique situation."

Ochi glared impatiently at the religious leader.

"I do believe this prisoner is a gift from God," Father Prodido said.

Patrida's leader placed his calloused hands on the back of his chair. With his eyebrows furrowed, he stared even more intensely at the religious leader awaiting his punchline.

"Patrida is not healthy," Father Prodido continued. "Each of us knows this to be true. The people are divided on almost every issue. They argue about which man will marry the next eligible servant, which foods we will grow for the next season and the decisions we make from this very council room."

While speaking, the religious leader stood in front of the single painting on the wall and stared at it. The tilt of his head indicated he must not have been satisfied it was completely level. Placing his thumbs on each side, he adjusted it to his exacting standards.

"Even earlier today," Father Prodido continued, still evaluating the painting, "a group was in the street arguing to the figurative death about the fitness of your leadership."

Ochi glared at the religious leader from behind, but Father Prodido could not see his face and continued without a pause.

"Our town has become an addict of complaint, feeding upon and deriving its energy from constant outrage. If we were to punish every offender daily, we would cease to have a community within weeks, maybe days."

"You're testing my patience. Tell me how any of this is a gift from God," Ochi demanded impatiently.

"Yes, yes, of course, your Excellency," said Father Prodido, turning from the painting to face the leader. "As Tyran alluded to earlier, this is an opportunity for us. Depending on how we handle the outsider, we may begin to heal the many ailments and disorders plaguing us. Our prisoner may very well be the sacrificial lamb, if you will, we need at this moment to heal our deep divisions and make Patrida great again. That is how he is a gift."

Ochi sat back at the table and rubbed the day-old, graying stubble on his chin. He knew precisely where Father Prodido was going with this argument. The gallows had always been an effective means of keeping order and preserving Patrida's culture in the past. But this situation was different. They had never had to make a decision about an outsider, someone not like them. This unique scenario had the potential to be even more powerful.

Getting information from the enemy and then executing him could eliminate the growing fear gripping Patrida. Even more, the situation was a unique gift in that it would give Patrida a common purpose to unite behind, reminding them who they are as a people. But Ochi also secretly knew there was an opportunity to strengthen their confidence in his leadership. Father Prodido's plan appeared to be a win-win scenario for everyone involved.

Patrida's leader again sat silently contemplating Father Prodido and Tyran's words but also thinking about how hungry he was. The religious leader sat back down at the table and looked at Tyran with wide eyes, indicating he wanted him to finish laying out the argument. Ochi, meanwhile, left the table to retrieve the tray of bread and cheeses Thura had prepared earlier.

"We'll execute him," Tyran said, his eyes following his father across the room. "End of the story. Done deal. We'll get the information we need from him first and then execute him. The people will love us. We haven't had an execution in a while. It'll be like feeding a bunch of ravenous wolves."

Ochi sat back down at the table without grabbing any food. Instead, he closed his eyes, partially from an oncoming headache and partially from listening to his son's blathering. Tyran's words sounded like the incoherent parroting of Father Prodido, and it nauseated him.

Seeing the leader's growing impatience, Father Prodido put his elbows on the table, linked his fingers prayerfully, and leaned in toward Ochi to close the deal.

"Of course, this plan is contingent upon how we sell it to the people. If we spin this the right way, it could truly be a catalyst toward revisiting greatness. Do you remember that morning nearly twenty years ago? The dreams. The aspirations. A holy and righteous community of God where people could experience peace and freedom," the religious leader said in hopes of appealing to a part of Ochi he sensed had been waning.

Pushing away the uneaten tray of food, Patrida's leader stood up decisively from his chair and moved toward the door. Father Prodido and Tyran looked at each other quizzically but then stood and followed behind.

"We'll address the entire town at Sanctuary tonight," Ochi said. "We'll announce our goal of getting information from the prisoner and then execute him within the next few days. That will satisfy them for now and put us in everyone's good graces."

"Ah yes. Brilliant decision as always, your Excellency," Father Prodido said. "The Lord has certainly provided for us on this day, and you are his hands."

Ochi left the room and headed down the dimly lit corridor toward his quarters to prepare for the public address. Father Prodido gently closed the door with only he and Tyran remaining.

"You performed exceedingly well in explaining exactly what's at stake for Patrida and why we need to be decisive," Father Prodido said, turning to his young protégé and motioning for him to sit back down at the table. "You remind me so much of your father when we first established Patrida. He was bold and strong and resolute. He was respected then. I see those same qualities in you, Tyran."

"Thank you, Father," Tyran said, tearing off a piece of bread. "You've helped me find my voice. You know I've always had ideas running through my head about what I believe and how we should do things. But I never had any real direction from my father. He was always too busy with other people and their problems. You've given me the direction he failed to give me. While I haven't always been able to speak with confidence, your guidance and trust have helped me. I am getting better at speaking what is on my mind and taking a stand for what I believe in. And hopefully, it will show in how I rule one day."

Father Prodido joined his protégé at the table and straightened his vestment. It was becoming evident the religious leader wanted more than idle chit-chat with Tyran.

"Yes, very good, Tyran. Very good," Father Prodido said. "We need a strong, god-fearing leader who will take a stand against the rampant ungodliness of Patrida, whether it be among the dissenters or those who speak ill against the council or the ignorant backbiters. Of course, you understand this."

"I do," Tyran said, attempting to speak with his mouth full, only to be interrupted by the religious leader.

"There have been too many recent trespasses the council has disregarded," said Father Prodido. "But you see, Tyran, compliance begins with a strong arm at the top. Compliance produces upright and virtuous people. What we need is a leader who is neither weak among his supporters nor his enemies. We need a leader who will lead us back to the faithfulness of our founding. Do you understand what I am saying?"

Father Prodido was not only known for his position and rigid moral code in Patrida, but also for the eloquence of his words and his cunning stratagem. If Patrida's council was a game of chess and Father Prodido's true intentions could be known, they would see that he was always thinking two to three steps ahead. However, no one knew his true intentions, only that he desired to be around the table of influence and close to the ear of leadership. For this reason, the religious leader always stayed close to Ochi. He took every opportunity to ingratiate him with his words.

But it was in his close proximity to Ochi that Father Prodido concluded something had changed with him. Twelve months prior, almost a year to the date, Ochi secretly confessed something to the religious leader he had never shared with anyone else. Father Prodido believed this confession was directly related to the stranger apprehended in the woods earlier. Sitting alone with Tyran in the council room, he thought it was the right moment to share this information with him.

As the young man sat unwittingly across the table from Father Prodido, the religious leader continued to wax poetic about bringing Patrida back to its former greatness. His genius was not in his directness but in selling an idea with colorful language and imaginative context.

"You and I have an opportunity of a lifetime, together, at this very moment, to restore the glory of this island," Father Prodido said. "And you, Tyran, will be the leader who will help us realize it."

Tyran looked at the religious leader leaning forward from across the table and watched the flame of the oil lamp dance in his aged but determined eyes. The young man understood precisely what his mentor was suggesting and realized the most obvious and glaring omission.

"But where is my father in this plan?" Tyran asked. "I haven't heard you say anything about him."

Father Prodido put his pale hands on the dark wood and stared at the young man intently.

"Oh, your father is fine, Tyran," the religious leader said. "But there is something you deserve to know about his past. In the first couple of years after we arrived on the island, when you were still a little boy, there was an uprising."

Tyran nodded his head hesitantly.

"You mean the Great Liberation."

"Yes, yes," said Father Prodido. "You know it quite well. It was our liberation from a hostile group in Patrida that profaned our beliefs and ideals. They challenged your father at every turn. When we could no longer take their heresy and divisiveness, we drove them into the forest and eliminated each one of them."

"I know all of this," Tyran said, reaching for a piece of cheese this time. "But what about my father?"

"Your father, filled with tremendous animus and rage, pursued the remaining remnant by himself because they would not fight back," Father Prodido continued. "He was determined to cut down every last person who had undermined his leadership as an act of personal retribution and vengeance. He took it all very personally. When he came face to face with the opposition leader, your father did not even give him a final word. He put a knife right through him."

"Father Prodido, with all due respect," Tyran replied. "There's nothing new in what you're telling me about my father. I grew up hearing these stories and knowing of my father's valor in battle. From the time I was a teenager, I heard about how he single-handedly slaughtered every remaining infidel."

"Yes, Tyran. You have," Father Prodido said. "But there is one thing about the Great Liberation and your father you do not know. Your father di … "

"Father Prodido! Tyran!" a voice called out. "If you're still up here, everyone has gathered at Sanctuary. They're demanding to know what's going on with the prisoner. Ochi needs you to join him immediately."

CHAPTER 3

Thura's bedroom appeared smaller than it ever had before. The momentary feeling of liberation she experienced in the corridor, only a few minutes prior, had vanquished behind the closed door of her room. From inside the four walls, it felt sealed and constricted, almost suffocating. The only thing separating Thura from the bright flicker of the small, white candle sitting on her desk was the blanket on her bed she hid beneath in darkness.

In many ways, the young woman's room was a microcosm of her life in Patrida. Her closed door represented her containment and restricted opportunity. The four walls reminded Thura she was limited, not only geographically on an island, but also ideologically in a strict and repressive religious system. The darkness surrounding her was symbolic of Patrida's darkness and her years of unknowing within the system. The single candle she lit was her present, feeble attempt at pushing back the shadows. From beneath her blanket, the young woman created the only space in Patrida where she felt safe to ask questions and consider possibilities.

Thura held her thoughts and questions close to her, however. Sharing them with others would do nothing but bring the severe disapproval of the council. While it was true that conflict was normal in Patrida, it only came from peripheral and inconsequential issues. The council hated dissension, but there was a threshold they seemed willing to tolerate, so long as it did not challenge Patrida's status quo. That is not to say there were no repercussions for stirring things up.

There certainly was. But petty conflicts did not result in heavy-handed punishment like those deemed more disruptive and treasonous.

For instance, if a person dissented by asking real, honest questions and challenging the religious or political order, the total weight of the council's justice would crush the offender for their offense. As a young girl, Thura witnessed servants standing up to their husbands, even Father Prodido, and protesting their subjugation. But the system permanently silenced them. The structural integrity of Patrida was wholly dependent upon the suppression of honest questions and the elimination of free-thinking.

Thura vividly remembered one young woman named Fayme who stood up while Father Prodido spoke at Sanctuary. On that day, he boasted of Patrida's greatness and how God had allowed freedom to flourish on the island. Interrupting the religious leader, the young woman asked him to define freedom. She asked that question specifically because she did not think he really knew what it meant. While her husband pulled at her arm to sit down, she remained standing until she received an answer. Father Prodido, indignant and burning with anger, told her that freedom comes only through adherence to God's law. He then motioned for the guards to arrest her. She never asked another question again.

At the time, Thura believed reckless martyrdom would neither benefit her nor anyone else. As she grew older, however, Thura often thought about Fayme's bravery. Not only did she stand up to Father Prodido, but she confronted the entire system that day in Sanctuary. As a result, Thura slowly began to understand why questions were dangerous to the religious and political system. That single, rebellious question about freedom was the one thing Father Prodido and the council feared most because it challenged the seemingly impenetrable walls of Patrida's control.

An honest question did not float in the air and dissipate into oblivion. It could land on fertile ground and take root in others, crumbling previously undisturbed soil in the process. That is precisely what happened within Thura all those years ago when Fayme decided to question Father Prodido publicly. The seeds Sophia had sown within Thura began to grow with Fayme's courage to question authority. They took root and sprouted into even more subversive questions that Thura regularly considered, even under her blanket in the dimly lit room that day.

What is Patrida? Thura wondered. Why is it controlled like a prison? If this is freedom, why do I hate it so much? I follow the rules, why do I not feel free? If there is such a thing as freedom, where is it?

Unfortunately for Thura, asking questions only increased her restlessness. They did not make her feel any more liberated. Questions alone cannot produce freedom, she realized. They can only begin to unsettle the status quo. Thura was certainly unsettled and hungered for more, although she could not quite put her finger on what that *more* was exactly. All she knew was that she no longer wanted the enslaving chains of Patrida holding her back. She no longer identified with the mindset and beliefs espoused by Patrida's leaders. In fact, she was beginning to resent them. She could no longer sit idly by tending to her work while watching the mistreatment of others from her window above.

Thura threw off her quilted blanket and stared at the lone candle straining in the darkness of her room. They shared the same struggle. This is not how life ought to be, she thought. Thura was done living in fear and hiding away her thoughts and questions. Searching throughout her room, the young woman found ten more candles, which she lined up on the nightstand in front of her window. One by one, she lit them and watched the first candle no longer strain by itself in the darkness as the other candles began to share their light.

Thura's room began to glow. Its radiance poured out her window onto the darkened Monon. But as she watched the last few people move along the street toward Sanctuary, not a single person noticed the brilliance emanating from above. This is so typical of these people, Thura thought. This magnificent light is literally shining out into the darkness, and not one of you can see it.

~

The Patridian guards lit the last few torches that emblazoned the center aisle of Sanctuary. On each side were rows of long, rectangular stone slab benches sitting directly on the ground, perfectly spaced and uniform. The visual design of the area epitomized the monolithic and rigid nature of Patrida.

At front and center was the holy shrine, the sacrarium, with three Patridian flags planted equidistantly in front of it. Each flag was embroidered with the image of the shrine. Centered in the middle were the words *Sacrarium Convenae* stitched below it, which meant *Sacred Community of Refugees*. This phrase captured the first inhabitants' heart and sentiment when they arrived on the island two decades prior as refugees themselves. But for everyone who had gathered in Sanctuary awaiting the presentation of their prisoner, it represented a sad irony completely lost on them.

One by one, Ochi, Father Prodido and Tyran walked down the center aisle in feigned solemnity. Hidden behind the singular emotion on each man's face were very different feelings about the occasion. Father Prodido and Tyran shared a sense of excitement in parading the criminal before the crowd and feeding into the frenzy. Ochi, on the other hand, was much more subdued. While he was marching down the aisle physically, his head was somewhere else. But from the outside looking in, the three men appeared unified and resolved.

Complete silence had arrested the crowd as they watched each council member take his place in front of his respective flag. Ochi and Tyran stood on each side, while Father Prodido stood in the middle with the most prominent flag behind him. The religious leader taking front and center was not an unusual arrangement for the council. He almost always took center stage since he did the majority of the talking. However, everyone secretly knew he wanted to be the focus of their attention.

The opaque backdrop of the forest's edge matched the starless sky above. The barely perceptible pop and crack of each torch's flame joined the muted gurgle of water flowing from the spring behind the flags. An eerie enthusiasm and anticipation temporarily suppressed the crowd's rage and fear.

Father Prodido meticulously straightened each sleeve of his religious attire, again brushing off the lint and dirt only visible to him. His simple but dignified, white, long-sleeved robe decorated with the gold necklace and medallion centered on his chest glowed from the surrounding orange flames. The imagery on Father Prodido's medallion perfectly represented the religious man and his aspirations. The depiction was of two swords crossed, overlaying praying hands. Inscribed around the image were the words *Peace Through Strength*. At last, deeming himself presentable, Father Prodido surveyed the audience with no visible expression on his face.

"Brothers and sisters," he began. "We… are not alone."

In unison, the crowd immediately jumped up from their silence and began to shout and scream, as they had done earlier along the Monon. While internally loving the animus he saw in front of him, the religious leader attempted to keep order by raising his hand for silence.

"The council convened, and our glorious leader will soon fill you in on what has been decided," Father Prodido said. "But first, a few reflections on the day. As you know, in Patrida, we operate by the providence of God and the rule of law. This truth has been made evident among us, from our past and into our present. As such, we will not allow a single person, nor faction, to tear apart the fabric of this holy community."

Off to the side, Ochi stood with his head down and eyes closed. The crowd could have mistaken it for a prayerful posture, but nausea had him disoriented and spinning. Ochi's headache had followed him from the council room to the front of Sanctuary, pounding more intensely in his forehead and between his eyes. Exacerbating the pain were Father Prodido's continued direct and indirect references to Patrida's past and the Great Liberation.

"But on this day," the religious leader continued, "we have entered a new era in the life of this sacred community of refugees. What once was a nascent and naive community, settled beyond the reaches of unholy, pagan influence, has become an attraction for corruption, a host for disease, a body for malignancy. On this day, an infidel has infiltrated our home and livelihood. A savage has threatened our peace and freedom. And this criminal could represent others like him who are surrounding this island or standing in these woods, readying to besiege us at any moment."

Father Prodido was not content with a subdued presentation. He preferred the emotion of theatrics and performance art. The religious leader calculatingly pushed buttons to stoke the crowd into a directed fury against the enemy while leading them toward a common purpose and uniting narrative. Smiling and nodding his head at each person's growing anger standing in front of him, Father Prodido raised his hand once again to silence the crowd.

"Thank God this council is committed to the strength of Patrida and the ideals that have made us great," he said. "Thank God for his protection from any potential enemy and the valiant service of the Patridian guard and its leaders. We commit to you, the faithful of Patrida, that your way of life will be preserved. No conformity. No compromises. No mercy. Our *no* will be a resounding *no!* We will not become a community of *yes*, lest we lose the very heart and character of what makes us great. Our peace will be preserved through our strength. Our freedom will be protected at all costs because freedom is never free."

The crowd stood and cheered in a wild and frenzied hysteria. Father Prodido closed his eyes and breathed in deeply, feeding off of their raw and unrestrained energy. Nodding his head in approval, the religious leader continued.

"Repeat after me," he shouted. "Our no is no!"

The crowd chanted his words in perfect accord, but it was not enough for the religious leader. Like an emcee readying the crowd for the prizefight, his eyes opened wide as he shouted to the top of his lungs.

"Our no is no! Our no is no! Our no is no!"

The crowd, now maniacal puppets feeding off the religious leader's unrestrained energy, chanted their protestation again and again.

"No! No! No! No! No!"

Clapping his hands perfectly to the crowd's syncopated chanting, Father Prodido laughed hysterically as the people continued. No longer needing to feed off of the religious leader's zeal, the people of Patrida, standing united in Sanctuary, discovered their common purpose and shared passion. What brought them together was not what they were for but what they were against.

∿

Thura discretely made her way alongside the standing crowd toward the front, where she slid in next to her mother, Velos. The matriarch looked at her daughter harshly, as if to communicate her displeasure for her significant tardiness. Sheepishly and somewhat apologetically, Thura held out her wine-stained arms, which now looked more ghoulish as they absorbed the scarlet, flickering light of the torches. Her mother's eyes opened widely, misunderstanding exactly what her daughter was showing her.

"It is only wine," Thura mouthed in an attempt to avoid a scene in the front row with people all around. "I had to change clothes."

Taking a deep breath, clearly holding back her frustration with her daughter, Velos turned toward the front once again. By this time, Father Prodido had already asked the audience to join him in the Patridian pledge, which was more of a mix between a pledge and prayer.

"I pledge my heart and my allegiance to Patrida and to the God who protects her," he began with every voice joining him. "For in this sacred community, I find my peace, my freedom, and my refuge. Amen."

With her head still down, examining the stains on her hands, Thura hoped no one had noticed her subtle act of defiance in not joining the crowd in their unitive pledge. If I no longer share this community's values, she thought, how can I give it my heart and allegiance. As much as Thura desired to keep peace with everyone around her, repeating words she no longer believed would be disingenuous. Trusting no one had noticed her silence, the young woman sat down with the crowd as her father stepped in front of Father Prodido and the center flag to give his address.

"We gather here in this place, in Sanctuary," Ochi began, "in the very spot that represents the freedom we enjoy as Patridians. As Father Prodido said, the freedom in which we gather and the freedom we celebrate each day is costly. And no freedom-loving community that desires peace can sit idly by while a mounting threat slowly begins to creep in among us. Nor can we turn a blind eye to this threat as it begins to surround us."

It was evident to everyone that their leader's affect was flat and monotone, almost rote and memorized. He sounded off. Ochi was not delivering with the same rousing, emotional punch as Father Prodido. Of course, the leader was always to the point and a matter-of-fact man, but this presentation lacked his regular energy. It did not come close to capturing the hysteria of the last few hours. Father Prodido, now standing to Ochi's left, glanced at Tyran under a quizzical brow and received a subtle nod in return. The pair seemed to be acknowledging Ochi's detachment and that their earlier conversation needed to resume as soon as possible.

"After a short deliberation this evening," Ochi continued, "the council and I have decided unanimously that we'll seek additional information from the prisoner about his intentions. We'll also try to determine who his people are and what their intentions could be."

The leader's pause at that exact moment did not serve him well. The crowd, which had been hanging on every word and riding the emotion of Father Prodido's inspiring words, grew into a ferocious beast whose insatiable appetite wanted more than an interrogation. It was not long before they began to roar in dissatisfaction. Raising his hand in hopes of taming the beast, Ochi shouted out above their growling in one last attempt to satisfy their hunger.

"But to make a statement on how we will deal with anyone outside of Patrida who poses a threat to our community and our way of life, we will execute the prisoner within the next few days, once we get the information we need from him."

The beast rumbled in delight as it jumped up in pandemonium. The macabre scene played out as if the entire performance had been perfectly choreographed. Ochi stared down the center aisle in a dream-like haze. His head throbbed, and a tunnel appeared before him, blocking out everything around him in darkness except what was directly in front of him. He could only see Pali and Machi marching down the center aisle, leading the prisoner with a rope around his neck to the people's thunderous and echoing chants.

"No! No! No! No! No! No! No! No!" they cried as the prisoner stumbled past them.

Like a father proudly observing his children's great accomplishment, Father Prodido looked at the brothers and then to the crowd, nodding his head in approval. Both Ochi and Tyran left their positions and joined Velos and Thura in the front row. The elder leader took the spot next to his daughter, mustering a meager half-smile after looking down at her arms. Despite the cacophony and madness surrounding them, Ochi reached for Thura's red wine-stained hand and squeezed it once before letting it go.

Standing back at the center with the two brothers and prisoner, Father Prodido slowly raised both hands and looked to the heavens. His white-clothed arms began to shake violently. His gold medallion bounced from its chain up and down on his chest. The religious leader closed his eyes as if summoning power from above. He was in full performance mode, and everyone cheered with approval at what they were witnessing. Father Prodido stayed in this pose and played the part for almost a full minute as, one by one, the crowd began to raise their hands and close their eyes with him.

That is, everyone but Thura, whose hands remained boldly by her side and her eyes rebelliously open. All she could do at that moment was stare at the bloodied and bruised face of a man she did not know. With the rope still tightly bound around his neck, in the most dehumanizing position possible, he stared helplessly at the ground. To Thura, it looked as if he had already given up and was resigned to his fate. She did not know exactly what to do, but her heart ached. All she could do was stare at him.

This man is surrounded by people who hate him, she thought. They mocked him and do not even know his name. And now, he is being sentenced to death. Yet, here we sit in our religious pageantry, raising ourselves up as holy and righteous people before God. Unable to turn her eyes away from the cuts on his bloodied face, Thura's thoughts turned to tears streaming down her cheeks. What in the world are we doing? Why am I a part of this?

Thura placed her hands in front of her face and wiped the tears from her eyes. But as she removed her hands, she noticed the prisoner's eyes staring back at her. Thura caught her breath in shock. But for some reason she could not look away. There was depth and kindness in his eyes. They seemed to be reassuring her that everything would be alright.

But as quickly as the young man glanced at her, his eyes darted back to the ground before the prayer ended. With rain beginning to fall and rapidly intensifying, the prayerful lowered their arms and turned their faces from the dark, precipitating sky back toward Father Prodido. A subtle nod from the religious leader released Pali and Machi. The brothers stepped forward and marched down the center aisle victoriously toward the Monon, dragging the prisoner behind them. The crowd hastily ran through the pouring rain to crashes of thunder. Order devolved into scattered and frantic mayhem. Unmoved by the chaos around her, Thura stood alone in the front row transfixed by torches refusing to yield to the rain.

CHAPTER 4

The outer edges of Patrida were not the meticulously ordered cobblestone of the Monon. While the main thoroughfare would have been the most direct route to the jail from Thura's house, located next to Sanctuary at the complete opposite end of town, Thura did not want anyone to see her. The gravelly route along the perimeter provided the necessary cover she needed to move discreetly from one side of town to the other, especially at night.

Walking along the slightly muddy alleyways for a little less than a half-hour, Thura cautiously began to approach the jail on the final side street. The young woman peered around the corner to ensure the guards had already retreated for the night. She stood in a dimly lit area, but it provided enough adequate cover in the shadows for her not to be seen. But between where she stood and the jail door at the other end was a dozen or more oil lamps gently casting their light on the narrow street.

For Thura, this final stretch would be precarious. It would involve her walking nearly the entire length of the alley to reach the jail door, which itself was only a couple dozen steps away from the Monon. At any moment, a person could turn onto the alleyway or walk out of their house and see her. To make the situation even more unnerving, she would be visible to anyone walking along the Monon near the gallows.

But Patrida was as silent as Thura could ever remember it. Her father's announcement of the prisoner's impending interrogation and execution had temporarily allayed the townspeople's passion. Combined with the sudden rain shower, it appeared as if everyone decided to make it a short night and turn in early. Fortunately for Thura, that meant little activity along the Monon. As she patiently waited and watched every window from her limited vantage point, the second-story lights gradually began to fade.

Thura did not want to expose herself by walking straight down the middle of the alley or immediately crossing to the other side. Instead, she would hug the edges of the buildings on her side of the road and walk a delicate tightrope until she was directly across from the prison cell. Clenching her fists, the young woman took a determined yet wary first step around the corner of the building onto the alleyway, eyeing the prison door.

Thura placed her back against the wall, balancing a thin line as she opened her hands and ran her palms against the cool, smooth stones for balance. Despite her nervousness, the young woman scurried through the shadows until she stood with her back up against a wooden storage door. She stared at the prisoner's darkened window across the street as she wiped the sweat from her shaking hands onto her dress. In an attempt to control her nervous breathing, which had been progressively intensifying, Thura closed her eyes, took one last deep breath, and then walked directly to the cell. As she stepped in front of the heavy, wooden door, between the gentle flicker of two oil lamps on each side, she peered into the darkened cell through the small, square opening.

"Hello?" she whispered, not quite sure what she might hear in response if anything at all.

No answer.

There were no movements or even subtle sounds in the black of the cell but the prisoner had to be inside, as this was the only holding area in Patrida. Placing the tips of her fingers on the small, rectangular wooden shelf below the window, the young woman leaned closer to the window and tried once more.

"Hello, friend," Thura whispered.

A bruised and dirty face appeared out of the darkness, almost as if the young woman's kindness summoned him. His face gradually illuminated with the hazy shimmer of streetlights as he stepped forward toward the window.

"My name is Odigo," he whispered back.

"It's nice to meet you, Odigo," Thura said. "But obviously not under these circumstances. I am so sorry for what they have done to you. My name is…"

"Thura," Odigo gently interrupted, his lips pressed together in a subtle smile. "I know who you are."

Thura stared at the young man in a disbelieving and somewhat stupefied silence. She should have been horrified that a stranger said her name. For only twelve hours earlier, the possibility of another person existing on the island outside of Patrida would have been inconceivable. But in her naïveté, or maybe it was the benevolent glance Odigo gave her during the prayer at Sanctuary, Thura was still more curious than scared.

"How do you know me?" Thura demanded. "How do you know my name? Why are you here? Where did you come from? Are there others here on the island? Did you come to Patrida for me?"

The young woman had nothing, if not a thousand questions, but too many questions for the limited amount of time and precariousness of their situation. Understanding the necessity of brevity at the moment, Odigo began.

"I am from a small community on the other side of the island that once existed as a part of Patrida."

Thura stared at Odigo but then at the ground in confusion. As much as the young woman tried to understand what he was saying, she could not comprehend how that was possible. While it was true she was only a little girl when they first arrived on the island, Thura had never heard anyone say a single word about another community. Searching the ground as if waiting for it to give her the answer, she concluded that no one in Patrida knew of this other community, or that they had purposefully kept it a secret from her.

But how has not one person in Patrida ever spoken about this? Thura thought. Someone has to know, right? Of all people, my father, the leader of Patrida, has to know about this other community, doesn't he? If they were a part of Patrida, he has to know. What about my mother or my brother or Father Prodido? Surely they have to know something. How can they not? They absolutely have to know. What are they trying to hide? Thura's heart began to beat faster as her nervous excitement began to fade into a feeling of betrayal.

"Despite being driven out of Patrida so long ago," Odigo continued, "We have continued to be present with your people over the years, although you have not been aware of it."

Thura did not acknowledge Odigo speaking to her. Every question running through her mind multiplied into more questions. Everything she thought she knew about life and how it worked began to crumble in front of the prison door. Thura began to wonder who the prisoner of Patrida actually was. Was it Odigo, or was it her? Could a person believe they are free, only to find out they have been the prisoner the entire time? Thura searched the ground desperately waiting for answers.

"We have been among you in hopes of finding an opening for peace with Patrida," Odigo said. "There are individuals, like me, who have constantly looked for an open door with your people. But it has become apparent that over the years, Patrida's door has closed."

Thura knew precisely the feeling Odigo expressed, as this was the same feeling she had been experiencing lately as well. If Patrida's door appeared to be closing before Odigo was apprehended, then it certainly had to be shut now. Everything Thura had been trying to hold together in tension throughout the day began to flow in tears streaming down her face. As she looked back at Odigo, Thura put her hands up to cover her face.

"Thura," Odigo whispered. "Do you suppose I got caught by the guards or that I purposefully gave myself up?"

Thura's quiet sobbing stopped, but her wine-stained hands remained in front of her face. Peering through a thin crack between her fingers, she could see the peaceful contentment on Odigo's face, which sharply contrasted the bleak obscurity of his holding cell. The coincidental symbolism was not lost on the young woman. In Odigo, she caught a glimpse of a young man who, despite his uncertain circumstances, appeared liberated and at peace. Thura had only known one other person in her life with that kind of contentment.

"Did you come here to rescue me then?" Thura asked. "If you know my name and know all about Patrida and came into this town on your own accord, then it must have been to save me from this place."

"I did not come here to rescue you, Thura," Odigo said.

"Then what are you doing here?" she asked in frustration. "Clearly, I am the only person you have spoken with. Everyone else in this town wants you dead. What do you want me to do? Just tell me."

"There was once a young woman named Dipsa," Odigo whispered. "Every morning, since Dipsa was a small girl, she would walk outside the city gates along a straight path to an old man who had jugs of water for sale. Week after week, year after year, Dipsa made this journey with her empty containers and paid the old man for more water before traveling back home."

Thura patiently listened to the story but began to nervously glance over her shoulder to make sure she was still alone.

"One particular morning," Odigo continued. "Dipsa decided to take another path to reach the old man. Her new route was along a winding trail that climbed a few small hills and ultimately dropped into a gully leading down to a large, blue pond. As Dipsa approached the pond, she heard someone moving around in the water. Still hidden from sight, she cautiously looked around the corner of a large rock and saw the old man filling jugs of water. Nervous at first, but then gaining courage, Dipsa confronted the old man."

"What did she say to him?" Thura pleaded in a whisper as Odigo paused for suspense.

"Dipsa said to the old man, 'Why have I been paying you for water that has always been so abundant and freely accessible to me?' The old man, still retrieving the water and never once looking up, replied to Dipsa, 'You only ever find that for which you are truly searching.'"

Thura thoughtfully considered Odigo's words, pondering the parable and trying to find the deeper meaning within the story.

Finally, she asked, "Am I Dipsa?"

"That is your question to answer," Odigo said.

A shuffle around the corner on the Monon startled Thura. Frightened, she turned and dashed behind a storage room door on the opposite side of the alleyway. She was careful to not make a noise or attract any potential attention. As Thura listened intently, the cadence of deliberate footsteps grew louder. They sounded as if they were approaching either Odigo's prison door or the door behind which she stood in fear.

There was a prolonged silence.

Thura held her breath behind the nearly closed storage room door and waited. On the other side were muted sounds, but no longer any footsteps. A faint shadow on the ground filled the narrow opening. The presence of a person leaning against the wooden door, only a few inches away from where she stood, almost made Thura pass out from not breathing. The door creaked but did not open. Whoever was standing on the other side backed away. The footsteps began again. As they slowly faded away, Thura gasped to catch her breath.

Discreetly peering out the prison door window, Odigo no longer saw Thura, nor the person who had visited them. After a few minutes of nothing but the lingering drips of water from the rooftops into the puddles below, the storage door across the alleyway slowly opened. Thura cautiously emerged from the darkness. Crossing with care to not make a noise, the young woman stepped between the delicate radiance of the oil lamps on each side of the prison entrance and gazed adamantly at Odigo.

"I am Dipsa," Thura whispered resolutely.

"Yes, you are, my dear. You have always been Dipsa," a voice called out from behind Odigo. The wrinkled and weathered face of an old woman became visible over the prisoner's shoulder as she stepped forward.

"Such great thirst, and always searching for a drinkable source," she said.

"I am sorry for waking you, Sophia. I was trying to be as quiet as possible," Thura said. "I came here because I was cur…"

"Curious who this prisoner is and who his people are?" Sophia interjected.

"Um, yes."

"While you, dear Thura, have been visiting with me for many years," Sophia said, "I have never fully revealed my story to you, for it was never the right time."

Thura tried to connect the dots between Sophia and Odigo but could not imagine any scenario in which the two knew each other. She briefly entertained the idea that Sophia was one of the people Odigo alluded to earlier. But for Thura's entire life, Sophia had always been Patrida's prisoner, locked away from the community.

The truth was that, while Thura had been visiting the old woman for nearly a decade, Sophia remained a mystery. As a young girl, she would frequently ask her family about the old woman and why she was in prison. But her questions were always met with the same curt response, "There are some things of which we do not speak, and Sophia is one of those things." Consequently, Thura grew up understanding that any discussion about Sophia was off-limits. However, everyone generally understood that Sophia had challenged the community's structure and order, which necessitated her imprisonment.

Throughout Thura's adolescence, the Patridian's did not view Sophia as a person but more of a depersonalized threat. And they needed to keep her contained and neutralized. But that was how Patrida always dealt with people who challenged the system. If the council could convince people to no longer view another person as a human being but as the embodiment of evil, it was always easier to discredit, discard, or kill them. Even more, as Father Prodido preached that they were the sole bearers of goodness and truth, the town presumed it was their responsibility to eradicate that which they deemed evil. To the Patridians, Sophia was not a human being. She was evil. She was a threatening set of disruptive ideals deserving to be locked away and forgotten.

"Before you were born, I was a part of the group that challenged Patrida," Sophia began. "We believed that for all our good intentions in coming to the island and rebirthing a community of life and virtue, we had very quickly lost our heart as a people. Everything we had envisioned for this community began to be distorted."

"I do not remember any of this," Thura said.

"You would not remember it, Thura," said Sophia. "You were too young. But at that time, Father Prodido was incredibly influential with your father. He believed the most effective way to create a virtuous and holy community was through a religious leadership establishing standards of morality. To your father, who was not quite the visionary, that appeared to be the most efficient way to order and structure the community."

Thura vaguely remembered parts of the story she had picked up over the years from other servants. But, Sophia told her version from a much more honest perspective than anything Thura had ever heard.

"So what did your group do, Sophia?" Thura asked.

"We believed the proverbial pendulum had gone too far in the other direction. One's virtue and morality could never come from the kind of heavy-handed legislation or governance that Patrida enforced. People have to pursue it for themselves. You cannot force virtue or morality on them. But the unfortunate trajectory of Patrida and where it would all end was apparent. So we began to speak up and challenge the leadership. However, it was not long before the system turned on us, before the leadership turned on us, and drove us out of Patrida by force."

At this point, Thura believed she knew where the story was going, but she was not entirely sure she wanted to know every detail. However, with so much hidden from her over the years, Thura wanted to finally understand the truth.

"Tell me exactly what happened, Sophia," Thura said. "I may not be ready to hear it, but I desperately need to know what happened. I can't live with blinders over my eyes any longer."

"The guards, headed by Pali and Machi, began to pursue us and then began to slaughter us. Your father was among them," Sophia said.

Thura already knew the part her father played in the onslaught, but it was still painful for her to hear.

"At one point," Sophia continued, "your father called off the guards and continued tracking us by himself. We could have continued running from him, but we stopped and faced him unarmed. All we wanted was peace. Neither his threats of violence nor the fear he tried to induce intimidated us. But he knew we would not fight back. Without hesitation, your father ran up to our leader, Numa, and stabbed him in his chest, directly into his heart. I stood there in shock and horror as he fell to his knees. Like the gentle soul he was, he looked up at your father in forgiveness and whispered his last words before falling over."

Tears began to stream down Sophia's chiseled cheeks as Odigo wrapped his slender but muscular arms around her in solace. Thura had never seen this side of Sophia before. But now, on the other side of the prison door, was an opening into her tender heart where she invited Thura to understand the deep love she had for her friends and the heartbreak she carried for Patrida. Thura reached in through the window and cradled the old woman's face, wiping her tears with her thumb.

"Numa was not just our leader," Sophia whispered. "He was my husband. For as long as I can remember, we were always together. From the time we were children until the day we married, we were always by each other's side. I never thought our time in Patrida would end in such calamity and sadness. I remember falling to the ground and holding him while he died, his blood all over my hands and arms. I kept repeating to him that I would never leave his side. But he was already gone. Your father callously grabbed me by the hair and dragged me away from him. That is when he hit me, and everything went black."

Thura began to cry. She stared deeply into Sophia's dark, pained eyes.

"That's all I remember of that night," Sophia said. "A night of confusion and madness. I was devastated and heartbroken. I had become the sole prisoner of Patrida, a Patrida I no longer recognized or identified with. I believed that they had killed every one of my dear friends and that no one had escaped alive. But then, Odigo came walking down the road today as a prisoner. And I knew, I just knew, some of them must have survived all those years ago. And guess what? They did. Some of them did survive. That is the secret your father has been carrying with him, and there is not a single person in Patrida who knows that he did not kill everyone that day."

Thura wiped away tears from her own face this time. She wondered how she would act normally around her father the following day. But even more, she wondered how she would get Sophia and Odigo out of Patrida before their execution. With the townspeople moving about the Monon throughout the day, any real chance of pulling off an escape would be nothing short of a miracle. But Thura had an idea and a slim chance of making it happen. The young woman was determined to get out of Patrida and discover this new community on the other side of the island.

CHAPTER 5

Anticipation accompanied the new day in Patrida. The sunrise seemed to summon more people to the Monon than a typical morning. Even sleepy-eyed children with bedhead ambled outside to eat their modest breakfasts in front of their houses. From behind Sanctuary, a single guard exited the woods and made his way toward Father Prodido's house, located across the street from Patrida's leader. Pali and Machi loitered outside the front door on the plain, white-painted porch and greeted him as he entered.

Father Prodido and Tyran stood from the small, square table where the pair had finished an early morning huddle with Ochi only a few minutes before. Their impromptu council meeting had been to discuss their detailed plans for the prisoner. But after only a few exchanges into their brief conversation, Ochi abruptly left the house.

"Father Prodido. Tyran," said the guard.

"Yes, fine sir," said Father Prodido. "An update, please."

"Yes, sir," said the guard. "As instructed, we set up a perimeter and kept watch overnight. There is currently no enemy activity to report."

"Very well then," said Father Prodido. "You are dismissed."

The guard turned toward the door to leave.

"But before you go," Father Prodido called out, "can I trust you will summon Fovos for me? Bring him here and then return to your outpost in the woods."

"Yes, sir," said the guard.

As the door closed behind him, Father Prodido and Tyran sat back down at the table, one across from the other. With a look of indifference evident on the religious leader's face, he straightened his vestment and cleared his throat before making eye contact with Tyran, who appeared quite relieved from the guard's report. But before Father Prodido could offer his first word to the young man, Tyran reached for a piece of nearly burnt toast and began to talk exuberantly.

"That's fantastic news, Father!" Tyran exclaimed. "I was anxious last night, not knowing what might be coming our way. No one has ever threatened us from the outside."

The religious leader patiently watched Tyran eat his darkened toast and saw an opportunity.

"You would be wise to remain anxious, Tyran," the religious leader replied dryly and at least an octave lower than his normal speaking voice. "The threat did not come last night. But make no mistake, it is imminent. We must be prepared for any eventuality."

The seriousness of Father Prodido's demeanor was apparent. While the religious leader had been unusually forward and assertive with Tyran, especially over the last few months without any real explanation, his presence across the table conveyed something deeper and more complex. To Tyran, the brief and highly unusual meeting with his father, a few minutes prior, seemed to have unlocked a part of Father Prodido he had never witnessed before.

"What do you mean, Father?" Tyran asked, bothered by the religious leader's tone and demeanor. "How do you know for sure that a threat is imminent? Are there more people like this prisoner on the way?"

"I do not want to be dramatic or cause any problems," Father Prodido said with the same seriousness as his previous comment. "But your father is not who you think he is, Tyran."

"I don't understand. What does that mean?" Tyran asked. "And what does any of this have to do with a potential attack from outsiders?"

"Your father came to me almost a year ago in confidence and told me there were many things he wanted to confess," Father Prodido began. "I believed it to be highly unusual because your father had always been a private man. And this was the first time he had ever approached me in this way since establishing Patrida."

Tyran agreed with the religious leader on this particular point. His father had always been a private man and very reserved. Unless he needed to speak, he listened. He observed. He took things in and would ruminate on them. But he typically never spoke unless the situation necessitated it. That was one of the reasons why so many people in Patrida loved him. He always seemed to be considering everything around him but was reluctant to say much. He let his actions speak for him.

Under normal circumstances, Tyran could not understand his father opening up like that for anyone. Unless there was something notable weighing on him for quite some time, it would be highly unusual and out of character for his father to approach Father Prodido to confess anything at all.

"He asked if we could meet privately one night, as there was something he had been holding deep within him since the Great Liberation," Father Prodido said. "He confided in me that he had personally pursued and single-handedly cut down many in the rebel faction group."

Tyran placed the half-eaten toast back on his plate and pushed it to the center of the table. The intense look on his face indicated he was slowly putting the pieces together.

"But my father didn't kill every infidel, did he?" Tyran asked.

"Your pursuit of truth has rewarded you, young Tyran," Father Prodido said with the morning light barely visible through the drawn curtains. "You are correct. Your father did not pursue them as they fled. And now these blasphemers and traitors live on this island cultivating their ungodly beliefs, no doubt looking for every opportunity to bring their heresy back to Patrida."

Tyran's eyes moved from Father Prodido to the table, where he began to pick at a stubborn hangnail on his left hand. The young leader did not have anything further to say in response to what he had heard. He clearly understood the implications for Patrida, for the leadership council, and for his father.

As Father Prodido adjusted in his seat and cleared his throat to continue, Tyran could already anticipate what the religious leader was about to say. The two spent so much time with each other over the last year their thoughts had grown increasingly similar. As Tyran thought about the timing of his father's confession, he understood why Father Prodido had been so insistent upon their mentoring relationship. Still staring down at his hands, Tyran doggedly removed the hangnail from his index finger but did not appear to feel the pain or notice the blood as he wiped it on his shirt and looked back to Father Prodido.

"Your father, our leader, who has always been hailed and lifted up by our community for his great conviction and valor, has deceived his people, Tyran," Father Prodido said. "I deeply apologize for burdening you with such heavy information. He has been concealing a lie and, as a result, has put the fine people of Patrida at increased risk for the last two decades, while a rogue community has continued to grow larger, stronger, and more dangerous."

Father Prodido knew the threat from the inhabitants was actually very low, likely nonexistent. But this kind of peaceful narrative did not play well for the type of future he envisioned for a strong and insulated Patrida. The religious leader needed a threat and an enemy. So with selective truths, Father Prodido continued his story to manipulate Tyran toward that end.

"We intentionally inhabited this island to escape the madness of the mainland," Father Prodido continued. "Yet, because of your father's laxity, he created the exact thing we once fled, a corrupt people with no regard for what is right or wrong and with no idea what is in their best interest."

Tyran sat silently with his head down, as he knew the religious leader had more to say.

"How now shall we live and contend with these savages and their radical ideas on our island?" Father Prodido asked rhetorically. "How shall we deal with these parasites who are hungry to consume our every resource? How shall we defend against vermin seeking to infiltrate our community and our way of life? How shall our peace and freedom be preserved against those who desire to upend it, Tyran? What if they bring their strange religious ideas back to Patrida? What happens when our children begin to hear their heresies? What does that do to the faith? What does it do to our pursuit of righteousness and holiness? What happens when they begin disrupting our very way of life? Do you not think this prisoner was sent here with ill-intentions?"

Tyran wiped the remaining blood from his finger on the lower part of his shirt and then asked Father Prodido the most obvious question.

"With all due respect, Father," Tyran began. "You know I agree with everything you've said. But why has it taken you so long to tell me this? Why did it take an outsider watching us from the woods for you to say something to me about my father's confession and this other community? You know, this is something you could've told me a long time before today."

Sensing a subtle resistance from his protégé, an annoyed Father Prodido quickly countered.

"Those are not the correct questions, Tyran," Father Prodido said. "The only question here is, 'Why has your father had such a reluctance in dealing with these people?' That is the real question. You know my affection toward your father, and you know I would stand by him through any fire, but he has changed in some way. He is not the same man. Not the same determined leader. Not the same fierce warrior. Not the same god-fearing man who first planted the Patridian flag in this sacred soil. You witnessed it yourself last night when he spoke at Sanctuary. And then this morning when he came into this very room and told us what he wanted to do with the prisoner."

Staring at the blackened toast, Tyran nodded.

The sound of footsteps on the front porch and an accompanying knock at the door caused the two leaders to stand abruptly. Fovos entered the room and bowed before Father Prodido.

"You sent for me, Father?"

~

Ochi sat at a nearly empty breakfast table with Velos facing him on the opposite side. Thura walked into the quiet room and noticed something was not right. Her father instantly picked up his cup of water and drank what was left in it, as Velos stared blankly at him. It was apparent to Thura that her mother was about to say something to her father before she walked in on them. The reprimanding look on her face conveyed that her thoughts had been interrupted. But despite the tension and the lingering silence, Thura nervously walked to the table and asked her father if she could fill up his cup with more water.

Ochi nodded without saying a word and smiled.

Breaking her icy stare at Ochi, Velos directed her attention toward her daughter, who was now standing to her father's right holding the pitcher of water.

"Why were you so late getting in last night?" asked Velos.

Thura had started pouring the water but stopped, only filling the cup halfway. The young woman caught a glimpse of her mother's stern face and froze. Velos had a natural beauty that did not necessarily match her personality or temperament. While her physical allure could easily draw the attention of both men and women in Patrida, her personality was blunt and dour. Thura experienced both as she wondered if the conversation she interrupted had been about her. The young woman's mind began to race.

What does she know? Thura wondered. Does she already know the answer to that question? What does my father know? Could it have been my mom or dad standing on the other side of the storage door last night? Could it have been Tyran? Did he tell them?

The sudden barrage of thoughts and questions left Thura momentarily paralyzed and stumbling for an answer. But before any words could materialize, Velos turned to her husband and asked him the same question.

Without hesitation, the leader responded.

"I stayed up late talking to Father Prodido at his house," Ochi said.

Seemingly satisfied with his answer, Velos turned back to her daughter, waiting expectantly for an answer. Thura was still unsure who knew what and was even more uncertain with what to say.

Was my dad really with Father Prodido last night? She wondered. Was my mom really at home during that time? Did either of them know I had been visiting with the prisoners?

Thura eventually answered so as not to attract any more suspicion.

"I needed to clear my head," she said. "Yesterday was so crazy that I went for a long walk after the town meeting at Sanctuary."

Velos and Ochi both sat in an uneasy silence. Her mother seemed unsure of her answer as if her motherly intuition told her something did not feel right. But after a brief pause, she stood up and left the room without saying another word.

"What is going on this morning?" Thura whispered to her father.

"It's a long story," he said, "but I went back over to Father Prodido's this morning and met with him and Tyran. I told them there was not going to be an execution. We will interrogate the prisoner, but that's it. When you walked in the room, I had told your mother my decision. As you can see, she's not at all happy with it."

With an indiscernible sigh of relief, Thura was thankful the conversation between her parents had not been about her. As far as she could tell, neither her mother nor father were suspicious of her meeting with Odigo and Sophia the night before. However, her mother still appeared to be off. Thura decided it must have been her father's abrupt decision to stay the execution. While she was still unsure who was with her in the alley the previous night, she was confident it was not her parents.

As Thura turned away from the table, she caught an unusual movement out of the corner of her eye. People were beginning to assemble in front of their house. As early as it was, the street's noise was louder than any ordinary day in Patrida. Within seconds, the riotous rumble was unmistakable. A growing mob surrounded the front of their house. Thura looked out the window petrified and then turned back to Ochi.

"Father!" she screamed. "Everyone is outside our door!"

Ochi jumped up and opened the door to a zealous mob that began to riotously chant his name. In front of them, standing arrogantly on the porch facing Ochi with a giant smile underneath his black handlebar mustache, was the man Father Prodido called for only a few minutes earlier.

Fovos had been quietly gaining notoriety in certain circles in Patrida for some time but had grown more influential as of late because of Father Prodido. People knew him for his comedic posture and his reputation for getting what he wanted through intimidation. He was a tall and slender man with a black, receding hairline. With a wild look always in his eyes, Fovos knew how to evoke fear in others. It was for that reason alone why Father Prodido had been working covertly through him since the previous summer.

The crowd quieted in anticipation of the confrontation.

"Good morning, leader," Fovos said but then turned to the crowd.

"Should I call him a leader if he's not really a leader?" he asked, looking out the corner of his eye and smiling.

The crowd roared with laughter and jeers.

"How about instead of leader, I call you Mr. Ochi?" Fovos quipped. "How's that sound to you, Mr. Ochi?"

The howling of the crowd grew louder.

"You see, you haven't been doing that much leadin' lately. In fact, we kinda feel like you're gettin' a little soft and the people are afraid, Mr. Ochi."

Ochi stepped through the doorway onto the porch a couple of feet away from Fovos. As he stepped out, Thura attempted to grab his shirt and hold him back but was unsuccessful. With the increasing commotion in front of their house, Velos ran from the back room and joined Thura at the door just in time to hear Ochi respond to his accuser.

"What can I do for you this morning, Fovos?" the leader asked calmly, although there was some history between the two men.

Putting his hands on his hips and smiling at Ochi, Fovos slowly turned again toward the crowd and smiled in manufactured astonishment before turning back to face him.

"We're here to bring you with us, Mr. Ochi," Fovos barked. "You know, so we can have a conversation if you know what I mean. The fine people of Patrida were cheerin' for you last night, ya know. But it didn't seem like your heart was in it too much, Mr. Ochi. At least not like Father Prodido. I'm guessin' maybe your son's heart might be into it more than yours. I don't know. Maybe we can help you get your heart into it? You know, give it a kickstart, if you know what I mean."

Fovos turned toward the crowd.

"Whaddya say?" Fovos shouted. "Can we help Mr. Ochi find his little heart?"

The crowd lapped up everything Fovos fed them and exploded in approval.

Ochi didn't respond. Part of him wanted to punch Fovos in his mustached mouth. But another part of him, which was much more rational and controlled at the moment, realized the angry crowd significantly outnumbered him.

"You see, there's a lot of fear floatin' around here, Mr. Ochi, and we don't see you takin' it very seriously. Who's in those woods anyway? And what's their plan with us? And what are they gonna do to these fine people you're supposed to be protectin'?"

The mob pushed closer to the front porch, with several more imposing goons jumping up next to Fovos on each side. Taking a well-chewed toothpick out of his mouth and staring at the ground for a few seconds, as if thinking about something important, Fovos gave his men the command.

"Why don't you boys help Mr. Ochi down from the porch?" Fovos said as he flicked his toothpick at the leader.

Ochi did his best to resist the men, but he was easily overwhelmed and then escorted forcefully toward the Monon. The crowd followed in a mix of uproarious cheering and maniacal laughter. While the group that had surrounded Ochi's house was only a tiny fraction of the town, more and more people began to emerge onto the street. Furiously screaming for Tyran and Father Prodido, Velos ran through the crowd to find them. But neither were anywhere to be found.

As terrified as Thura was for her father, she had also been impatiently waiting for her parents to leave the house since early morning. She had tossed and turned throughout the night, thinking about how to get them out at the same time. As bizarre and unexpected as the morning turned out to be, Thura was finally home alone and needed to act quickly.

With a quick peek out the window to make sure no one was lingering around the house, Thura ran into her parent's bedroom. As she approached her father's closet, she remembered the games she used to play as a child with her close friend. While her parents would sit on the front porch every late afternoon, the children would run aimlessly throughout the house, playing hide and seek with each other.

The images cycled over in her mind as she thought about the first time she hid in her father's closet. Thura remembered how dark the closet used to be when the door closed, but how the light would creep in through the crack at its base. She remembered how she would see the shadow of her friend and hear her soft footfall, knowing she was seconds from being found. Then, there was the smell of her father's clothes and how they would hang down and surround her. When she would close her eyes, she imagined they were closer. While their relationship had always been good, a distance always separated them.

Throughout Thura's childhood, there had been moments when she felt close to her father. However, there were even more times when she felt far away from him. Of course, there had always been the subtle smiles and the squeezing of her hand throughout her childhood. But no matter how intimate those moments appeared, there always seemed to be a distance with him.

Despite hints of her father's goodness, they were eclipsed by moments when a darker part of him emerged. Thura could never reconcile these two people she saw in him. She often wondered how he could have moments of such goodness yet feel no remorse for lying to everyone in Patrida or killing and imprisoning good people.

On the other hand, she wondered why he stopped the execution and what his motivation could have possibly been. Could it have been his goodness breaking through, or was it something else? Thura honestly did not know what to believe about her father. All she knew was the kind of relationship she wanted with him, but that he could never reciprocate for some reason. Despite his stark inconsistencies as a father and a human being, she loved him and felt empathy toward him.

Thura opened her father's closet door and got down on her hands and knees. She moved aside a pair of his old sandals and pushed down on one of the loose floorboards in the front corner, the same way she had when she was seven years old. As the floorboard moved out of place, it revealed a handcrafted and intricately designed cedar box with the Patridian flag carved into the top.

Thura had only opened the box briefly one other time but had been too terrified of being caught to inspect everything in it thoroughly. She only remembered three items inside of it- her father's weathered, leather journal, a curved hand-carved knife with the words *Live By the Sword* etched into it, and a large, unused, commemorative key Thura believed could be used for the prison door. While she knew one of the guards held the usage key, she deduced that her father had been given the commemorative key, along with the knife, as symbols of his leadership and Patrida's values.

Thura closed the box and started to put it back below the floorboard when the front door opened. Immediately grabbing the piece of wood, Thura slid it back into place. As she stood up, Tyran walked into their parent's room.

"What are you doing in father's closet?" Tyran demanded.

Thura put her hands behind her back. Her brother's sudden appearance shook her.

"Are you hiding something from me, sister?" Tyran asked. "What do you have in your hands?"

Thura, who had somewhat regained her composure, calmly responded to her brother.

"It is just a shirt for father," she said.

"Then why is it behind your back?" he asked.

Tyran stepped toward Thura and grabbed both of her arms, pulling them out from behind her back. Ripping away from her brother, Thura held out both hands to reveal one of her father's shirts.

"When the crowd seized father, they tore his shirt," Thura explained. "I thought I would get another one for him before leaving the house."

Suspicious of his sister's story but not having time to interrogate her at the moment, Tyran grabbed her arm, pulling her from the room and then out of the house onto the Monon.

"You need to come immediately, Thura," he yelled. "I've been told to bring you with me."

CHAPTER 6

As the procession made its way down the Monon and approached the gallows, the spectacle attracted nearly every person in Patrida. The intense clamor of the evolving crowd drew even those who lived on the outskirts and edges of town. Children ran along each side of the street. They cheered and laughed without any idea what was transpiring. The sheer madness of the moment tore at the fabric of order in Patrida and left many staring in disbelief. While the number of detractors that opposed Ochi had slowly been growing at the behest of Fovos and his inner circle, there were still more citizens that supported their leader and had confidence in his leadership. So while many chanted in opposition, more people stood staring in shock.

Fovos, stopping in front of the gallows, turned to face the crowd. Imitating the religious leader, who was still nowhere to be seen, he raised one hand to the sky to quiet the crowd and smiled. As Fovos surveyed the audience he had attracted, he nodded in the direction of Patrida's leader. At once, the men surrounding Ochi forcibly strong-armed the fully resistant leader up thirteen steps to the wooden platform that was visible to everyone along the entire length of the Monon. The crowd grew deathly silent, except for the cries of Thura, who had finally pulled away from Tyran. She was attempting to push her way through the compactness of the crowd.

"What is happening! Father! Please, someone!" Thura cried loudly, pushing through the people.

Upon hearing his daughter's voice, Ochi violently began to wrestle the men again to no avail. A mountainous, heavyset man, who looked to be twice Ochi's size, put him in a bear hug from behind, while two men on each side grabbed his seizing arms. Ochi had been known for his brute, physical strength and endurance when he was younger, but he was no longer that strong, nor did he have the stamina he once did.

The men wrestled him toward one of the square hatches on the wooden platform. Thura's cries intensified. In an attempt to get closer to the gallows, the young woman began to forcefully push her way through the maze of people. She knocked both men and women to the side. At last close enough to catch a glimpse of her father's face, Thura locked eyes with him. He was desperate.

"What are you doing to my father!" Thura screamed. "What are you doing to him! Where is my mother? Where is Father Prodido? Please, someone! Pali! Machi! Anyone, help!"

Amidst the chaos, no one had noticed the absence of the religious leader or the brothers. That is until they heard Thura's desperate cries among them. The crowd's deafening quiet transformed into an eruption of murmuring and chatter that echoed off the buildings on each side of the street, making it even louder than it really was.

People could be heard asking about Father Prodido. Many of them speculated that he must be the one behind the stunt. Fovos, still standing with his hand raised, received the same speculation from those close to the front. With a nervous smile growing beneath his mustache, the opposition leader gently moved his arm up and down, trying to quiet the crowd.

Not to be silenced, especially by Fovos, Thura shouted louder. Her voice was too distracting for anyone to pay attention to anything Fovos tried to say. Finally, toward the front of the crowd, Thura broke through the last few people and stood face to face with her father's captor.

Fovos, avoiding eye contact, glanced over the young woman's shoulder to a few of his men in the crowd and nodded. As the men grabbed her, Thura went into a frenzy of screaming and shouting. She desperately tried to rip away from their restraint.

In response, Ochi began to struggle more violently, this time from the platform. But with three men still holding him down, one the size of a small elephant, his rebellion was in vain. Receiving a final gasp of restrained profanities from Ochi, the opposition leader turned his attention toward his audience.

"My good people!" Fovos called out. "You may be wonderin' why your Excellency is here on stage this morning. Well, you're in luck, because I'm gonna tell you. As you fine people know, we have savages marchin' toward Patrida, aka toward your children and your homes."

A visible terror covered the face of every person along the Monon. If there had been any noise at all when Fovos first began to speak, silence and fear now gripped the entire town of Patrida. While everyone had been nervous and afraid at the first sight of the prisoner being led through town the evening prior, the words of Fovos were even more ominous and terrifying. Someone had at last admitted to them that a threat was truly imminent. But the gravity of the moment could not fully restrain the subtle comedic sarcasm of the opposition leader.

"Your Excellency here wanted me to gather you fine folks together so that he could tell you why he's not been taking this threat very seriously," Fovos said, staring daggers through Ochi. As his smile faded, it was evident that Fovos' comedic routine had run its course. Stern hostility erupted without warning.

"We're waiting! Speak!" Fovos screamed at Ochi.

The guards picked up Patrida's leader and shook him down as if their coercion would provoke him to speak.

While Ochi was not afraid to play nice to save his neck, he would not be humiliated in front of the entire town. Although the odds appeared unevenly stacked against him, he would not be told by some idiotic lackey what he was going to do or how he was going to do it. He was still the leader of Patrida and would not be giving some no-name cartoon character the satisfaction of his compliance.

But as Ochi attempted to piece together a response to the madness surrounding him on the gallows, he realized he had been abandoned by those closest to him. He could not find Velos, Father Prodido, Tyran, nor the brothers anywhere along the Monon. Bewildered and betrayed by their absence, Ochi was sure someone had set him up. However, he could not understand what their motives could have been.

His immediate impulse of anger quickly became anxiety and despair that moved from his neck and chest throughout his entire body. A profound sense of isolation and fear paralyzed him. His heart began to beat rapidly in his chest, which was immediately accompanied by a sharp ringing in his ears that only intensified by the second. Suddenly, Ochi became disoriented. His eyes manically surveyed the crowd, desperate to find anyone. His frantic searching ended with the only one who had not abandoned him. Although he knew his daughter had been there all along, he finally saw her.

~

The quiet that lined the Monon became a low rumble as the people toward the back and those comprising the middle began moving their bodies intently to make a center aisle. At once, like the parting of the Red Sea, a direct route opened progressively through the masses. Pali and Machi forcefully moved those lingering in the center out of the way. Velos, Tyran, and Father Prodido followed closely behind. Not a single person on the Monon could make sense of their sudden appearance. Some wondered if they were arriving to formally condemn Ochi or if they had arrived just in time to save him from the subterfuge of Fovos and his mob.

The brothers, lacking any visible emotion, marched resolutely up the steps and stood on each side of the platform facing the crowd. Velos walked over to where Thura was being held and stood beside them. Father Prodido calmly took center stage and stood right beside Fovos.

This was the kind of melodrama the people of Patrida loved. It was a real-life soap opera of conflict and emotion. It was titillating, satisfying their every carnal craving because it was so easy to consume. But the great sadness of the people was that they could not see the forest for the trees. They could not comprehend that every leader was playing them.

They were people easily blown from side to side by the ever-changing winds. They were consumers who devoured whatever someone put in front of them without discernment. They were inhabitants of houses built upon foundations of sinking sand. They were plants without roots, suffering from a significant lack of nourishment.

But from their narrow vantage point, they could not see it. Truth was nothing more than the next narrative to be believed. Their eagerness to blindly follow and their gullibility in being so easily manipulated proved their bondage and their desperate need for liberation, although they already claimed to be free.

Father Prodido stood before the crowd like Moses before the Israelites and raised his staff above his head.

"Brothers and sisters of Patrida," the religious leader cried. "As your humble servant, may I be so bold to ask what exactly is going on here?"

Mass confusion led to yet another significant uproar, which Father Prodido had been expecting with his initial question. While everyone was preoccupied with trying to understand what was happening, the religious leader leaned in toward Fovos and whispered in his ear. It appeared to everyone as if Father Prodido spoke with Fovos to understand the situation. But up close, it was something entirely different.

"You imbecile!" Father Prodido screamed in a hushed tone. "I said a little fear and then Sanctuary! For the love of god, you idiot! Look at what you have created!"

Fovos, unfazed by the religious leader's tone and still enjoying the chaotic charade he had created, whispered back.

"I thought the gallows was a nice touch," he said.

Frustrated by the incompetence of his accomplice, Father Prodido continued before the crowd.

"I regret to say that there have been some significant misunderstandings. These mistakes should have been settled in person rather than turned into a public spectacle. While we believe there is reason to stay alert and ready ourselves for an impending attack, be assured that our forces are still deployed in the woods around Patrida and are giving us regular updates. Lastly, the council will sit down with Fovos to discuss these misunderstandings as soon as we adjourn. So please, go about your day and trust that you are in good hands. Let us meet back at Sanctuary this evening. May God bless you all."

As everyone began to depart, Prodido turned and nodded at Pali. The head guard, without hesitation, vigorously pushed away Ochi's captors on the platform. Irritated and embarrassed, Ochi straightened his ripped shirt as best he could and walked down the stairs toward Father Prodido and Fovos. His brown eyes locked in on Fovos, and he charged. Summoning the strength of his youth, Ochi knocked his adversary to the ground and covered him. The two men grappled and rolled around in the dirt, kicking up dust that was as prominent as their shouting and grunting.

Unamused, Father Prodido watched but let it continue longer than he usually would have. Pali and Machi even began to run toward the scuttle to break it up, but the religious leader gave them a look, indicating a few more seconds. It was difficult to determine precisely what Father Prodido's motives were in letting Ochi knock around his antagonizer. Either he believed Fovos needed to be pummeled for creating a bigger circus than he had intended. Or, he thought Ochi might be less likely to execute Fovos if he was able to rough him up a bit. Both were likely true. But Father Prodido did not need Fovos dead no matter the real reason. He was too valuable of an asset at the moment.

Those who had not already dispersed began to congregate again, this time to watch Ochi and Fovos settle the matter for themselves. But as the small crowd began to cheer, Father Prodido released the brothers to rip them apart. The last thing he needed was another big crowd requiring another speech. Without stopping or even acknowledging the two men, Father Prodido walked solemnly between them.

"Now, you gentlemen will follow me," he said. "We will finish this in the council room."

As the men walked together along the Monon toward the council room, Tyran rushed up from behind and followed them. Still standing at the gallows with her daughter, Velos turned her attention from the leaders to Thura. The matriarch, as stern as Thura had ever seen her, grabbed the front of her daughter's dress and pulled her close. Her mother's face was no more than an inch from her own. She could feel her intensity.

"Where were you?" Velos said. "You abandoned me when they took your father. I ran after them and thought you were right behind me the entire time. But you were nowhere to be found, just like the rest of them! I didn't have anyone, except your brother, who I found walking around aimlessly in the crowd."

"I am sorry," Thura mouthed, though not meaning it.

"Do you think I had time to worry about what you were doing, Thura?" Velos asked, not expecting an answer. "Your father was being taken to the gallows, for god's sake! How did I know that someone had not taken you as well! Did you think about that! When I should have been only concerned about your father, I had to send Tyran off to find you! And what were you doing? He told me that you were in my room doing god knows what."

Thura remembered she was holding her father's shirt. She knew, however, that using it as an excuse with her mother was super thin and bordered on ridiculous. There was no way it would convince her mother or stand up to her intense scrutiny. So rather than answering her, Thura put her hand on top of her mother's tight grip and gently lowered her hand. As the young woman pulled away, she held the shirt high in the air and took off running down the Monon.

"Father's shirt!" Thura shouted out. "I forgot to give it to him!"

~

A palpable unease permeated the council room as the men sat down at the table. Father Prodido placed himself directly across from Fovos while Ochi and Tyran sat opposing one another. This configuration meant that Ochi had to sit right beside his adversary. Without waiting for the religious leader's proper formalities, Ochi, still full of raw, unfiltered emotion, began to speak.

"Does anyone want to tell me what the hell is going on here?" Ochi said, raising his voice to an uncomfortable level.

Startled, the men raised their eyes from the table. But no one immediately responded so Ochi continued.

"I have to tell you, from where I sit, this looks like some kind of conspiracy," he said. "Pretty convenient for every person I consider to be a friend, or a part of my family, to be mysteriously absent while this jackass tries to hang me!"

While Father Prodido desperately wanted to offer perspective, he knew he should let Ochi continue to burn off his anger before speaking.

"Where were you, Father?" Ochi asked. "Pretty amazing that you were nowhere to be found. And you, Tyran. My own son. You finally show up when he shows up. You see how this looks?"

Ochi paused and stared at the men, who could not even return eye contact with the leader.

"You guys show up at the last second to save the day," Ochi said. "Isn't that convenient? All this was ironically happening right after I met with you guys at your house, Father, and told you that I was reconsidering what to do with the prisoner."

Ochi then turned to his nemesis.

"And you. It's not Mr. Ochi, nor will it ever be Mr. Ochi to you again. Do you understand?" he demanded. "I am your leader, and you will address me as such. You know nothing of a threat because you are an ignorant fool. All you know is how to scare people and work them into a frenzy."

It had been a while since the men had seen this kind of energy and aggression from Ochi. Of course, it was justified, and Father Prodido knew it. But at the same time, he also knew he needed to interject before the leader went any further. Ochi was getting precariously close to punishing Fovos, and if that happened, Father Prodido believed Fovos might expose their relationship and their brief, early morning conversation.

"Your Excellency, if I may," Father Prodido gently interrupted.

Ochi immediately stopped speaking and turned toward the religious leader, as if giving him permission, but signaling that he was walking on thin ice.

"I know that the circumstantial evidence appears to point toward our guilt," Father Prodido began, "but I can assure you there really has been a significant misunderstanding."

Ochi sat up straight in his chair and opened his eyes wider, communicating that he was moments from jumping out of his chair at the religious leader.

"You are testing my patience, Father," Ochi warned, "but I am curious what kind of story you're concocting."

"When you left my house this morning," Father Prodido continued, "I told Tyran that I was going to take my usual early morning walk by the creek. But I have to admit that I was deeply bothered by your decision to not execute the prisoner immediately."

Ochi leaned forward and put his muscular arms on the table, slowly cracking each knuckle of both hands.

"As I told you at the time," Father Prodido continued. "I believed that delaying the execution would send the wrong message to the townspeople. They need to feel safe and protected from outsiders. But again, as I told you this morning, you are my leader, and I will humbly follow your lead. So I went into the woods to clear my head. I walked through Sanctuary and then along the route I normally follow. I was not so far away that I did not hear the commotion in town, but I also was not close enough to be there immediately. I turned and began my trek back, but as you know, I do not move as swiftly as I once did."

"I ran to get him from the woods," Tyran interjected. "Well, I was in the bathroom in my house at first, but then I ran outside and saw mother frantically looking for anyone to help her. I knew I couldn't stop the mob all by myself, so I ran into the woods to find him. But before reaching him, I saw a guard and told him what was happening. He told me that both Pali and Machi were doing rounds in the woods like they do every day. We agreed that I would find Father Prodido, and he would go find the brothers."

It appeared that Ochi was buying the story, or at a minimum, had not stopped its telling.

"Yes, and that is when Tyran located me, and the guard located the brothers," Father Prodido said. "As we exited the woods, we all came together in Sanctuary and began our march down the Monon. We understand how conspiratorial this all appeared to you, and we are sincerely sorry. We are all deeply remorseful that we were not there for you, your Excellency. You are our leader, and you have our sincere and utmost allegiance."

Ochi turned and looked directly at Fovos, who had remained deathly silent as Father Prodido and Tyran recounted their stories.

"Well, it looks like this all comes back to you," Ochi said, "and I can't wait to hear what you come up with."

Father Prodido and Tyran prayed for a contrite and apologetic Fovos. But they were about to witness the opposite. Realizing he was virtually untouchable, Fovos leaned back in his chair, put his hands behind his head, and smiled from ear to ear.

"I don't know, leader. See, I can still say leader. Did you hear it? That should count for somethin', right? What do you gentlemen think?" Fovos asked as he looked at his accomplices.

Father Prodido and Tyran froze in fear of what he might say next.

"But I digress," Fovos said. "I'm not sure any of this comes back to me at all. In fact, if I may be so bold, Mr. Ochi, I think it all comes back to you."

Ochi stood abruptly from his chair and waited for Fovos to stand up before taking him out.

"Let's go! Stand up!" Ochi yelled. "You're nothing but a rodeo clown! I'm going to personally take you to the gallows with my own two hands and put that damn rope around your neck."

"Sit down, leader," Fovos said, putting both of his feet on the council room table and rocking back in his chair. "We're not done talkin' here. If you still want to break my neck after this, I will gladly walk up those thirteen steps and put that old noose around my neck all by myself."

Ochi looked at Father Prodido, who raised his eyebrows, indicating that maybe he should at least hear what his adversary had to say. Ochi remained standing and ready to aggress but allowed Fovos to continue.

"Listen, leader," Fovos said, reaching for a toothpick out of his shirt pocket. "We're all wantin' the same thing around here in Patrida. These fine people just want to be safe. That's all. But how can these fine people enjoy their freedoms if they're always lookin' over their shoulders worryin' about savages comin' out of the woods? They can't. Do you guys have any firewater? I'm gettin' thirsty here."

Glaring at Father Prodido, Ochi's red face indicated that he had reached his limit.

"How many of these fine people have you talked to lately, leader?" Fovos asked before Ochi had a chance to make a move. "They're afraid. Now I know you're a busy man and can't talk to everyone. But all I'm sayin' is that we need to see some good ol' fashioned Patrida resolve from you about now. Cause the way I see it, you really don't have a choice in the matter. So here's my ultimatum to you … "

Ochi went for Fovos' throat with both hands. As the leader hit his neck, Fovos fell backwards out of his chair. Scrambling under the table to the other side of the room, Fovos moved as if that was part of his plan. He deftly danced back and forth from one side of the room to the other like a wild animal to avoid being caught.

"You're going to die either way, Ochi!" Fovos shouted. "Don't you understand that? The people are turning against you. You're going to die!"

The room suddenly stopped.

"Listen to me, leader," Fovos continued, breathing heavily. "Not only are you going to hang that savage tomorrow at high noon, but you're also going to hang the old woman with him. And if you don't, I will turn this town upside-down in a fear you have never had the privilege to behold. And I can guarantee that if you don't oblige, the fine people of Patrida will be happy to throw a necktie party for you as well, dear leader. Do you understand me!"

Ochi remained silent but burning.

"Oh, and one more thing," Fovos shouted. "You try to hurt ol' Fovos, or even think about laying a finger on ol' Fovos, and every single one of these fine people will know it's you. You got me?"

Seething with anger, Ochi had no interest in dignifying Fovos with a response.

"In fact, my little second-rate concierge service will be delighted to make reservations for your wife and daughter, as well," Fovos continued. "Yes, sir! We might just have ourselves a party if you know what I mean. On second thought, no reservations needed! If you don't execute those prisoners, your wife and daughter will be hanging right there with you! Do you understand me! So how about you just play nice and announce your plan for an execution tomorrow. You do that, and ol' Fovos will be happy to tell everybody around Patrida how great a leader you are. You see? It's a win-win, your Excellency. And you know, I am always lookin' out for those win-wins."

Fovos had backed Ochi into a corner, but the leader was not going to give him the satisfaction of knowing it. While he was not completely sold on Father Prodido or Tyran's stories earlier, he knew Fovos was the fulcrum of turmoil. He even supposed that it was Fovos who had manipulated Father Prodido and Tyran against him. As Ochi circled back to his seat at the table, he could not turn around and face the men. He stared at the empty wall with an intense heat radiating from within.

"Get out of here!" Ochi screamed at Fovos without turning around. "Get out of here now! Before I take my chances with killing you with my bare hands!"

Unfazed by the leader's tone and threat, Fovos slowly made his way to the door. With his hand on the doorknob, he turned toward Ochi with a half cartoonish, half villainous smile and offered one more knife to the gut.

"You've got until this evening to make your decision," Fovos said. "I'll be eager to hear what you decide, Mr. Ochi."

CHAPTER 7

From a distance, the island was a tiny dot immersed in vast blue. Below, the azure sea cradled it. Above, the cloudless, cerulean sky enveloped it. The invitation was not so much what could be seen but what was below the surface. An uninhabited paradise was the allure, but the real bounty could only be found from within.

The welcoming aberration danced softly on the horizon as the calm sea found its rhythm. Wood creaked, and the waters coaxed the boat closer toward the shoreline, with the only resistance being the salty brine mist blowing delicately on sun-cracked lips and overexposed faces. The passengers were in a trance-like state, partially from the steady cadence, but more so from the opportunity of freedom that lay ahead.

Tyran rested his wet and weary head on his father's sunburnt arm as his mother ran her long fingers through his wavy, black hair. The boy had traveled remarkably well, complaining very little, during their three-day voyage. While this particular trip was certainly different in the number of people joining them, Tyran had already been to this island at least three other times over the last three years with his father.

"What will we do when we first get there, Kala?" the young boy whispered to his father in an almost inaudible voice, but still loud enough to be heard over the crashing waves.

"Just like our trips, Tyran. We will need to have water, fire, and basic shelter first," Ochi said. "And then, we will make time to lie on the beach together. The skies are clear, and the stars should be delightful tonight."

Tyran smiled lovingly at his dad.

Kala was the family name, but Tyran called his dad Kala since he could first speak. When others said "Ochi Kala," the young boy thought his dad's name was Kala, and he would repeat it over and over. Even when his mother tried to correct him by saying, "No Tyran. Daddy's name is Oh-Chee," the boy would yell, "Kala!" and laugh hysterically.

The name caught on with family and friends when Tyran was young. Everyone loved the boy erupting in a wild and nonsensical toddler laughter every time they said the name. They did it for Tyran. So while the entire family was technically Kala, only one person would go by that name throughout Tyran's childhood… his dad.

Kala delighted in sharing his love of the outdoors with his son, and the island was his regular escape for what it offered. While solitude was a lost commodity on the mainland, it was in precious abundance on the island. Despite having the entire landmass to themselves, the father and son had found their perfect spot where they set up camp each year. It was on the west side of the island closest to the mainland. The area was wide open, flat, and perfectly accommodating. A freshwater spring hugged a beautifully forested area, creating a creek that flowed into the woods. It was ideal for hiking and exploring.

As the boats landed on the shore, the boy lifted his head and looked up to his father. Without words, Tyran appeared to be communicating that he was not ready to share their island with others. Kala could see it in his eyes. Down deep, his father was not prepared to share it either. While their situation necessitated this move to the island, he also knew they would be sacrificing something special between them.

The island was where he first taught Tyran how to build a fire with a flint and know the difference between edible and inedible berries. It was in those woods where the two ran animal trails and first discovered the towering megalith jutting out of the mossy ground where they would sit for hours talking and eating their lunch together. It was where the father and son discovered the largest and broadest tree they had ever seen, with branches extending like a canopy over an intricately exposed root system on the ground. The two would lie under it among the roots. With Tyran's head nestled between his father's arm and chest, the two would gaze up into the dense network of branches and watch the small animals scurry aimlessly through the maze. The island was indeed their place.

Kala's strong-arm reached into the boat, welcoming his son and then his wife and young daughter to their new permanent home. Surrounding them was the busyness and chaos of boats crashing into the shore and people pouring out en masse, many of whom they did not know. Men yelled and directed other vessels approaching. Women carried their children and supplies from the boats toward the open area next to the woods and immediately began filling their freshwater containers. Children ran around screaming at each other as if discovering another dimension of freedom they had never known. Amidst the madness, Tyran stayed close to his dad.

"How are you doing?" Kala asked as he placed his hand behind Tyran's head.

Tyran's pause told him everything he needed to know.

"How about you and I walk down to our rock and have a snack together?" Kala asked.

Tyran looked up at his father with a smile. It was a small consolation for their new normal, for the mass intrusion of "their place." But at the moment, he would do anything to escape the people. He would do anything to hike alone with his dad down to their rock. There would be plenty of daylight remaining to build a temporary shelter when they returned from their excursion.

As the family dropped off their supplies in the area where they would eventually set up camp, Tyran and Kala eagerly made their way toward the wood's edge. That was when they heard a cry that sounded like a woman in distress. Velos was screaming at someone. But it was not immediately apparent who she was yelling at or what the situation was. Kala instructed his son to stay put as he ran frantically toward his wife. Approaching the area, he saw a man grabbing Velos' arm and pulling her close as she tried unsuccessfully to tear away. When the man saw Kala running toward them, he abruptly let go of her arm and backed away with both hands in the air.

"Whoa! Whoa! Whoa! Easy there, friend!" the man called out.

Rather than promptly tackling him, Kala stopped abruptly in front of the aggressor to see what the problem was.

"Explain yourself," Kala demanded.

"Is this your old lady?" the man asked. "Oh, well, I beg your pardon, mister. I was just tellin' your lady friend here that if she were by herself, ol' Fovos would be happy to show her a good time tonight."

Kala took a step forward and got right in the man's face.

"She has a husband," Kala said. "From this point forward, if you come within fifty feet of her, you'll wish you had never landed on this island. Understand?"

"Well, yes, sir. We don't need to start off like this, do we?" the mustached man asked, putting his hand out in apology, his smile extending from ear to ear.

Kala turned his back on the man and began walking toward where Tyran had been standing. But he was no longer there. Kala's walk became a full-on manic sprint toward the woods as he nervously began shouting his son's name. He could not find Tyran anywhere. He ran into the woods alongside the stream and continued to cry out. While Kala thought it would be highly unusual for someone to have abducted Tyran, he could not be entirely sure of anything at the moment. As he approached a fork in the stream, he continued to shout out Tyran's name until he heard a response back. With a sigh of relief, he knew Tyran was okay and was already at their rock.

Kala walked down the embankment and saw Tyran standing in front of the megalith next to another man. Unsure of what to do or what to say because he did not recognize the gentleman, Kala stopped and stared at him. The man looked up slowly with a smile on his face and walked toward him.

"This blessed child is your son. Is that correct, Kala?" the man asked. "I have heard so much about you from my sister before arriving on the island. Let me formally introduce myself. My name is Prodido, and I am humbled to meet you and be of service in any way possible."

~

The council room was as constricted as it ever had been for Ochi. Despite no one having placed the noose over his head at the gallows earlier, he felt an increasing tightness around his neck. The thoughts of their first arrival on the island replayed in his mind as he sat back down at the table with Father Prodido and Tyran.

Ochi remained in somber silence without caring to look at either one of the men. Instead, he stared at the single, old painting on the wall of a man in a wooden fishing boat sitting beside a young child, each with their hands gripping the row, preparing to go to sea. On the child's face was a solemn but nervous expression, while the man gazed at the child with a loving reassurance.

For minutes, Ochi stared at the portrait, looking back and forth at the faces of the young child and older man. It evoked both sadness and longing within him. He remembered the emotions of first being on the boat and the hope he had for a new life with his family on the island. However, those sentiments had long past, as he considered the decline of Patrida and evaluated his current situation.

Still staring at the painting, Ochi turned his attention from their faces to the hazy horizon where other sailboats disappeared in the distance. He closed his eyes and imagined following those boats and

sailing away from his problems in hopes of discovering peace else-
where. But as he opened his eyes and looked back one last time at
the child and the older man, he saw their sail already lowered in their
boat. They would not be following the other boats out to sea.

Ochi knew Patrida had become something he could have never
envisioned when he took his first step out of the boat onto the beach.
He often wondered if making different decisions would have changed
anything. What if he had trusted his gut instinct from the beginning
and insisted on sending Fovos back to the mainland after their first
encounter? What if he had not created so much distance between
himself and Tyran over the years? What if their relationship had
remained as close as when Tyran was a young boy? Would their relationship be different today if the inconsequential affairs of Patrida had
not preoccupied him for years? Would Father Prodido have had such a
profound influence on Tyran had Ochi been closer to him as he grew
older? He could not help but think about how he had contributed to
these problems.

Recognizing Ochi was not in any condition to discuss the issue
of the executions, the religious leader stood up quietly and left with
Tyran following behind him. However, Ochi continued to sit alone
at the table in deep regret, not taking his eyes off the picture. Minute
after minute, he continued to stare at the child and the older man.
Again, he looked at the child's face and then back at the older man's
face and then back again. He wondered what the point of the painting
was and what the painter was trying to convey.

Ochi knew the child and older man were not going anywhere, so
he wondered what exactly he was missing. He looked at the older man
intently one last time and stared at the expression on his face. At that
moment, Ochi realized the painting was not about the horizon or
sailing off into the distance to find something else. It was about what
was in the boat.

For Ochi, it was about the man in the painting. He saw something in him he desired for himself. He did not see a man constantly looking to the horizon hoping to discover peace somewhere else, but a man experiencing it as he sat in the boat with the young child. Ochi desired to find that kind of peace. But at the same time, he understood the near impossibility of finding it in Patrida.

~

From around the corner of the hallway, Thura knew her father must still be in the council room because she had not seen him leave with the other two men. Not only was she curious as to how the meeting went with Fovos and what they had discussed, she desperately needed to give her father the shirt she had been carrying around since he was apprehended. At this point, giving him the shirt had way more to do with Thura selling her story than her father having a fresh shirt, so she made her way down the dimly lit hallway toward the council room door and opened it.

Ochi walked out of the room and faced his daughter. She could tell that something was on his mind. But she could also tell from his demeanor and red eyes that it was not a good idea to ask him about the meeting. She put her arm out and offered him the shirt. Ochi's eyes glistened as he took it and hugged his daughter. He then turned and defeatedly walked down the stairway and out the door toward the Monon.

There were so many unanswered questions and so much lingering intrigue that Thura could not help but follow her father. But as soon as she got to the base of the stairs and exited the doorway leading to the Monon, she saw her father enter Tyran's house. Thura, as casually as possible, walked across the street, attempting to avoid any suspicion she could potentially attract. Convinced no one was watching her, she slipped between Tyran's house and the house next door.

Since the houses were so close to one another, likely less than a few feet, Thura was virtually imperceptible unless someone was intentionally trying to see her. The young woman edged up close to one of the side windows but was too terrified to look inside. She was fearful Tyran or her father would see her. Instead, Thura tried to listen, although most of the conversation was muted and indiscernible.

As Thura was about to give up, she heard her father begin to cry. While his eyes had been red earlier when he exited the council room, she had never seen nor heard her father cry before. Whatever was going on, she knew something was not right, and it left her aching for him.

Thura knew she had to peer around the edge of the window and see him, even if it was the only bit of solidarity she could offer. Desperately desiring to know what was going on inside, she took a deep breath and cautiously turned her head toward the room in which they were still talking. Her brother was standing with his back to her, but she could see her father's face. His eyes were closed as he embraced Tyran. When the two separated, Thura looked into his tired, red eyes and read the words that came off his lips.

"This madness has got to stop," Ochi said, "and an execution is the only solution."

Although her father was still talking, Thura turned away from the window and could no longer see his face. She did not want to see her father's face. The sound coming from the window were the deadened tones of a man who represented everything wrong with Patrida. Whatever glimpses of humanity Thura believed she saw in her father over the years, or even as recently as the hug outside the council room, it was eclipsed by a darkness that continued to suffocate the entire community. Thura knew without question her father was at the center of Patrida's problem.

Shuffling between the houses, Thura exited the backside without being noticed. She sprinted down the side street as fast as she could toward Odigo and Sophia's cell at the other end of the Monon. The young woman hastily flew past the edge dwellers, and other people pushed to the margins of Patrida. Thura began crying as she ran. Her heart ached so badly for her family and everyone who lived in her town, but she did not know what to do to help them. All she wanted to do was leave everything behind. With every stride, she believed she was running into a different future, a future far away from Patrida. Tears ran down her cheeks as the wind blew them off of her face.

As Thura turned down the alleyway and sprinted toward their cell, she stopped short of the entrance because the jail door had been propped slightly open. Hesitant to look through the crack of the door to see who was on the other side, Thura inched forward and spotted a guard who had finished cleaning the cell. At once, the guard turned, but Thura promptly stepped out of sight. Immediately from behind, several people began to shuffle down a short, adjacent alleyway. Thura believed she had no choice but to run toward the Monon and hopefully avoid being caught for loitering near the cell.

But as the young woman began to sprint toward the thoroughfare, she suddenly stopped. Thura had always run away in the past. But this time she would not let fear dictate what she did. Turning around, she defiantly faced the guard leading Odigo and Sophia out of the alleyway and back to their cell. The guard, surprised by the young woman's assertive stance, held Odigo and Sophia back so he could ascertain precisely what the girl was doing. Thura put her hand in her pocket, clutched her father's jail key, and walked directly at them.

The guard's shouting grew louder with Thura's each step, but her eyes were locked on Odigo and Sophia. They could tell by her determined gaze that something had changed. They watched as Thura marched and rebelliously brushed past the guard on his left, bumping him and almost knocking him back. As they turned and followed the young woman, she began to run. Sophia glanced at Odigo, who nodded back with a smile.

CHAPTER 8

The repetitive clanking of chains swaying to and fro accompanied the wafts of frankincense and myrrh permeating the Monon. With each step down the center of the thoroughfare, the swinging gold censer signaled the beginning of a purification ritual, which the religious leader performed before every execution. Looking straight forward, Father Prodido walked in full regalia with patience, placing each foot methodically in front of the other.

The religious leader's slow and deliberate march toward the gallows could have been easily mistaken for somber holiness rooted in a desire to cleanse Patrida and wash her in righteousness. But this dark performance art was nothing less than a power play by the religious leader. Despite the ultimatum Fovos gave Ochi earlier in the council room, Father Prodido did not believe Patrida's leader had the fortitude to take a hard stand before the entire town and execute the prisoners. From the religious leader's perspective, beginning the purification ritual was the perfect move to force Ochi's hand and expose him for what he had become.

Facing Father Prodido, as he gradually made his way westward, were six perfectly formed lines of guards awaiting him. Each guard was cloaked in a black robe, as dark as a moonless night, with hoods draped over their heads so their faces were hidden. In their right hands they held Patridian flags, which were planted firmly in the ground. The scene playing out in front of the gallows could not have been any more exciting or ghoulish, depending on one's perspective. But from the vantage point of those who began lining the Monon, it was undoubtedly the former.

As the religious leader stopped in front of the guards, the gold censer ceased its swinging.

Father Prodido shouted aloud, "Sacrarium Convenae!"

"Sacrarium Convenae!" the guards shouted back louder and in unison.

Resolutely turning, Father Prodido faced eastward toward Sanctuary, his head raised slightly higher in pomp. He began marching with the guards following perfectly behind him. The religious leader had devised the subversive plan earlier, while Ochi remained in the council room following their meeting with Fovos and then while the leader was at Tyran's house. During that time, both Father Prodido and Fovos feverishly moved every piece into place. One mobilized guards in town who were not currently in the field. The other spread the word for everyone else to meet along the Monon. Interestingly, not a single guard nor citizen knew Father Prodido and Fovos had orchestrated the plan without Ochi's knowledge or consent. They all believed Ochi had been the one who initiated the purification ceremony and execution.

As the somber and growing movement continued down the cobblestone road, Ochi ran from the side of his house in a semi-controlled rage. Internally he could have torn Father Prodido to shreds for pulling such a stunt without consulting him first. But externally, he remained calm so as not to stir the passions of the people once again. He was walking a delicate line and needed to play it the right way.

As Ochi walked up next to Father Prodido at the head of the parade, the crowd began to cheer wildly for him, but only because they believed an execution was imminent. For the moment, Ochi was their hero. Father Prodido's powerplay to force Ochi's hand was a brilliant masterstroke and even more diabolical in its execution. It would

either lead to the hanging of Patrida's enemies or expose their leader
as a sympathizer to the enemy.

〜

Sanctuary appeared more peaceful and picturesque than ever. The
rows of stone slab seating artfully contrasted the palette of natural
greens. Abundant waters swelled from the earth beneath the trium-
phant arcs and filled the sacrarium. Sunlight danced on the flow and
revealed a spectrum of luminous colors throughout the water like the
turning of a prism.

Like specters moving into an unsuspecting home, the darkly
cloaked guards floated along the edges and down the center aisle ahead
of Patrida's leaders and townspeople. Each guard successively stopped
in their assigned position and planted their flags into the ground, signaling the area was ready to be occupied. As Ochi and Father Prodido
took their first steps, Tyran rushed forward and joined them from
the side. Instead of standing next to his father while walking down
the aisle, he stood on the opposite side of the religious leader, taking
Father Prodido's right side while his father took the left.

These power dynamics were likely unintentional on the part of the
leaders. However, the image of Father Prodido always being at the
center and Tyran always standing to his right conveyed the real leadership hierarchy of Patrida. Their positioning told the tragic story of a
leader falling from favor. Even more, it was the story of a man and his
son and the growing distance between them.

Though walking as three among hundreds, Ochi felt like he was
walking utterly alone. With each labored step forward, he carried
the heavy weight of Patrida and her transgressions on his shoulders.
The chains of his past misgivings and current regrets shackled him.
Ochi knew there would be no mercy granted, nor forgiveness given,
to a leader who wanted to guide Patrida along a different path. Any

decision acquitting the prisoners and allowing them to go free would be his death sentence. But Ochi could no longer carry his burdens alone and could no longer walk with shackled feet. He would rather die a free man than remain a prisoner from within.

As the crowd hastily took their seats and silence spread among them, Father Prodido took center stage.

"Brothers and sisters, I greet you this splendid evening," he began. "I trust that, despite the uncertainties of the last forty-eight hours, you have been assured by, and remained confident in, God's unwavering providence and your Leadership Council's steadfast resolve. While your continued favor, along with the humble service of the Patridian guard, have certainly blessed us, I would be remiss if I did not take this opportunity to magnify and lift up our glorious leader and his steadfast resilience in these trying times."

Each word uttered by the religious leader was an arrow hitting the target. And Ochi was the target. The leader had to bite his lower lip so he would not call out the charlatan's lies. At this point, Ochi was confident Father Prodido, Fovos, and possibly even Tyran had conspired together to turn the entire town against him. He raged internally with festering anger toward the backstabbing leader. Father Prodido had turned his son against him. Now he was setting the stage to make Ochi an outcast in his own town and the enemy of his own people.

Ochi nauseously closed his eyes and once again saw the painting hanging on the council room wall. He stared at the face of the man sitting in the boat and then looked at the child's face. Ochi had always envisioned that child being Tyran, preparing for yet another trip to the island with him. However, he realized he had been forcing something onto the painting that had never been there. He had only seen the picture for what he thought it ought to be, rather than for what it was. The older man in the boat looked, not at a young boy sitting beside him, but a young girl whose hands joined his on the paddle.

Ochi stared at the young girl in his mind's eye as if she was sitting right next to him in the boat. Despite refusing to see her before, he finally saw her. Regret had ravaged Ochi for so many years that he had neglected what had been with him all along. The painting began to take on an entirely different meaning for him.

Ochi no longer wanted to be consumed with anger toward Patrida or live in constant regret for his mistakes, even his mistakes with Tyran. He no longer wanted to look to the horizon in hopes of his life changing one day. Despite the confines of the small boat, or in his case, the confines of Patrida, he wanted what the older man in the painting had found. Before opening his eyes, Ochi whispered a prayer under his breath.

"As you well know, there was a grave misunderstanding this morning," Father Prodido continued. "But I am happy to report that the Leadership Council gathered together with Fovos. Everyone aired their grievances, cleared their offenses, and agreed upon a new way forward. I now call upon our leader, your Excellency, as he will share with you these exciting developments."

Putting an exclamation mark on his performance for the people, Father Prodido bowed before Ochi in phony submission and then stood off to one side next to Pali and Tyran. As Ochi took his place in the center and faced the crowd, he slowly looked from side to side to locate Thura. Not only was she not sitting next to Velos in the front row, but Ochi could neither find her sitting in the crowd nor trying to sneak in along the side. He desperately wished he could make eye contact with her. There was no way she would begin to understand what he was about to say or why he would say it.

"Greetings, friends and family," the leader began hesitantly.

A blanket of unease covered the crowd with those first words. If they had been unconvinced of Ochi's resolve the last time he stood before them, he was more monotone, unemotional, and detached this time. To the side, Father Prodido discreetly made eye contact with

Fovos. Both men knew what the other was thinking at that moment. Ochi's time as Patrida's leader was expiring. His body language and tone made it evident to everyone. And not a single person suspected either one of them had anything to do with it.

Ochi meagerly continued.

"As the leader of Patrida over the last two decades," he said, "I have always worked for the best interest of our community. You know I've never been as eloquent with my words as Father Prodido. But I have always led with my heart and have always had the best intentions for everyone."

Once again playing to the crowd, the overly animated religious leader looked with astonishment at specific individuals sitting in the audience, shrugging his shoulders quizzically, indicating he had no idea where Ochi was going with his speech.

"With that being said," the leader continued, "to protect the values and integrity of Patrida, I hereby announce the execution by hanging of our two prisoners, which will take place tomorrow at high noon."

Half of the crowd booed, while the other half cheered in jubilation. The difference in reaction had nothing to do with the execution itself but the timing of it. Those who made their disdain known were those closest to Fovos, and predictably, he was the first person who stood up and began shouting at Ochi. Within seconds, dozens more joined him and stood up shouting at the leader. Within a half-minute, Fovos had persuaded the entire crowd, and they began to rage.

Before joining Ochi at center stage, Father Prodido leaned forward and whispered in Pali's ear. At once, both Pali and Machi ran down the center aisle and onto the Monon in a full sprint. The religious leader then nodded at a couple of the guards dressed in black who subsequently stood on each side of him and Ochi. Father Prodido stepped forward and raised his hand to silence the boisterous crowd, but they could not be silenced, not even by the hand of the religious leader.

"Brothers and sisters! Please!" Father Prodido shouted. "Please! Quiet! Everyone quiet! Please!"

The religious leader pleaded with the crowd for minutes before they ultimately quieted enough to hear what he had to say.

Still raising his hand in the air, as if he was holding their silence by sheer will, the religious leader began to speak.

"It is apparent the hand of God is truly upon us at this moment," Father Prodido began. "Not only will justice prevail in Patrida, but we will also ensure our values are maintained, and our future secured. The only way we remain pure as a community is to cleanse ourselves of all unrighteousness. If there are those among us who threaten our beliefs or try to pervert our traditions, we must take a stand. Your Heavenly Father and your Patridian Council both hear your cries to make this land holy once again. Shall we now be the hands, your Excellency?"

Before turning toward Father Prodido, Ochi once again scanned the crowd in vain to locate Thura. He could not find her anywhere. At once, shouts roared the length of the Monon, instantly transforming the quiet of Sanctuary into complete disarray. Pali and Machi tore down the road in wild hysteria and charged the center aisle in unconstrained madness.

Everyone was immediately panic-stricken and terrified by the shocking irrationality of the moment. Fearing for their lives, the crowd stood up and rushed away from the center aisle. No one had ever seen the brothers in such a furor. Even the guards who lined the center aisle believed someone was chasing the brothers and took defensive positions. Not a single person could discern what Pali and Machi were screaming about until they reached the front, and then it became apparent to everyone. The prisoners had escaped.

The woods behind Sanctuary, which had previously given the people of Patrida some sense of security because of the guard outposts, began to hauntingly produce its own shouts and screams. If there had been terror among the people when the brothers ran down the center aisle, it was now exponentially compounded with the sound of people running through the forest and approaching Sanctuary.

Scrambling and haphazardly falling over one another to escape the area, no one really knew what the threat of danger was to them. Women were wailing while grabbing their children. The children were crying in response to their frightened mothers. Fear had been pumped into their minds for so long that their first inclination was an enemy attack.

As the guards and Tyran ran toward the woods to confront the approaching enemy, neither Father Prodido nor Ochi moved an inch from where they had been standing. Both knew there was no threat, nor were they being attacked by anyone. Those who had been shouting from the woods ran out and faced Tyran and his band of shrouded guards. Staring at one another in disbelief, Tyran quickly realized they were not the enemy, only the guards stationed in the wooded outposts.

Amidst the pandemonium and utter disbelief at what had transpired, both Father Prodido and Ochi knew immediately that someone had carefully orchestrated the charade. The only difference between the two men was that Father Prodido had no idea how it happened, while Ochi believed he knew exactly how it happened.

Patrida's leader instantly took off and ran through the maze of people who had not yet figured out there was no threat. Along the Monon, Ochi ran as fast as he could toward the prisoner's cell. He desperately wanted to know if the door had been forced open in some way by the prisoners or if someone had unlocked it.

Since he had not been able to find Thura in the crowd, Ochi believed he already knew the answer, but he wanted to make sure. As he approached the open door, it was apparent there was no damage or forced exit. Someone had clearly unlocked it. And he was nearly certain it had been Thura who unlocked it. But there was only one way to find out definitively. Ochi needed to get back to his house to see if his key was missing. Thura should not have known about the box or the key, but he could not imagine this being any more coincidental.

In Sanctuary, everyone had figured out that no enemy was attacking them, but they remained perplexed by all that had happened. Father Prodido, Tyran, and the Patridian guards assembled and subsequently began to walk the length of the Monon toward the jail so they could investigate and make an assessment of how the prisoners had escaped.

Peering around the corner at the other end of the Monon, Ochi could see they were making their way toward him. Determined to avoid a confrontation at all cost, he turned back and ran down the short alley adjacent to the cell. Within a couple of minutes, the entourage, led by Father Prodido and Tyran, turned from the Monon and approached the open cell door. Ochi, sweating profusely from nervousness, his heart palpitating from fear, walked briskly past the gallows and then turned down a side alley running parallel to the Monon on the other side.

Ochi ran as fast as he could down the alleyway toward the backside of his house, where he took a side door to enter. As he ran up the wooden stairs and reached the last few steps, the door was cracked open. He could see light coming from behind it. He was worried Velos was already in the house searching for Thura herself.

Nervously pushing the door open the rest of the way, Ochi walked into the room with cautious feet. Every candle and oil lamp they owned had been lit, illuminating the room. He paused, anticipating Velos in the house. But the only sound was the gentle crack of each candle's flame.

Ochi called out for both his wife and daughter to no response. Deciding he was in the clear, the leader ran into his room and promptly opened his closet door. As he fell to his knees, Ochi moved everything out of the way and expertly removed the floorboard, which revealed his wooden box below the surface. Opening it, he noticed his commemorative key was indeed missing. In its place, there was a folded piece of paper with his name on it. Ochi carefully put the box down on the floor and removed the letter. With apprehension, he unfolded the note and began to read.

Father,

I guess you figured out I was the one who took your key. I am sure everyone is upset at the moment. At least, that is what I have come to expect from all of you. That is why I took it. There is a sickness in Patrida that has been here since I was young, but I have only recently begun to see it. The other night, after talking to Sophia and your prisoner, whose name is Odigo, by the way, I saw what life could be like, and I really wanted that for myself. But at the same time, I began to see how hopeless and lost Patrida really is and how hopeless and lost you are, as well. You pretend this is the home of freedom, yet you fail to realize you remain its prisoner. You say you fight to protect your values, yet you compromise those values by what you think of others and how you treat them. You try to create virtue by following the rules and by demanding others follow them, yet you have only made compliant people who follow the rules while they die on the inside. I know you can't see it, but Patrida is in total darkness. As their leader, you are completely responsible. You have been and continue to be the problem. You are the sickness of Patrida.

—Thura

Tears fell from Ochi's swollen eyes and covered every heartbreaking word he read. He was devastated. A tightness moved from his heart up through his neck. He felt like someone was gently strangling him with no way to stop it. Rather than holding a letter from his daughter, he wished she was with him instead. If only he could explain to her what he had been feeling over the last year. If only he could share with her the regret and pain he had been carrying with him. If only he had not been so fearful, so private, so isolated. If only she knew he was the one standing on the other side of the storage door in the alleyway. If only he had opened it, he could have told her how proud he was of her for being everything he was too afraid to be himself. If only he could tell her what he finally saw in the painting.

Ochi wiped the tears from his cheeks with his shirt and began to fold the letter when he heard footsteps coming from the stairway. The noise stopped as the person reached the top of the stairs, no doubt taking in the fully illuminated room. Ochi closed the cedar box and hastily placed it back in the corner of the closet before anyone saw what he was doing.

"Thura? Are you in here?" Velos called out.

Ochi stood up and began moving about the room to create enough noise not to startle his wife.

"No. It's me. I'm in the bedroom," Ochi called out with trepidation.

Walking into the bedroom, Velos stared at her husband with stone-faced suspicion.

"What are you doing?" she interrogated with an irritated intensity.

No matter what Ochi could have told her in response, Velos was not going to believe it. She did not fully understand everything that had been going on with him, but she did know that he had not been honest with her at breakfast. Despite what he had initially told her, Ochi had not been out late with Father Prodido the night before. In fact, and in direct contradiction to what Ochi had previously told her, Tyran told her he had seen his father walking the previous night along the Monon. He told her it appeared as if he was going to the gallows. But to Velos, it was not only the lies. His strange and erratic behavior accompanied his shifting, noncommittal attitude toward the prisoner that made her distrust him. She was beginning to believe he had something to do with the prisoners escaping.

Ochi could tell that no matter his response, he would be walking on thin ice. The best he could do was divert his wife's attention onto his missing daughter and away from himself.

"Velos, I'm looking desperately for Thura," Ochi said. "I saw the candles and lanterns burning and noticed the stairway door open, so I thought she was somewhere in the house."

"Have you checked her room?" Velos asked, unrelenting in her skepticism.

A tingling sensation ran up his spine. A million thoughts instantaneously raced through his mind as he tried to merge them into a quick and appropriate response. Ochi anticipated that Father Prodido would demand search parties to retrieve the prisoners. But he had so much at stake with his daughter that he could not risk them apprehending her. With Thura already believing he was the center of Patrida's problems, she would never forgive him, nor would she ever talk to him again if she thought he had anything to do with bringing her back. He knew there was only one way to answer Velos.

"I've looked throughout the entire house, including her room, but can't find her," Ochi said with a hint of desperation in his voice. "I believe someone has abducted her, and she may be in danger."

Velos did not immediately buy his story, but Ochi kept selling it.

"That boy was sent here for a reason, Velos!" Ochi cried out in all the concocted rage he could muster. "Do you not think he hasn't been calculating this very moment when he would make his move? Do you not think he hasn't been looking for the perfect person to take with him? So his people can use her as leverage? Are you seriously going to doubt me in this when the life of our daughter could very well be on the line?"

A crack had surfaced in Velos' disposition, but Ochi's story was interrupted by the sound of more steps in the stairway. Both Ochi and Velos ran into the main room and saw Father Prodido, Tyran, and Pali standing together.

"The jail door was intact, Ochi," Father Prodido said. "We could not find any apparent damage to it. It looks as if someone unlocked it."

"Father, there is a more pressing concern at the moment," Ochi cried, attempting to redirect. "Velos and I believe Thura has been taken against her will by the prisoner. She may be in danger. For all we know, the guard's key could have been picked by the hostile. We can't even guarantee the guards locked the door after taking the prisoners out for the last time. We can investigate later but must absolutely focus on Thura and get her back safely."

Father Prodido glanced at Velos. The religious leader was searching for any reason at all to immediately dismiss Ochi's story. While he thought the leader was grasping for anything within reach to keep from falling, Velos appeared to be bothered enough by the story to at least make him pause for the moment.

"I am sorry to hear of this development with your dear daughter," Father Prodido said, playing along with Ochi's narrative. "We will investigate later. If this is true, how do you propose we proceed?"

"If the hostile believes the guards are hunting him down," Ochi began, "it will only put Thura in more danger. That's the last thing we need right now. They don't need to feel threatened. I propose I go by myself to get her back. I'll track them from a safe distance. When I determine it's safe enough to move in, I'll negotiate her release. It's the least threatening option we have at this point, in my humble opinion."

Father Prodido looked to the ground, stroked his chin contemplatively, and acted as if he was seriously considering Ochi's plan. The truth was that he did not believe the story in the first place. He was not quite sure how it all happened, but the facts of an abduction did not appear to add up.

Father Prodido knew Thura spent way too much time at the jail over the last few years when taking food to Sophia. While he could not completely rule out the possibility the prisoner had somehow manipulated Thura and taken her as a hostage as potential leverage, he did not believe she was really in danger. The people they had driven out of Patrida would not even fight back when attacked. There was no way they would send someone into Patrida to abduct the leader's daughter.

However, Ochi's plan was intriguing to Father Prodido. Not only had the enemies fled, but Ochi would soon be leaving Patrida to join them. This evolving situation would give the religious leader unprecedented and unrestricted space to turn the town completely against him. Father Prodido would carefully paint Ochi as a colluder and sympathizer to the enemy. This very subtle move would ultimately give him the power to fulfill his religious vision for Patrida and eradicate the unrighteous from the island.

Nodding his head while still looking down and attempting to cloak his excitement in a somber seriousness, Father Prodido, still smelling of frankincense and myrrh, responded.

"I like your plan, your Excellency," he said. "Go humbly and bring your daughter home safely. You have our blessing. Know our prayers will go before you on your journey."

"Thank you, Father," Ochi said, relieved that the religious leader bought his story. "As leaving now would only create undue fear if I approach them in the dark. I'll gather my things and leave at first light. Pali, have the guards secure the Monon and ensure every townsperson is outside. I'll let them know of Thura's abduction and then inform them of my plans to bring her home."

CHAPTER 9

Thura's racing heart intensified with each stride perfectly timed to the sound of crunching gravel beneath her feet. Every sharp breath flirted with hyperventilation. The young woman could already feel the sweat on her palms while squeezing each hand tightly into a fist. She had never been so scared in her entire life.

Conformity in Patrida had a way of keeping people in line, especially the servants. Those in power constantly retold stories of the Great Liberation to remind them what happens to those who veer from the straight and narrow. They could very easily experience the weight of social isolation or death if they got too close to that line.

Thura and the other servants heard these harsh lines daily. The teenage girls and young women were frequently reminded by those they served that the consequences of pushing back against Patrida's religious beliefs and community values could mean their lives. Living under constant threat dissuaded anyone from ever challenging the status quo. When Thura turned from the Monon to face the Patridian guard near the jail cell, it was not only the most pivotal and symbolic moment of her life. Thura was making a life or death decision.

Still attempting to catch her breath, Thura bent over and put her hands on her knees. But instead of breathing, she began to dry heave. Since she was little, any confrontation Thura ever experienced had always produced this kind of anxious response in her. But her anxiety had become more prominent since her atonement ceremony when she turned the unfortunate age of thirteen. It was at this so-called sacred event where Thura's questioning of the ritual in front of the towns-people could have closed the metaphorical door of her life forever.

In Patrida, the atonement ceremony was the rite of passage for each new teenager. It was a special celebration in which the entire community would gather together in Sanctuary to participate. The ritual involved the teenager being covered in mud, repeating the atonement vow, and then standing in front of the sacrarium. At the same time, Father Prodido threw bowls of consecrated water on the child. They believed full inclusion into the community could never happen until one was cleansed of their unrighteousness and then fully immersed in the values of Patrida.

Thura walked alone down the center aisle wearing a white robe with her arms outstretched and her palms up. The onlookers began to throw mud at the teenager with every step she took. Despite this part of the ceremony appearing to be antagonistic and slightly aggressive, it was a normal practice within Patrida and never bothered any of the participants. It was understood to be the one thing a person had to do to enter the community. At least that was what Father Prodido told them, as he was the one who created the ritual. He said mud symbolized a person's trespasses and served as a tangible reminder of their uncleanliness when thrown at them. From his perspective, only he could wash them away with the holy waters of the sacrarium. From that point forward, as each citizen remained in good standing and abided by the ideals of Patrida, they were accepted by God and the community.

When young Thura finally made it to the front of Sanctuary, covered from head to toe in mud, she faced Father Prodido, who greeted her in sober melancholy.

"Oh child, you are so dirty. Look at yourself," the religious leader began. "There is nothing good here. I see only transgression."

The religious leader turned and faced the crowd.

"Brothers and sisters, what do you see?" he asked.

"Transgression," they responded in unison.

The religious leader turned back toward Thura and stared at her as if her sight repulsed him.

"Child, you enter Patrida only by word and water, for this is the only way," he said. "Unless you make this declaration and receive this washing, you remain stained forever in transgression and isolated from the community of God. Do you understand?"

"Yes, Father," young Thura said.

"Then please, let these words I say become your own words by repeating them after me," Father Prodido commanded. "I, Thura Kala."

"I, Thura Kala," she repeated slowly.

"In the presence of God and Patrida."

"In the presence of God and Patrida."

"Declare today."

"Declare today."

"There is nothing good in me."

Thura paused and refused to immediately repeat Father Prodido's words.

"Child, please, continue," said the religious leader. "There is nothing good in me."

The contrast between the night sky and the blazing flames of each torch surrounding Sanctuary never seemed more stark. The westerly wind began to blow in from across the waters and over the beach along the Monon. The flames of Sanctuary started to flicker, and many of them went dark. Thura stood calmly before Father Prodido and continued her hesitation in repeating his words. The religious leader, irritated by the teenager's seeming contempt and noncompliance, looked toward her parents as if summoning them to intervene. But before they could do anything, Thura responded.

"What is goodness, Father?" Thura asked.

"Excuse me?" Father Prodido responded in shock.

"What is goodness?" Thura asked again.

"Goodness only comes from God when you have been washed of your unrighteousness!" Father Prodido said, raising his voice with indignancy. "But this is not the time for questions! There is nothing good in me. Repeat it!"

"But if God is good and I came from God," Thura pressed, "then how is there nothing good in me?"

Enraged, Father Prodido raised his voice.

"Repeat the words, girl!" the religious leader yelled.

Undaunted, Thura continued questioning as a naive teenager who acted as if she knew nothing of fear.

"But what happens when others repeat those words and nothing changes in their lives?" Thura continued. "Are they considered good only because they have repeated the words? What if I do not repeat them? Are you saying I will never be good?"

Father Prodido took a step forward, his countenance towered over Thura. The religious leader spoke in a deep, malevolent tone.

"Look at yourself. You are filthy," he growled. "You … are … not … good. The goodness of God shall never reside in anyone unless they are washed and made clean."

The crowd joined Prodido's verdict by hissing in displeasure at Thura's offensive and ill-timed questioning. From their perspective, the young girl's questions cavalierly profaned both her ceremony and the position of Father Prodido, which were both held in high esteem in Patrida. Father Prodido, attempting to regain his composure and some sort of control over the ceremony, turned back toward Ochi and Velos. He stared at them in exasperated disbelief. Then, looking back toward the crowd, he made an announcement.

"Among us is one. One who remains unrepentantly unclean," Father Prodido said. "One who remains purposefully isolated. By Patridian law, no one shall speak to her, nor shall she be washed clean. This punishment shall be a sign of her defiance. It shall also be a lesson for all who choose to walk in adamant unrighteousness. For the next forty days, let this mud she wears remind her of every transgression she has chosen to carry in isolation as she walks among us each day on the Monon."

In silence, Father Prodido put out his hand, inviting Ochi, Velos, and young Tyran to join him in walking down the aisle to conclude the ceremony. The Patridian guards and then each row from the front to the back successively fell in line behind the leaders. Thura was left standing in the front by herself in the fading light of Sanctuary. Looking down at the dimly lit grass and then upward toward the brilliantly starred sky, Thura already knew goodness. She also knew her question about goodness had been answered, not in eloquent or convincing words from the religious leader, but by the fact that she stood alone covered in mud.

～

The fortieth day arrived with a spectrum of grays and overcast skies hanging over Sanctuary. With the ceremony being held first thing in the morning, rather than at sundown with the light of burning torches, the area was devoid of its typical ambiance and dramatic effect. It had the feeling of a necessary formality rather than a joyous celebration.

The townspeople lined each row with subdued eagerness, awaiting the commencement of Thura's second atonement ceremony. The anticipation was not so much for the ceremony itself as it was for Thura and the attitude she might bring with her. The crowd stared at the young girl standing in the back as she began her sheepish and despondent walk down the center aisle toward Father Prodido. He stood solemnly in the front without any apparent emotion on his face. No mud was being thrown at the young girl this time because she still wore the faded, light brown flakes and dust of dried mud covering her clothes and exposed skin. Thura's head remained pitifully bowed as she walked toward the religious leader. It wasn't a prayerful disposition. She was broken.

For forty days, silence had followed Thura closely like a shadow haunting her. Not only had no one spoken to her, but she also was not acknowledged by anyone, not even with a simple glance. Thura was surrounded by so many people each day, but the profound isolation and loneliness she experienced taught her to never again ask a question publicly that challenged the system. She may have questions, even essential questions, but for fear of being completely cut off from her community, she would never ask one again.

For anyone, but especially a thirteen-year-old, this kind of social and emotional punishment was devastating. There had been too many sleepless and heartbroken nights on the hard, wooden floor of Thura's room, which is where she slept to keep her bed clean, to ever convince Thura she ought to stand up for anything again. So as she walked down the center aisle of Sanctuary that disheartening morning, Thura committed to herself that she would no longer stand up for herself when faced with any conflict.

Approaching Father Prodido, Thura positioned herself directly in front of him while still staring at the ground. The religious leader looked down on her and attempted to make eye contact, but she would not look up at him. The crowd held their breath in suspense, waiting to see what Thura was planning to do.

Despite the young girl still looking at the ground, Father Prodido began.

"Repeat after me. I, Thura Kala."

Thura hesitated but finally whispered, "I, Thura Kala."

"In the presence of God and Patrida."

"In the presence of God and Patrida," she whispered again.

"Declare today."

"Declare today," she whispered, but this time in a barely audible tone.

"There is nothing good in me," Father Prodido said, hovering above the girl like a vulture spreading its wings over a kill.

Thura's gaze slowly moved from the sturdy and lush ground beneath her to her mud-caked feet and then continued gradually over the rest of her body. She examined every inch of the cracked and flaking mud hanging onto her legs, arms, and hands. She then closed her eyes. Beneath her dirty exterior, she saw a person who delighted in the sunset, freshly cut spring flowers, and the laughter of little children.

But even more, she saw a person who cared about people and always helped others. She saw a person who talked to those who lived on the edges of Patrida. She knew she wasn't perfect, but there was good in her.

Thura's soft eyes met the hard stare of Father Prodido. From the back, looking down the aisle, the two were perfectly centered and opposing one another in a strange paradox. Not a single person watching the ceremony could appreciate the ironic dichotomy. On one side was the outwardly clean, polished, and pristine religious leader in full regalia who insisted a person's goodness only comes through strict adherence to Patrida's ritual but who was bereft of goodness himself. On the other side was the outwardly bedraggled, unkempt, and filthy teenager in silted clothing who knew divine goodness had always been within her regardless of pretense or ritual.

As Father Prodido was about to call off the ceremony once again and summon Thura's parents to the front for further disciplinary measures, she responded. While the teenager had learned her lesson to avoid conflict at all costs moving forward, she could not help but put forth one last rebellious jab. At that moment, Sanctuary's complete silence threatened to expose the teenager's nearly imperceptible whisper.

"There is something good in me," Thura breathed.

Father Prodido looked to Ochi and Velos and nodded approvingly. Neither he nor anyone else in Sanctuary heard Thura's subtle subversion. Realizing no one caught what she said, Thura looked back at the ground and smiled. The religious leader gave his final impartations and poured the holy water over her head and then the rest of her body.

"By the power vested in me, Thura Kala, you have been made clean," he announced. "You have been received by God and Patrida. Go forth in peace."

Thura watched the water run in slow motion over the dirt on her arms and legs, which gradually began to reveal her skin once again. The young girl had never been so happy to be washed from head to toe, especially knowing she had not compromised what she believed about herself. It was even more gratifying that she did it with Father Prodido standing two feet away from her. With every eye in Patrida still watching the teenager, Thura turned toward the crowd with her head still bowed. First, one person stood up, then two, and then the entire crowd followed suit. They began to roar in approval. This final irony was not lost on her.

~

Thura's breathing returned to its natural rhythm as she took her hands off of her knees and stood up. She still could not believe what she had done. Even more, she could not believe what she was about to do. While Father Prodido had almost extinguished the young woman's fire nearly a decade prior, it now raged within her, burning away her fear and timidity.

Peering around the corner, she noticed the guard was no longer in the area and the cell door was closed. While Thura's plan had always been to break them out under the cover of darkness, the situation was proving to be increasingly fluid, as the pieces seemed to be moving more quickly than she had anticipated.

Working her way along the perimeter of the town, Thura made her way toward a group loitering on the porch of a run-down house. On Patrida's outskirts lived those excluded from the elite social order. Since Thura had taken meals to Sophia over the years along this particular route, she knew many of the people who lived there quite well.

"Have any of you seen Kaleo?" Thura asked.

"Yeah, he's inside," one of the ladies responded.

"Do you think I could go in and talk to him?" Thura asked.

The lady looked at a man sitting beside the door, who gave a barely noticeable shake of his head, indicating it was not okay for Thura to go in the house.

"Kaleo! The girl's here," the lady shouted out instead of getting up.

Thura was taken aback by her volume but was not necessarily concerned with being seen by anyone she knew. She had never once seen a familiar face from the Monon on these roads, not even a guard.

"Kaleo!" the lady shouted again, this time louder, causing Thura to cringe.

The door opened, and a man, the same age as her father, walked out of the house. To Thura, he looked as if he could have been sleeping, but she also knew he wore a tired, worn-down look on his face when fully rested. Being a social outcast in Patrida had taken its toll on him emotionally, but even more so physically, as his head was now entirely gray and the creases on his face were deep. Kaleo walked toward Thura, smiling, and gave her a big hug.

"Thura, it's so good to see you," Kaleo said. "It's been a while. Where have you been?"

Not really having the time to engage in a conversation or pleasantries for that matter, Thura jumped right into what was happening in Patrida.

"I am sorry to be so abrupt, Kaleo," she said, "but I have a very important favor to ask of you."

She had his full attention.

"What's wrong, Thura? What's going on?" Kaleo asked.

"A young man was apprehended in the woods the other day, and it turns out he lives on the other side of the island with a small community," Thura explained.

With interest, Kaleo leaned in closer to Thura to hear every word of her story.

"Evidently, during the Great Liberation when my father killed Numa and took Sophia captive," Thura continued, "there were several others who got away. They have been living on the other side of the island this entire time."

The older man closed his eyes and shook his head as if he understood precisely what Thura was telling him. While Kaleo now lived on the edges of Patrida as an outcast, he was once very close to Thura's father.

"From everything people told me," he responded, "I believed your father killed every remaining insurgent, as well. In fact, all these years later, I still believed it. So you're telling me one of them came back, and he's here?"

"Yes, he is a young man named Odigo, and they have locked him up with Sophia," Thura said. "But listen, I need you to trust me. I do not have time to tell you every detail, but my father will have them executed soon. I have taken a key to the cell door and am getting ready to break them out within the hour."

Kaleo smiled at Thura, his creases stretched across his face under his gray stubble. Not only was he impressed with her bravery and determination, but Kaleo was also delighted that someone was finally pushing back against the system. It made him even more thrilled that it was Ochi's daughter.

"What can we do to help?" Kaleo asked. "I know my wife and friends here will be happy to help in any way possible."

"I'm going to grab a few things for the journey first, and then I am going to come back and hopefully get them out," Thura said. "There are a half dozen guards in the woods on lookout. I need you to run out there and tell them there has been an uprising in town and everything is on fire."

By this time, everyone on the porch had surrounded Thura and listened to her plan.

"We've got this, Thura," Kaleo responded emphatically. "Every single one of us. We're in this with you."

~

Fortunately for Thura, she had already packed a satchel and hid it away the same night she first talked to Odigo and Sophia at their cell. All it would take was her sneaking into the house to retrieve it from her room. Thura climbed the stairway located at the side entrance of her house and tip-toed her way down the hallway without making a sound. Opening her bedroom door, she dashed across the room and grabbed her satchel from underneath her bed. Not hearing another sound in the house, Thura ran down the hallway and then down the stairs.

"Hey! Whoa! What's the rush, young lady?" Ochi inquired from the top of the stairs as she tried to race out the door.

Thura hesitatingly stopped and looked up toward her curious father.

"Nothing," Thura muttered. "Just uh… well… I'm just… um."

The young woman searched desperately for anything at all to give him. Turning her attention toward a growing commotion along the Monon, Thura saw a large contingency moving in the direction of Sanctuary. A crowd walking eastward on the thoroughfare at that time of day struck Thura as peculiar.

"Um… hey dad… what's going on over there?" Thura asked, redirecting their conversation to the passing parade.

Ochi walked casually down the stairs and stood beside Thura, as they both watched each passerby with interest. At once, the father and daughter looked at each other in disbelief.

"Do you smell that, father?" Thura asked, knowing exactly what it was.

Ochi did not answer. He knew precisely what the scent was, as well. It was the burning of frankincense and myrrh, which could only be from one person doing one thing. Ochi left Thura in haste and immediately ran toward the Monon.

With no time to spare, Thura rushed behind her house and along the alleyway westward toward the gallows. Each stride carried her past the narrow gaps between houses from where she could see the crowd continuing to walk toward Sanctuary. Thura had an idea of what was happening and what Father Prodido was doing. But all she cared about at that moment was the crowd moving in the right direction, away from Sophia and Odigo.

When Thura reached the gallows, she stood still for a second behind the monstrous contraption to catch her breath and to make sure no threats were in sight. When she took in the entire length of the Monon and saw the crowd settling into their seats, she was frightened by what she saw. Each aisle, including the perimeter of Sanctuary, was lined with hooded guards wearing their black robes. While she had seen executions in the past, she had never seen the guards wearing their formal attire.

At the front, Thura saw Father Prodido standing triumphantly beside her father. The scene broke her heart for him and the cowardly path he had chosen for himself. Every word the young woman had written to him and placed in his cedar box was true. He was reaping all he had sown in Patrida all these years. Without question, Thura knew she was making the right decision by releasing her friends and fleeing from a truly godforsaken place.

Convinced every guard in Patrida was either at Sanctuary or in the woods, Thura darted toward the cell. Odigo and Sophia were already standing at the door, looking out the window and smiling as she approached. Without saying a word, Thura hurriedly took the key out of her satchel, placed it in the keyhole, and tried to turn it. The key did not move. Frantically, she removed it from the slot, but it slipped out of her nervous hand to the ground. Beginning to sweat and breathe rapidly, Thura scrambled to pick up the key and try once again. Putting the key in the hole, she tried to turn it. But it did not budge.

Watching Thura fumble through the window, Odigo gently offered a suggestion.

"Thura, it is going to be okay," he said. "Just calm down and take a deep breath. Try turning the key the other way."

Thura stepped back and looked at Odigo. She inhaled and then exhaled before stepping forward and placing the key into the door one last time. Turning the key the other direction, it finally began to move, then suddenly clicked. The door unlocked.

Thura pulled the door open as Sophia and Odigo stepped through. The trio walked briskly away from the Monon toward the back alleyway. When they turned the corner, Sophia stopped abruptly and looked around the corner back at the cell.

"Sophia, we have to get moving," Thura said, gently pulling at the old woman's arm. "I have friends helping me create a diversion in the woods so we can make a safe escape."

Caught up in the urgency of her plan, Thura failed to consider the fact that Sophia had been locked away in Patrida for nearly two decades. The old woman had spent a little less than a third of her life narrowly looking out the cell door window. She had seen people come and go. She had watched children like Thura grow up. She had no reason to feel anything but complete exhilaration for her escape, yet she turned to Thura and Odigo with tears in her eyes.

"I am not finished here," the old woman said. "There is still so much to do. So many people. So many lives and relationships. I have gotten to know more of them than you can imagine over the years from within those four walls. I know their stories. I have heard about their families. They need me here."

Despite her urgency, Thura paused to listen to her old friend.

"When you spend so much time in captivity," Sophia continued, "you have to decide what you will do with your time and who you want to be. This has been my home, and I have tried to make everyone I meet a part of my family. It is true I could only do so much from my cell, but I did all I could. Yet, there is so much left undone."

Sophia put her wrinkled hand over her face and cried.

"For the hand you were dealt, you have done so much, Sophia. You have done enough. Look what you have done for me," Thura whispered as she pulled Sophia close and stroked her white hair. "And there is still so much more you are going to do now that you are free."

"I was free when I was imprisoned, Thura," Sophia said. "Am I now supposed to abandon those who are truly imprisoned?"

Thura released Sophia as Odigo interrupted.

"I am sorry to interrupt," he said, 'but we really need to get to the woods before someone sees us, or we miss our window of opportunity. Sophia, may we continue this conversation once we are in the clear?"

The old woman nodded her head in humble agreement and walked at her own unhurried pace down the dusty alleyway ahead of the other two. Thura and Odigo quickly fell in behind her. Despite having been locked away with minimal movement for all those years, Sophia moved at a surprisingly brisk pace. While Thura and Odigo may have mistakenly believed the adage that a group can only move as fast as the slowest person, it was, in fact, Sophia who slowed her pace so they could catch up with her.

CHAPTER 10

The forceful hands of the Patridian guard had at last silenced the panicked hysteria of Patrida. Under the loud and commanding leadership of Machi, the guards turned every house upside-down in search of the prisoners while at the same time pulling everyone else out into the streets. Gradually and painstakingly, the guards encircled Patrida, moving inward, successfully corralling the townspeople on the Monon.

An eerie and uncertain hush befell everyone as the guards carried out a directive to line each side of the Monon. This directive included each end, essentially securing the entire length of the main thoroughfare. For all the citizens knew, a threat remained. But the safest place at the moment was in the middle of those tasked to protect them. The word on the street was that Ochi and Father Prodido would soon be giving an update on the prisoner escape and their plan moving forward. There had also been a rumor, spreading like wildfire, that someone had abducted Thura during the escape.

As would be expected during a crisis in the town, there was a higher concentration of guards protecting the front entrance of Ochi's house. The restlessness along the Monon necessitated it. Being that the people had been enclosed like sheep and treated as if they were the real threat, several factions close to one another became significantly loud and unruly, shouting profanities at the guards.

Like the grand conductor of a disjointed and discordant symphony, the epicenter of the contentious scene was none other than Fovos. The fear-mongering maestro stood on a wooden crate, uniting his band of brigands in a song of rebellion. While he certainly drew the Patridian guards' attention with his barking and animated gestures, his tirade had not yet reached a level of concern, so he continued unimpeded.

"We're not barnyard animals here! And this is not some kind of petting zoo for your amusement! Are we free-range chickens! Are we dairy cows!" Fovos shouted to the laughs and cheers of those surrounding him. He then turned contentiously to the guards closest to him, and the joking immediately ceased.

"What's the price of admission, boys?" he asked. "How much are they payin' you to turn on your own kin? To turn on your fellow man? Who'd ya sell your soul to, anyway?"

Fovos' sharp turn from comedic routine to a more serious tone prompted a similar change in the crowd surrounding him, which had been quickly attracting more people. One moment they nervously laughed at Fovos' jokes. In the next moment, unsettled displeasure erupted among them, as they remembered the Patridian guards corralling them like animals. Fovos knew how to direct the crowd masterfully from one emotion to another without anyone ever suspecting that his sole motivation was manipulating and turning them against Ochi. Summoning his inner thespian, Fovos put his thumbs behind his suspenders and launched into another tirade.

"Look around, sheep!" Fovos shouted. "Who outnumbers who here? Oh yeah, that's right. We outnumber them. But looky there! Look who sits up in that little comfortable council room while we're caged down here like animals! Who's controlling who here? Who's controlling who! What do you think they care about more? You or remaining in power! I'm startin' to think…"

Suddenly, interrupting Fovos and emerging from the house, Ochi, Father Prodido, and Tyran walked out and stood behind the guards before the sea of onlookers. As Ochi raised his hand to summon the crowd's attention, a mob rolled across the Monon like a wave moving toward the leader.

The guards, still clothed in their midnight black attire and armed with their staffs, took a defensive stance in front of Ochi. Their sudden movement subsequently set off a domino effect with every guard on the perimeter. The majority of the citizens could not determine whether the guards caused the sudden rush of people in the crowd or if the movement provoked the guards. Either way, people began to scream and move frantically away from the guards, which forced everyone to huddle more closely together in the middle of the Monon.

Standing in the newly created gap between the compressed, uncertain masses and Ochi, who was still calmly holding his hand in the air, was Fovos. The man glared directly into the soft yet tired eyes of Patrida's leader and dared him to say or do anything. If there was a moment that perfectly captured the deteriorating and free-falling state of Patrida, in what they had lost and what remained in its place, it was that exact moment. Wisdom had abandoned them, and fear stood in her place.

"Why don't you come down from your perch, dear leader, and talk to me mano a mano," Fovos impatiently shouted at Ochi, disregarding pleasantries.

The leader didn't immediately respond, which caused Fovos to take a step forward before barking at Ochi a second time. Although his step forward was nothing close to an attack, the guards lunged forward with their staffs.

"Get down here and face me like a man, you coward!" Fovos screamed. "This is why you've lost the people! Quit hiding behind your guards and look me in the eyes when I talk to you!"

At that point, no one in Patrida knew the motives of anyone else or what was happening in general. Father Prodido stood beside Tyran, and neither of them could discern what Fovos was doing. Had he gone rogue? Was he no longer serving the interest of the religious leader? There was no way they could be sure of anything with him amidst the pandemonium, so they continued to watch hesitantly.

Ochi, unfazed by his adversary's tone and aggressiveness, brought his hand down and waved it toward the guards standing in front of him. Each guard stepped aside, faced the leader, and stood at attention. Unarmed yet confident, Ochi passed through the pathway created for him and stopped a few feet in front of Fovos. It appeared as if every eye was upon the men. The quiet along the Monon added to the tension and suspense of the staredown. Neither man wanted to be the first to speak, but at last, Ochi broke the silence.

"Fovos," he said, "I understand many of you are upset with the escape of the prisoners and for the intrusive measures we have taken to secure you. But for the time being, may I kindly ask for your patience and cooperation? The infidel took Thura hostage when making his escape."

Fovos reached into his pants pocket, fished around for a minute, and then pulled out an already chewed toothpick, which he then placed in his mouth. Putting his thumbs behind his suspenders and smiling from ear to ear while leaning back and shaking his head at the crowd, Fovos said the unthinkable.

"Listen here, your majesty, and listen close to what I have to say," he began. "Cause I'm only gonna say this one time. I know you all must be worried sick about your little princess, but I don't give a good goddamn about you or your daughter. Really your whole family for that matter. Did I just say that out loud? Hmm. I guess I did. But see, the truth here is that Ol' Fovos knows a snake oil salesman when he sees one, and you been sellin' a lot of that snake oil these last few days."

Ochi was emotionless and nonreactive as Fovos turned toward the crowd and continued to blather and bloviate.

"The reason they took this fool's daughter," he shouted, "is because he didn't have the cajonés to walk our little savage visitor down to hang town. Do you people know what I'm sayin' here? Your majesty sits all high and mighty in his throne room barkin' out orders about how this is gonna be or how that's gonna be, but he kept that poor bastard alive just so he could scare us and keep every one of us under his thumb!"

Smiling with his handlebar mustache as big as it had ever appeared, Fovos turned back to face Ochi and continued.

"Isn't that right, your majesty?" he asked. "Ol' Ochi feels like he's done lost control here in the Fatherland, and the best way to keep the people on your big kingly teat is to scare 'em a little bit! Isn't it!"

Of course, nothing Fovos said was based on facts or evidence. Every word he spoke was conjecture and a creation of his own ill-informed opinion. Nonetheless, he believed every single word that came out of his mouth was the truth. What he did not know, however, was that Father Prodido had purposefully kept him in the dark on many important details, even more than he had Tyran. Fovos was way too reactionary and volatile to trust as anything more than a useful idiot. Father Prodido knew any real information given to Fovos would immediately guarantee its weaponization, and he was much too calculating than to ever throw such valuable pearls before such a swine of a man.

However, in this unplanned and somewhat fortuitous moment along the Monon, Father Prodido saw how his useful idiot appeared to be selling the drama and successfully turning the crowd against Ochi, and it intrigued him. Despite having his own subversive plan to undermine Ochi once he left Patrida, Father Prodido was content watching Fovos make his case to the people against their leader. The thought of expediting public opinion against Ochi without having to sway them slowly and methodically in his absence seemed ideal.

With the Patridian guard's full force standing ready at his command, Ochi was happy to let Fovos blow off some steam. From his perspective, knowing precisely what Fovos had against him and having it aired publicly, rather than behind closed doors, seemed worth the small sacrifice of listening to his incessant barking.

But Pali and Machi, who both stood behind Ochi, interpreted the situation much differently. In Fovos, they saw a wild animal pacing back and forth, readying to bite the handler if his hand got too close to the cage. The brothers gave a quick glance over their shoulders to Father Prodido, who signaled for them to remain patient and watch the situation play out.

"You see, there was this mother hen that had some eggs she was carin' for," Fovos announced. "Now the problem was that the ol' mother hen was sick, you see. And there was a cunning ol' wolf that knew she wasn't doin' well and, boy oh boy, he was hungry. Now would you believe that the ol' wolf killed that sickly mother hen just as those little chicks hatched! And those little critters thought he was their mother! Yessir! They sure did. But he had himself a full belly and didn't have the heart to eat those youngins. I'll have you know that those little boogers followed him around every day not knowin' any better. For all they knew, that ol' wolf was their momma! And you know what? He took care of 'em! You see what I'm saying, your majesty?"

A smile crossed Ochi's face, but he refused to respond to Fovos' question.

"Wipe that smile off your face!" Fovos shouted. "You're the sick mother hen! And these chicks want to follow a mother with some teeth, you son of a bitch!"

In a violent rage, Fovos charged Ochi and tackled him to the ground. The brothers, once again, looked back at Father Prodido, who rolled his eyes and nodded his head for them to pull the men apart. Together, the guards rushed in and immediately ripped Fovos off of the leader. Unfazed by the assault, Ochi stood up, dusted his shirt, and wiped the blood from his smiling lip.

"Looks like the ol' wolf is going to bed with an empty belly tonight," said Ochi. "We have an open cell now. Put him in it. I will deal with him upon my return home with Thura."

The guards carted off a bellicose and rambunctious Fovos, but all eyes remained on Ochi as the brothers took their places on each side of him. Only those close in proximity heard what the two men had said during the earlier exchange. For most onlookers, Thura being taken hostage was still a rumor continuing to circulate and not an officially corroborated fact.

"Brothers and sisters, these have been trying times for our community over the last few days," Ochi announced. "I understand there continue to be rumors and conjecture floating around about everything that's been going on. So please, bear with me as I lay out the facts in the order they happened."

From behind the leader, Father Prodido put his head down and rolled his eyes, sighing loudly enough for those around him to hear it.

"As you know, Pali and Machi captured an infidel in the woods," Ochi continued. "We locked him up while we assessed the situation and fortified our defenses. While we assumed there could be more insurgents in the woods, we determined the threat remained low and the situation stable. We gave the guards orders to establish outposts and keep watch for any potential enemy activity. As you also know, there was a discussion if we should execute the prisoner. So, you may be wondering where we are now. While we have yet to determine the events and potential oversights leading to both prisoners' escape, we now know they took my daughter hostage. They abducted Thura."

Ochi expected shock but did not anticipate such outrage. The short fuse of the citizenry burned quickly and exploded mightily. To make the situation even more unstable, his casualness and perceived lack of urgency again conveyed a message he did not intend. The problem was that Ochi knew Thura was not in any danger, and his posture was way too relaxed, composed, and unemotional. In other words, Ochi's performance lacked the conviction and salesmanship of Father Prodido, or Fovos for that matter. He began to pay the price for it as the crowd directed angry shouts at him.

"Why are you not more outraged, you fool!"

"Where's the man who started this community!"

"Why are you not fighting for your family!"

"Why don't you mobilize the guard and destroy them!"

"How are you going to make this right!"

Ochi realized he seriously miscalculated where he stood with the people. While he may have retained a few ardent supporters scattered sparsely throughout the crowd, the scale of public sentiment appeared to have tipped heavily against him, and it was more significant than he could have imagined. His detachment from what had been happening at the ground level led to this sentiment change.

As Ochi had isolated himself and had been spending way too much time in the council room talking and making decisions behind closed doors, Fovos had been on the ground, looking people in the eyes and persuading them against the leader. The words of Fovos continued to echo in his head. *This is why you've lost the people!* Ochi had lost the people, and he knew it. But at the same time, he also knew he needed to figure out how to salvage his plan of retrieving Thura before everything turned entirely against him.

While Father Prodido had intervened on behalf of Ochi in the past, the religious leader remained unphased by the crowd's protests this time. He would not be stepping in to save Ochi again. Instead, he leaned toward Tyran and whispered what could have been an entire speech into his ear. One wonders what the religious leader said to the young man. But it must have certainly been something about his father's reluctance in dealing with Thura's captor, as Tyran's demeanor appeared to change.

The young man still believed his father was a traitor of the community. Not only had he let the insurgents go free during the Great Liberation and enabled them to start a new community, but he had also been utterly impotent in dealing with the prisoner. For these reasons, Tyran held his father solely responsible for every weak and reckless decision that put Thura's life at stake.

But even while Prodido whispered in his ear, Tyran looked at his father standing before the crowd and had empathy for him. The unexpected visit from his father earlier in the day brought a flood of emotions he had not experienced since he was a young boy. When Ochi showed up at his house, Tyran saw a side of his father he had never seen before. He appeared as a man weighed down and shackled by chains, a man struggling to break free from the pain of regret.

Through tears, his father talked about the painting in the council room and how he finally realized he was the older man sitting in the boat. He said the painting had always reminded him of their adventures to the island. He even shared with Tyran that the painting finally showed him that his peace had never been on the horizon to be found another day. It had been with him the whole time. However, the most heartbreaking thing he told Tyran was that he did not think he was capable of ever fully finding that peace, although he desired it.

Tyran understood for the first time how deeply his father regretted their distance over the years. He could see the remorse his father carried for not keeping their relationship close and for allowing the affairs of Patrida to get in the way. Even more, he discovered how much his father hated the influence of Father Prodido and how he wished he would have done more to keep the religious leader at a distance as Tyran grew older.

Breaking his gaze from his father and interrupting the religious leader who was still whispering in his ear, Tyran leaned into Father Prodido this time and responded with a whisper of his own, which elicited wide-eyed shock and dismay. Something Tyran said to him was enough to visibly unsettle the religious leader. But before their conversation could go any further, Ochi made an unexpected move in front of them by pushing Pali out of the way and grabbing Velos, pulling her close to him as he began to yell above the shouts of the crowd.

"I will go! I will go all by myself!" Ochi said manically. "We cannot put Thura's life in danger by sending in our warriors! With the support of my wife, and of course, the council, I will make the journey myself! I will journey alone! I will get our daughter back! And then, once she is safely home, we will mobilize the full might and strength of the Patridian guard and bring a reckoning upon the enemy!"

The crowd cheered a little more than half-heartedly. Ochi sensed he had only bought enough time to get his things together and catch a quick nap before beginning his journey. Still unsure of her husband's story, Velos pulled away from Ochi's half-hug in front of the crowd and walked back to join Father Prodido and Tyran, leaving him standing alone. The leader, surrounded in awkward silence, really did not know what else to say. The guards remained encircled around the citizens as they continued to wait for some sort of direction.

Finally, Ochi spoke.

"Okay. Thank you," he said. "You can go home now. We are done here. The guards will keep watch overnight. May you all rest in peace."

Relieved the day was over, the leader immediately turned, put his head down, and smiled as he walked up the steps past Velos, Tyran, and Father Prodido. While he had genuinely wanted to dismiss everyone for the night and wish them a peaceful rest, he realized that what he had uttered was a phrase meant for dead people. May you rest in peace, Ochi thought, as he began to chuckle and then laugh out loud. The irony of the situation made him belly laugh all the way back to his room.

Hanging from a small hook on his bedroom wall, Ochi grabbed his old, worn leather satchel. The truth was that he had not thought through this journey and did not know what he should be taking. He did not even know where he was going, for that matter. He imagined his pace would be quicker than their pace, as Sophia would slow them down. He decided on a couple of shirts, another pair of pants, and maybe some bread and hard cheese.

Ochi walked over to his closet to grab his clothes. As he opened the door, he took a quick peek in the direction of the floorboard, but something did not look right. In his haste earlier, he thought he had placed the box in the corner of the closet and thrown clothes over top of it. At least that was the way he remembered it. Everything had happened so hurriedly he was not sure exactly how he left it. As he stared down at the corner of his closet, the floorboard was back in place and the box was nowhere in sight. Fear ran through his body. Had someone else been in my closet? He thought. Did they get into the box and see my journal?

As he stood there with his questions, Ochi felt the presence of another person standing behind him in the room. Frozen, but too afraid to turn around, Ochi stood at his open closet and pretended to stare at his clothes. He wondered how he could have been so careless in not putting the box back below the floorboard. His mistake was obvious. The journal not only had information pertinent to Patrida and his leadership position, but the pages also contained everything he had been feeling over the last year. His words would be damning if someone were to read it.

Ochi looked over his shoulder, but no one was there. Breathing a sigh of relief, he got down on his hands and knees and removed the floorboard. The box was there. At this point, Ochi was again unsure if he was the one who replaced it or not. Maybe he did, and everything was fine. Either way, he still wanted to look in the box to make sure everything was in it. Reaching below the floor, Ochi grabbed the box. But as he was pulling it out, the presence returned to the room.

"Readying for your journey?" Velos inquired.

Ochi slowly lowered it back in place before answering.

"Yes," he said. "I thought a couple of shirts and a pair of pants would do. Have you seen my other pair of sandals by chance?"

As Velos answered him, Ochi pretended to look around for the sandals. But he was quietly securing the board back in place. He figured he would have to trust his gut that everything was in the box and that he had indeed replaced the floorboard earlier. Grabbing his sandals and the rest of his clothes, Ochi put them in his satchel and placed it by his bed for an early morning.

～

At first light, Ochi walked out of his house and stepped onto the Monon with a profound sense of adventure and excitement. The skies were welcoming and already brilliantly blue, with the most magnificently white cumulus clouds adding a perfect contrast. As Ochi turned toward Sanctuary with a figurative skip in his step, he could see the entire town had already gathered together and was eagerly awaiting him. He was unsure how they had all assembled without him knowing, but their thoughtfulness deeply moved him.

Ochi noticed that someone had dug a trench leading from the flowing sacrarium down the center aisle. He moved forward until his feet met the water's edge. Looking up from the water, Ochi saw Father Prodido, Tyran, Pali, and Velos, each standing beside an arch of the shrine. They looked as if they were awaiting him. Ochi placed one foot into the stream and then the other. The cold, clear water came up to his knees. He began to slowly walk down the aisle with the accompaniment of cheers and applause from the people.

Ochi looked forward at Pali, who nodded his head in approval at the leader. He then turned his attention to Velos, who offered both of her hands together, palms up, as if welcoming her husband. Ochi could not fathom what had transpired overnight while he had been asleep, but he was glad he was leaving on good terms with everyone.

The leader then looked at Tyran, who looked back at his father and placed his hand over his heart. Tears filled Ochi's eyes as he looked at his beautiful son. That was when he saw Father Prodido standing by one of the front arches on the left side with his hands prayerfully together. The religious leader momentarily closed his eyes and nodded humbly at Ochi.

Wading his hands through the water, he walked closer to the sacrarium. Ochi could see there was one more person in front of him standing in the shadows of the shrine. As he approached, he noticed it was a young woman with long red hair. He could not see her face as she had her back to him. Ochi stepped hesitantly into the entrance of the sacrarium. As the young woman heard his approach from behind, she turned and faced him. It was Thura.

Ochi ran through the water toward the center of the shrine and embraced his daughter. But she did not return his embrace. Instead, she took her hands and grabbed his arms, pulling them forcefully off of her.

"Father, will you help me tear down this structure?" Thura asked.

Confused, Ochi looked around at each person standing beside their respective arch. Their faces conveyed no emotion. They silently stared at the father and daughter. Perplexed as to what was happening and why Thura wanted to knock down the sacrarium, Ochi turned back to his daughter and found her pushing against one of the massive, white curved pillars from inside.

"Thura, what are you doing?" Ochi cried. "These arches were set by dozens of men. You cannot move them by your strength alone. They cannot even be moved by our strength together."

Ignoring her father's skepticism and his reluctance in joining her endeavor, Thura began to scream wildly and push the arch more violently.

"Thura, please!" Ochi called out. "This is crazy behavior! All of your pushing is futile! Can't you see everyone is bothered by what you are doing! Look around! Please, come with me, and let's dry off."

Amidst Ochi's pleas and Thura's commotion, Father Prodido rushed into the water and grabbed Thura. Quick to follow the religious leader's lead, Tyran, Velos, and Pali immediately ran into the water and helped him hold Thura down. Ochi was paralyzed. He could not move or make a sound. All he could do was helplessly watch them push the young woman down and hold her under the water. Thura began to struggle. She could not overpower their collective strength. From outside the sacrarium, the townspeople started to resoundingly sing a refrain over and over in unison, "This is why you've lost the people."

Ochi could not move. He could not breathe. Even though they held his daughter underwater, he felt as if he was the one dying by their hands. Thura's suffocation became his suffocation. Thura's struggle became his struggle. Praying for the ability to move or shout before it was too late, Ochi rushed forward, punching and knocking over everyone in the way. With every bit of strength he could summon, he tore them off of his daughter. Sobbing, Ochi fell to his knees and wailed uncontrollably.

"My God, what did you monsters do!" Ochi cried. "Why did you have to kill her! Why did you have to kill her! For pushing up against your shrine!"

Ochi began to hit the water forcefully and scream at everyone around him. Anger pulsated through his fists with each strike until he could no longer hit it. He was exhausted and consumed by grief. Ochi could do nothing but stare listlessly at the water as tears fell from his face. He had not noticed that the singing had stopped or that he was the only one left in the sacrarium. Everything was deathly quiet around him. As Ochi began to look even more intently at the still water, his head began to shake back and forth in disbelief at what he saw in front of him. In terror, he lifted the head of the lifeless body out of the water and screamed. The face he was looking at was his own.

The sudden sound of stone cracking and its palpable rumbles caused the leader to look up from his horror. On one side, he saw Father Prodido and Pali pushing against their arches. On the other side, Velos and Tyran were doing the same. Ochi attempted to get up from the water, but a hand grabbed his wrist and would not let him go. He struggled to get away and began screaming at the top of his lungs for them to stop. But as the sacrarium lost integrity and started to fall on him, he opened his eyes in a cold sweat. It was still dark outside and way too early to leave. But he decided he could no longer delay his journey.

CHAPTER 11

Thura pulled her tingling hand out from under her chest and examined the specks of brownish moss pressed into the length of her arm. The smell of wood smoke and muffled chatter disoriented her. She could not quite remember where she was. Thura slowly raised her head and gently brushed the dirt off her face, which had been flat against the ground the entire night. It was not the cleanest spot she had ever slept, but she rested soundly her first night away from Patrida.

Odigo and Kaleo chatted in quiet tones and grins off to one side, but Sophia was nowhere in sight. Thura remembered she had been sitting with Sophia the night before after they had collected firewood but realized she must have fallen asleep next to the older woman right after they made the fire. The fact that Sophia had been awake when Thura fell asleep and left before Thura awoke was not surprising at all. Sophia rarely slept. At least Thura never recalled her sleeping. Sophia meditated with her eyes closed, but that was the closest thing to sleep Thura could remember. Even at that, she was always fully present and alert when spoken to.

Thura thought about the magnitude of what she had pulled off in Patrida. She rubbed her eyes and attempted to find her bearings. A part of her wanted to jump up and down and scream with joy for finally being free. However, another part of her wondered about her family and what they must be thinking and feeling.

She remembered how she used to sit at the table for dinner as a young child and hold up four fingers, smiling at her dad, mom, and Tyran. Her mom would ask her what the four fingers represented, and she would gleefully shout, "Our family!" In her little mind, there was something special about the four of them together. But that was a long time ago. So much had changed in their family dynamics since then, even over the last few days.

Thura stared at one of her hands resting on her lap. She noticed how dirty she was as she opened her hand and spat on her fingers to clean them off. Thura rubbed her thumb in a circular motion over the three largest stained brown fingers, but the dirt would not come off.

"It is pine resin," a voice called out from behind. "You must have gotten it on your fingers while collecting wood last night."

Thura glanced over her shoulder to see Sophia slowly limping toward her. She stood up to greet the old woman.

"It takes me a while to get moving in the mornings, but I eventually get there. These legs walked more miles last night than they have for a long time," Sophia said, smiling while speaking loud enough for Odigo and Kaleo to hear her as well.

"Well, you kept pace with me, and that's saying something," Odigo added.

Sophia walked up to Thura, who was still working diligently on her fingers, and cusped the young woman's hands with her soft, wrinkled hands.

"There are some things you have to let be," Sophia said.

Thura looked blankly at her old friend, unsure as to what she was saying. Sophia released her hands and hobbled toward Odigo and Kaleo, who were both still standing near the humble fire they had rekindled.

"I was telling Odigo that I really need to get back to Patrida," Kaleo said, turning toward Sophia as she approached. "I hope you know that it would've been a real honor for me to accompany you to

Salome. And you should also know that I sure appreciate the invite. But after our conversation last night, I realized that Patrida needs me there. As much as I hate to admit it, I've been checked out for a long while, and I'm not sure if that was the best thing."

"If they had treated me half the way they treated you, I would have done the same thing," Thura said, as she joined the group around the fire. "But that is how my father has always been. Everyone is an enemy and needs to be dealt with harshly."

"That's not true, Thura," Kaleo countered.

"It is true! Look at the three of you! He stood by and let them push you out of your position. He imprisoned you for nearly two decades. And he was set to execute you before I got you out of there. So don't tell me it is not true," Thura said as she raised her voice and became more animated, pointing at each person as she made her point.

"I understand, Thura, I do," Kaleo said. "I'm not trying to make excuses for your dad. He's a big boy and makes his own decisions, always has. He's a strong personality, and it's always been his way or no way. But you hardly knew your dad before we came to this island. The man you know now wasn't the man I stood beside for years."

"I do not understand how you can make excuses for him," Thura said. "You used to be his head guard. His head guard! You were his most trusted companion and friend! But look what he did to you! They stripped you of your position, your respect, and your dignity. So tell me, should I really care who he used to be when I can see clearly who he is now?"

Thura's question silenced Kaleo and abruptly ended the discussion. He could have told her more about the man he used to know, but Thura was not in a place where she could receive it. For all the years they had conversed on Thura's way to visit Sophia, Kaleo had never seen this side of the young woman. Of course, he had known about her frustrations and general restlessness within Patrida, which he attributed to her unenviable position as a servant. Still, he had never heard her speak with so much bitterness, especially about her father. However, this was neither the time nor place to try changing her mind.

Attempting to break the long and uncomfortable silence, Odigo smiled and turned toward Sophia.

"Well, the path is never a straight line, is it?" he asked.

Without responding, Sophia walked over to Kaleo, placed her right hand on his cheek, and gently patted it. The man put his calloused hand over her wrinkled hand and held it against his weathered face.

"Thank you, my friend," Kaleo offered as he turned and made his way back toward the long and circuitous route they traveled the night before.

Still smiling, this time from being a bit perplexed, Odigo tilted his head and raised his eyebrow at the older woman.

"Um. Okay. So no goodbyes?" Odigo asked. "What in the world was that all about anyway? It was like you two were having your own private conversation without words. And we were standing here like, hello?"

Odigo's lightheartedness and injection of humor brought a much-needed change of energy to the group. Thura's emotional eruption, coupled with Sophia's sudden goodbye with Kaleo, left an uneasiness lingering amongst them. But Odigo had succeeded in eliciting some laughter from both women.

"My work is done here," he exclaimed as he walked away in the same direction Kaleo had exited.

"Are you serious? What do you mean your work is done here? Are you really going somewhere?" Thura asked quizzically.

Odigo turned and faced Thura, laughing while confidently walking backward.

"I'm kidding," he said. "But seriously, you two should get moving. I will keep a lookout to see if anyone is following us. I will catch up with the two of you a little later."

A thin blanket of brown, dried needles covered the forest floor, pro-
viding soft footing for Thura and Sophia as they walked through the
maze of scattered black pines. Despite overcast skies, the two women
could tell it was not quite noon, although they had been moving for
several hours without so much as a break. Sophia ambled toward a
mature tree that appeared as if someone had sheared off the lower
branches. It was perfect for her to sit beneath for a few minutes and
catch her breath.

"Oh, how I have missed these pines," the old woman said. "Nothing
against your beautiful ocean views in Patrida, but have you ever been
wrapped in such splendor, Thura? Close your eyes and breathe it in."

Thura sat down beside Sophia with her back up against the tree
and closed her eyes.

"Unless you close your eyes," she continued, "you will never fully
appreciate its splendor."

"I don't understand. How can I appreciate its splendor with my
eyes closed?" Thura asked.

"A person can rely so much on what they see with their eyes that
it becomes the only way they perceive and understand the world,"
Sophia said.

Still closing her eyes, Thura thought for a second and then
attempted to clarify.

"So you are saying there is more to seeing than looking with my
eyes?" Thura asked inquisitively.

"Precisely, Thura," Sophia responded. "There is always so much
more that can be seen, but rarely with your eyes. Tell me what you
see."

"I see a mix of old pine trees and saplings scattered around us,"
Thura said with her eyes tightly closed. "I see their needled branches
blowing in the wind. I see hundreds of ants running every which way,

building their little hills. I see an eagle's nest in one of the trees with the mother perched on it looking at us intently."

Sophia sat in silence for several minutes with her eyes still closed. She appeared to be basking in the few rays of sunlight evading the gray cloud cover.

"You have a keen sense of knowing what is around you," she said, breaking the silence. "That is a good first step for now. We should probably get moving."

Sophia's comment about it being a *good first step* perplexed Thura, who thought she had brilliantly, and very perceptively, described what was around them. From her perspective, which inched precariously close to a subtle arrogance, she believed the average person in Patrida would never have noticed half as much as she had. She wondered if Sophia was looking for more detail. Because if that was what she wanted, Thura could have been significantly more specific.

They were black pines with dark green needles, she thought. There were two separate sandy mounds with brown ants working at each. It was a white-breasted, brown-streaked eagle sitting atop the nest with two young eagles peeking out beside her.

"What do you mean by a *good first step*?" Thura asked, her mild frustration apparent. "I have always been aware of what was around me and have always noticed things others easily miss. I see the beauty of the sky and the way the sun shimmers on the waters. I notice the honeybees collecting pollen, and I appreciate their hard work in making honey. I recognize the people others have pushed aside. Were you looking for more detail? What more could I have told you?"

"Thura, sweet Thura. Yes, of course, it was a good first step," Sophia counseled, "but we are only ever taking first steps. Even now, in my old age, I only take first steps. Do you understand what that means?"

"I don't think so," Thura said.

"No one can be any farther along on this journey than another," Sophia said. "We are all students, always taking our first step together into greater knowing. But in that first step, the vastness of what we do not know becomes even more apparent. It is a strange and humbling paradox. That is why this road of knowing for a humble student never ends and why we are always taking first steps together, Thura."

"I am not sure I completely understand everything you just said, Sophia. But if you are still a student, then I cannot be anything but a student either, right?" Thura said with a smile, looking out of the corner of her eye at the old woman.

Sophia did not move or respond. Her heavy lids remained peacefully closed. The expanding and contracting of her chest was nearly imperceptible. Thura could not discern whether her friend was in deep meditation or if she had actually died while Thura was talking to her.

"Sophia?" Thura quietly asked.

"Yes?" Sophia whispered.

"I just wanted to make sure you were still with me," Thura said.

"I am here. Are you with me?" Sophia asked with intention.

"Yes, of course," Thura replied but then paused. "Um. I know we have to get moving, but what is my next first step, if you don't mind me asking?"

Still in a profoundly meditative posture, Sophia responded in a low monotone voice.

"Look at your three largest fingers," she said.

Thura curiously turned over her hand and, with intense scrutiny, examined the fingers she had so vigorously attempted to clean earlier in the morning.

"What do you see when you look at those fingers?" Sophia asked.

"Stains," Thura said.

"Is that really what you see, Thura?" Sophia asked.

"Well," Thura began, "you told me it was pine resin from…"

"From a pine tree," Sophia interrupted. "Is pine resin bad or good?"

Thura looked again at her three fingers but did not say a word. An immense heaviness expanded throughout the area behind Thura's ribcage, resulting in the unmistakable sting of saline in her eyes. The heaviness, unsatisfied with occupying only space in Thura's chest, began to creep upward and tighten around her neck, forcing out tears that fell like cleansing waters onto her stained fingers. While the young woman was not entirely sure where Sophia was going with her questioning, she realized she might not be ready for another first step.

"You see, Thura, what we see is not nearly as important as how we see," Sophia counseled. "While our first impulse is to always judge and label certain things as bad and other things as good, what if in the process of judging and labeling everything, we miss seeing what truly lies beneath the surface?"

Thura wiped her eyes but continued to look at her three fingers.

"Take the pine resin, for example," Sophia continued. "We never see it unless a pine tree is injured or broken. But then, it moves from within and works for the repairing, healing, and general well-being of the tree at the right time when the tree needs it."

"This isn't about the pine resin, though, is it?" Thura asked, although she knew the answer to her question. "This is about how I see people in Patrida and how I see my family."

"Keep going," Sophia gently coaxed.

"I see myself as someone who has figured out what I want and what I do not want for my life," Thura admitted. "I see myself as more enlightened than my family. So much so I view them as lost causes, especially my father."

Thura put her hands in front of her face, while Sophia was content letting Thura's last words sit with them. At last, the young woman continued.

"I only see their stains and blemishes and believe they are deserving of my judgment. I refuse to see the possibility of anything good within them. I am no different than anyone in Patrida who threw mud at me during my atonement ceremony and demanded that I say there was nothing good in me," Thura said.

This moment was the first time Thura had ever really looked at herself in this way. Before her conversation with Sophia, she had only been able to see her rightness and everyone else's wrongness. Her goodness, and everyone else's blemishes. But there was a more incredible irony in what she discovered. Thura realized the self-righteousness she so despised in Patrida was the same self-righteousness by which she judged her own family.

In an attempt to not end on a down note with Thura, Sophia gently coaxed her again.

"But you are learning that … "

"I am learning that we are all taking first steps and that I am right there with them," Thura said, finishing Sophia's sentence. "They are students just as I am and just as you are."

"And even though our first inclination is to see their stains," Sophia added, "there is something that lies below the surface of everyone that continues to work toward our healing and wholeness. Not just mine, not just yours, but their healing and wholeness, as well."

This time it was Sophia's eyes that glistened when she opened them and faced Thura. The old woman reached for Thura's hand and held it with the palm up, grasping Thura's fingers with her other hand.

"It's so easy to see stains, Thura," Sophia said. "But it takes grace and patience to see the possibility of wholeness in people and to not give up on them."

"Is that how you survived for so long imprisoned in Patrida?" Thura asked.

"Yes, it was," she said. "Anger, resentment, and pride can keep a person imprisoned. I had to find that deep reservoir of peace for myself before I could see anyone else differently. It was that peace, that deep abiding source that works for our good, Thura, that allowed me to first talk to you. While it would have been easier to hate you for what your father did to us, that peace helped me see you differently. I was able to see your beauty and humanity."

Thura put her other hand on top of Sophia's and squeezed it firmly.

"I know you are in this place as well, Thura," Sophia continued. "I could see it in you when you stood outside the prison door in that soft, yellow light coming from the oil lamp and said you were Dipsa. I saw your potential. You are not satisfied with jugs of water someone else attempts to fill up for you. You long for depths and abundance into which only you can dive headfirst. That is where you will find freedom, Thura."

"But you were able to discover that for yourself when you were imprisoned!" Thura said. "What hope do I have? I have been imprisoned in Patrida my whole life, and it did not come close to giving me the same sense of freedom. It did not make me want to stay there a second longer. The best I could do was light every candle and lamp in my house as an act of rebellion. Nothing changed in me at all except my resolve to get out of there. The truth is that my so-called prison only made me bitter and resentful, and ultimately judgmental toward the community and my family."

"Do you hear yourself, Thura?" Sophia asked. "That is not your truth at all. You are focusing on what you see and not on how you are seeing. Truth is not what you see on the surface of things. Truth is the underlying reality of all things. It is that which holds all things together and animates all life and gives it all the same value. Do you understand?"

Thura continued listening, as she knew the old woman had so much more to say.

"It cannot be earned or owned or labeled," Sophia continued. "It is that which can't be hidden, that which refuses to be concealed. This underlying truth of reality is always trying to break through the surface and manifest to all. This truth is divine love, Thura. But it is not something you go to find. It is that which has already found you and accepted you as you are. When the ocean surrounds you, you dive into it."

In the distance, a strange noise cried out like a bird. Frightened it was not a bird, but possibly the Patridian guards, Thura jumped up and hid behind another, more densely branched pine. Sophia, unfazed by the unseemly noise, put her hands to her face and returned the same strange bird call to Odigo. Within minutes, the young man appeared and greeted the women.

"You haven't traveled as far as I would have expected. Of course, you were probably waiting on Thura to catch up with you the entire time, right?" Odigo said with a sly smile.

"No. We were moving together the whole time," Sophia said, walking directly past Odigo without looking at him.

The young man raised his eyebrows and looked at Thura, who in turn raised her shoulders and hands in bewilderment at the old woman leaving them.

"Call out to her, Odigo. Ask her where she's going!" Thura said.

"What do you mean? Why me?" Odigo asked. "You've been with her the whole time."

The young woman gave the young man a light-hearted but menacing look.

"Okay, okay," Odigo said in resignation. "Sophia! You are going the wrong way! Where in the world are you going!"

Without stopping or even turning around to acknowledge the question, the old woman continued to hobble away into the woods before shouting back.

"Where I belong!"

CHAPTER 12

P rodido stood alone in the center of the dirt road running directly through the nearly year-old town. Staring westward toward an ocean veiled in darkness, his only sense was the warmth of the passing breeze. The windows of each house lining both sides of the road remained lightless, the townspeople still fast asleep, as the religious leader awaited Ochi for their early morning meeting.

From behind, the sun's first rays began to disproportionately break through the uneven density of the woods on the east end. Remaining perfectly oblivious to his surroundings, Prodido only considered the possibilities of his imminent conversation. Savage cries piercing through the silence startled the religious leader. Prodido, turning toward the disturbance, noticed the dark shadows of what appeared to be three or four vultures and a lone wolf closing in on the carcass of a small animal. He could not help but watch the unending back and forth between the animals but then appreciate the reward of the wolf's persistence.

"Good morning," a voice called out from behind.

"Oh! Good morning, Ochi," Prodido said, turning back quickly. "I was just admiring these wonderful creatures, and how dogged and relentless they are in satisfying their most primal and insatiable instinct. Ah! Praise God for his handiwork!"

Putting his arm around Ochi, the religious leader continued.

"Velos was the one who was instrumental in setting up this time for us," Prodido began. "It seems we never have an opportune time to connect without others around. It is either at the family dinner table or after services. So this is genuinely a blessing to spend some time with you."

"Likewise. What's been on your mind?" Ochi asked.

"I have been thinking about this infant community of ours, Ochi," the religious leader began, "and the amazing progress we have made in such a short amount of time through your leadership and hard work. But I cannot help but wonder if this infant community of yours is not ready to move from milk to solid foods if you know what I mean."

"That's certainly an interesting way of putting it," Ochi said. "I'm not quite sure I would have described our town that way myself. But I have to admit you've intrigued me. Go on."

Abruptly positioning himself in front of the leader, causing him to stop in his tracks, Prodido faced Ochi with a seriousness commensurate with the opportunity he perceived.

"The Lord has blessed you, your Excellency, if I may call you that," Prodido said. "You are a principled leader with a strong sense of right and wrong, and the people see that in you. That is precisely why they respect you and have continued to follow you. You have given them the milk they have needed in this season. But the children are rapidly growing and demanding the kind of food you cannot provide. They need real sustenance, your Excellency."

Ochi began to laugh as he found amusement, not only in Prodido's unusual metaphor but more so in his early morning sobriety.

"I haven't even had my first cup of coffee," Ochi chuckled. "You sure know how to get really serious, really fast, don't you? I like that."

Sensing the opportunity in front of him, Prodido excitedly continued.

"A community cannot be made holy by virtue of a principled leader," he explained. "You may guide them and give them direction, both of which you have done exceedingly well. But like branches of a tree, a people can only grow in holiness as they are rooted in holiness.

So my question to you, your Excellency, is how will these branches ultimately grow and flourish if someone does not order this community in a way that leads to holiness?"

Ochi remained quiet and pensive. While he proudly carried the weight and responsibility of being the de facto leader of this fledgling community, he was coming to realize his complete inadequacy as a visionary. But it was not a result of negligence on his part.

Ochi operated in a world of organization and function. He understood structure and found comfort in its rigidness and predictability. He had been the perfect leader to execute a detailed plan of building a community physically from the ground up and leading people through it. But seeing a future painted with possibilities and then navigating people toward that future was way out of his wheelhouse. So the thought of being their visionary was a weight he did not wish to carry.

"As you know, your Excellency," Prodido persisted, "and speaking strictly as a man of God, the Lord judges those whom he places in positions of authority more severely. Whether you like it or not, or whether you are even willing to acknowledge it or not, you will be held to account by the Almighty for how you decide … "

"Good morning, gentleman," Kaleo interrupted from behind. "I want to apologize for my tardiness. Would you mind catching me up on what I've missed?"

Attempting to make light of the conversation, Ochi immediately turned and smiled.

"Well, my friend, you've missed quite a bit," he said. "Prodido was just about to enlighten me on his spectacular vision for the future of this community."

Raising an eyebrow, Kaleo rebuffed.

"You don't say. Well, I think we're doing a pretty darn good job of leading the people at the present. Don't you think, Ochi?" he asked.

"Everyone seems to be getting along just fine, if you don't mind me saying so."

Prodido's irritation with Kaleo being a part of their meeting was readily apparent. By meeting at sunrise, he had hoped to speak freely with Ochi without Kaleo constantly offering his own two-cent opinions on everything. But as Prodido well knew, Kaleo believed he should be by the leader's side every waking hour as his head guard.

"As I was saying, Ochi," Prodido began again, ignoring their new third wheel. "It is your responsibility to order this entire island in a way that calls it to holiness. Walk with me."

The men walked westward toward the open space at the end of the dusty road. Their fleet of battered boats still lining the shore below. Prodido turned, facing the long stretch that ran directly between the newly constructed houses, as Ochi and Kaleo turned with him.

"This," Prodido announced emphatically with a penchant for the dramatic," is Patrida."

The men stood in silence.

"What's a Patrida?" Kaleo blurted out.

Closing his eyes in utter frustration, Prodido answered in a disgusted monotone.

"It means fatherland. This island shall be the land of God our Father," he explained.

"Oh," Kaleo mouthed.

"I like the sound of that," Ochi added. "It has the sound of seriousness and sophistication like we're a real town with a real identity. I even like the hidden meaning of it, too. Tell me more."

"Well, the area in which we are standing will display a criminal's gallows," Prodido continued. "No matter where one stands in Patrida, they will be reminded of God's justice for the wrongdoer."

The whites of Kaleo's eyes grew along with his disbelief. He expected Ochi to return the same reaction. But Prodido had already captivated the leader.

"Seems pretty gruesome and unnecessary. Don't you think, Ochi?" Kaleo asked in an attempt to inject some common sense into the conversation. "Can you imagine people waking up one day with some sort of death contraption in their face? We have a good thing going here, and we're doing things the right way. There's no need to threaten people to be good. That's not the way you do it."

"Good morning!" a young boy called out, running up from behind the men.

"Tyran! What are you doing up so early?" Ochi asked.

"There's my little buddy," Kaleo said as he put his hand on Tyran's head, messing up his morning hair even more. "You've got a good kid here, Ochi."

"We're discussing some important business right now, Tyran. Why don't you go back to the house and see what your mother is doing," Ochi instructed.

"The boy can stay here with us, Ochi. He's no problem," Prodido offered. "It is never too early to begin instructing a young boy in how to be godly, you know."

"I appreciate the offer, but he can join us another time. Off you go, Tyran," Ochi demanded.

"Very well then," Prodido responded. "But back to your comment, Kaleo, before young Tyran joined us. And I say this with all due respect. One can only understand the riches of God's mercy and forgiveness when they first understand the fiery rage by which God's wrath and judgment burn toward the unrepentant. That is why the criminal's gallows are essential. If the people do not understand judgment, how will they ever understand the path to freedom? Let's continue."

Prodido walked in a straight line down the center of the dirt road ahead of the two other men and opened his arms wide. Rising above the tree line and centered directly in front of the religious man, the sun's brilliance appeared to be summoning them and calling them forth.

"There is only one way to freedom," Prodido cried aloud, "and the people will know it intuitively as they walk along this road. The only way to travel from death to life, from enslavement to freedom, is along the straight and narrow path. This road shall be known as the Monon, for it is the only way."

With Prodido still walking ahead, wholly lost in his plan's grandiosity, Kaleo attempted to reason with Ochi.

"Does this not sound the least bit bizarre to you?" Kaleo whispered.

"Maybe from the outside looking in," Ochi said without regard to the volume of his speaking voice, "but his logic is sound. People need to know right and wrong. They need to understand justice and punishment. Once I explain how this vision will help preserve peace and create greater freedom, everyone will be fine with it."

Still whispering, but this time raising his voice, Kaleo responded.

"You mean you're seriously considering doing this?" he asked. "Have you not listened to a single word at our gatherings? And what others have been saying to Prodido? The way some of them have started to challenge him and his ideas of faith and…"

"What are we talking about here?" Prodido interrupted. "Did I hear my name, Kaleo?"

"You sure did," Kaleo announced. "I don't like one bit of what you're talking about, to be honest. I think it's backwards the way you talk about God. I was just saying that people like Numa and Sophia talk about a God that changes people through love, not fear and punishment."

His blood boiling at Kaleo's constant distraction and interference, but careful to remain patient and composed in front of Ochi, Prodido invited the men to join him at the spring.

"This is where we shall experience the God of love, Kaleo," the religious leader said. "We shall call it Sanctuary. For it is in this place of freedom where we shall gather each evening as a community to worship and experience the presence of the Almighty. And around these waters, we will build a sacrarium, a holy monument, to wash the repentant and make them holy."

"I like it. I like it a lot. Maybe we should start calling you Father Prodido," Ochi joked.

"Well, I want to go on record to say that I don't like it at all," Kaleo announced. "I'm not a religious scholar, but it doesn't feel right to me. People can be holy without all the pomp and dramatic effect. I would go so far as to say that we can experience God anywhere, anytime. So yeah. This feels like a bit of a power grab to me, if I'm being honest."

~

Prodido patiently watched the blood-red sunset fade into the vast black waters as darkness draped around him. Turning his back on the final light emanating from the horizon, the religious man walked along shadows while keeping an eye out for his new acquaintance. From a few houses away, Prodido saw the silhouette of a man standing at his doorstep.

"Heard you got your hands full, preacher man," the man barked out.

"You have no idea," Prodido said as he stepped onto his porch. "And please, call me Father. Father Prodido. Now, come in and have a seat at the table. I am going to call for my boys to join us."

The tall, slender man walked over to the dark wood table and pulled out one of the matching chairs. But before he could sit down, Father Prodido returned with his two sons.

"This is my oldest son, Pali," he said. "And this is my younger son, Machi."

The man shook their hands and took a seat.

"Boys, this is Fovos," Father Prodido said. "We have gotten to know each other over the last couple of weeks, and I find him to be equally comedic and resourceful. Now, while he and I chat, will the two of you do what I asked of you earlier?"

Without hesitation or a single word spoken, Pali and Machi promptly headed toward the door and exited.

"So tell me about this Kaleo character and what he's all about," Fovos said.

"Yes, yes, Kaleo," Father Prodido responded. "Well, as you know, he is Ochi's head guardsman, but I say that in jest. He neither has the legitimacy nor fortitude to be in such a position. He assumed it solely by merit of proximity to the leader. And as you have seen for yourself, his dozen or so guardsmen, if we can even call them guardsmen, are more helpful servants of the people than enforcers of the law."

"So he's the kind of guy that would put his foot in the doorway when you're trying to close it, huh?" Fovos scoffed.

"That is precisely how I would describe him," Father Prodido said. "And I am convinced that the way you get him to move his foot is by removing the man from the doorway entirely."

Fovos, who had placed an old toothpick in the corner of his mouth, rocked back in his chair, put both hands behind his head, and nodded.

"I sure am liking the way you think, Father," Fovos said. "While there's always more ways to skin a cat than one, I appreciate a man who's not afraid to just rip the damn skin off!"

Three knocks at the door preceded its opening, with Kaleo entering first and the brothers following closely behind. Father Prodido stood and greeted his guest.

"Kaleo, please, come have a seat," the religious leader said. "I have been ruminating on our time together this morning. I believe we have unfortunately been moving in two very different and opposing directions in how we see this fine community's future. I have called you here because I am desirous of us aligning our priorities. In fact, there is nothing that would make me more joyful than for us to get on the same page."

"I agree," Kaleo heartily replied. "When you have a good thing going, the best thing for everybody is to get along and then come together to work out their differences. So I sure apprecia…"

"That's why I have asked Fovos here to join us this evening," Prodido interrupted. "I am not sure if the two of you have officially met, but I can assure you he is a fabulous mediator."

Fovos put down his chair and leaned forward, placing his elbows on his knees. With a subtle tilt of his head, Fovos motioned for the brothers to take their place. Pali and Machi moved behind Kaleo's chair, each putting a hand on a shoulder.

"Here's the way ol' Fovos mediates," he said. "I say, and you do. See how that works?"

Kaleo sat unmoved in nervous silence.

"Here's what you're gonna do," Fovos began. "You're going to step down as head guard and move out of that fancy little house of yours. Where you take up residence is your own business, as long as it isn't along this road. Alright, boys, we're done here."

"I'm not stepping down just because you say so," Kaleo challenged. "And you're crazy if you think I'm moving out of the house I built with my own two hands."

"Oh. He wants to know the *why*," Fovos said as he laughed and looked at the others. "Father, this guy's a sharp one. He isn't gonna do it just because we say so. No! This ol' boy wants to know *why!*"

The four men surrounded Kaleo and began laughing riotously.

"You see, you're gonna do it because today Ochi's wife announced to the town that she's pregnant with their third child," Fovos said. "Now, is she really pregnant? Of course not. Does ol' Ochi think he's going to be a daddy? Of course he does. But no one has to know that she's not really pregnant, you see. And I'm doggone certain she'll announce her miscarriage after a few months."

"Why are you telling me this?" Kaleo demanded.

"Well, as far as the boys and I are concerned," Fovos said, "that's your baby! And I'll be happy to tell the whole damn town that you're the daddy. Now, is that the *why* you were looking for?"

"You have got to be kidding me! That's absurd! What's wrong with you!" Kaleo shouted as he attempted to stand up, only to be pushed back down by Pali and Machi. "No one would believe such an idiotic accusation! Ochi himself wouldn't even believe this garbage! Let alone Velos! She would laugh right in your face because she knows it's not true!"

Fovos leaned back in his chair, assuming his earlier position, grinning from ear to ear.

"Would she?" he asked rhetorically, looking up to the ceiling.

Stepping out from the darkened bedroom in the back, Velos walked toward the table and stared at Kaleo.

"I would absolutely tell my husband this is your child," Velos said with an unemotional resolve. "I will do whatever it takes to help bring order to Patrida and make us holy and presentable before God."

Perplexed and bewildered by the bizarre situation, Kaleo lost the ability to speak. A single word failed to materialize.

"Here, let me say it for you ol' boy," Fovos mocked. "Velos, how could you do such a thing!"

The room erupted again in boisterous laughter.

"Whoa! Whoa! Whoa! Quiet! Quiet! He doesn't know, does he?" Fovos manically shouted as he looked around the table at Prodido, Velos, and the brothers. "He doesn't know, does he? He doesn't know! He really doesn't know! Velos is Father Prodido's sister, you fool!"

The room exploded.

"How could you not know that!" Fovos screamed. "I tell you what! Ol' Fovos is just full of surprises tonight, isn't he! Father, I believe everyone's agreed to the terms here. Back to you!"

Fovos abruptly stood up from his chair and busted out of the house without saying another word. Exiting closely behind him was Velos, whose work, too, was complete. If Fovos had been a sentence in this dramatic episode, Velos was the exclamation mark. And no one felt the impact of it more than Kaleo, who sat nauseated and listless from the figurative punch to his gut.

"In the morning," Father Prodido began, "you will send a servant to Ochi requesting a meeting with him. In the request, you will ask that I be present along with my oldest, Pali. Once we gather together, you will step down from your position, a position never formally given to you, and recommend that Pali take over the head guard's position. You will tell him that, while you are slowly warming to the future vision of Patrida and the part you may play in it one day, you realize you are not the right person for this important position. Do you understand?"

"Yes," Kaleo whispered, looking down at the table.

"Excellent," Father Prodido said. "Lastly, you will need to vacate your house within the next thirty days. Do not draw attention to yourself or make it a big ceremony. You are moving. That is it. If there are questions, you are light on answers. Do you understand this?"

"Yes."

"Perfect. Now, you may be dismissed," the religious leader said. "And please, make sure you close the door on your way out."

CHAPTER 13

Nestling a ball of hardened pine resin within a bed of wood shavings, Ochi placed the tinder on the ground and began to strike his flint with fatigued resolve. Within minutes, one tiny spark ignited the shavings and set the resin aflame, around which he quickly added the kindling and larger pieces of wood he had collected.

Weary from waking so early that morning and then trying to determine the best route to reach the other side of the island, Ochi hypnotically watched oranges and reds dance across the embers. The day had been emotionally draining, and his exhaustion had almost entirely overtaken his gnawing hunger. Ochi reached into his leather satchel to grab anything edible, but instead, he pulled out a folded piece of paper. Opening it slowly, for fear of what could be written inside, the man held it in the light of the struggling fire.

I know what you are doing, Ochi. FP

Ochi's heart began to race, and every forest noise was suddenly magnified. In his mind, men hiding in the dark of the woods surrounded and watched him. But as every second grew longer and the soft, sedative glow slowly faded, Ochi closed his weary eyes and immediately fell asleep on a thick bed of pine needles.

Voices of men began to cry out in the woods, shouting his name. The distant shouts grew louder as the men drew closer, each coming from a different direction as if attempting to surround him. Ochi began to run but felt something holding his legs back. He looked down and saw the dense ground cover transform into weeds attempting to wrap around his ankles. With even more intensity as the men got closer and shouted his name louder, Ochi ripped away from the weeds and began to move freely once again. As he looked over his shoulder, the three men had converged and closed their distance on him. Ochi began to slow down, however, as he heard what they were shouting at him.

"You have turned away from God, Ochi!" the first man yelled.

"You have betrayed Patrida, Ochi!" the second man screamed.

"You have failed your family, Ochi!" the third man shouted.

The men continued to repeat their accusations over and over. As Ochi turned his head away from them, he noticed he was approaching a dead end. Within a dozen strides, Ochi reached a steep cliff atop a large body of water. He stood gazing at the hundred-foot drop as the men surrounded him. Turning to face them, Ochi firmly stood his ground without fear, despite the men not having faces. Each wore a black gown with a single word embroidered across their chests.

God.

Country.

Family.

Ochi could feel the loose ground beneath his heels. As the men closed in around him, they lifted their arms with knives in their hands. First, one foot began to slip and then the other. Ochi started to fall, but a hand reached down and grabbed his outstretched and desperate arm. Thura held him. But her grip was only momentary, as the blood on their arms caused his hand to slip.

"Who is bleeding, Thura? Who is bleeding?" Ochi cried as he began to slip.

"Ochi! Ochi!" Thura shouted.

The wind rushed past him violently as he fell, but it felt like slow motion. Why is my daughter calling out my name? he thought. Why does she not call me father? The distance between Ochi and Thura widened as he neared the water's surface.

"Ochi!" the voice cried out but was nearly inaudible.

Opening his eyes, Ochi saw the last wisp of smoke rising from the circulating ash dust. The pounding of his head, likely from inhaling smoke all night, joined the ache of his heart as he sat up and thought about his second bizarre dream. Just then, a voice cried out from the woods, shouting his name.

"Ochi! Ochi!"

He realized it had not been Thura shouting his name in the dream.

"Ochi!" the voice cried out again.

"Yes. I am here," he shouted back.

"There you are," Sophia said. "Why are you journeying alone?"

Completely disregarding the question, Ochi jumped up and ran toward the old woman, searching desperately for Thura.

"Where is she? Where's Thura?" he pleaded. "Is she okay?"

"She's fine. She's fine," Sophia responded in a motherly voice. "Thura is on her own journey. And your prisoner, a fine young man by the name of Odigo, is accompanying her. I thought you might want to know his name."

Ochi only heard the first part of what Sophia said because he was so preoccupied with looking past her to find Thura. Despite having told the people of Patrida that his daughter's life was in danger, he knew no one had harmed her. He asked only in hopes that Thura was standing somewhere nearby. He desperately wanted to make things right with her.

But the truth was that Ochi had no idea what he was doing. He left Patrida on a whim without any idea where he was going or what he would do when he first saw Thura. He did not even know what his ultimate goal was for returning to Patrida with her. Despite the unknowns surrounding him, the question that genuinely demanded an answer from him at the moment was Sophia's. Why was Ochi traveling alone? It was that one question, however, he was least prepared to answer.

Still searching in vain for Thura among the maze of pines, but mostly trying to avoid facing the old woman, Ochi barked out at her.

"So what do you want?" he asked. "Why are you here?"

"Why do you keep asking the wrong questions?" Sophia responded with a sly grin on her face.

"What's that supposed to mean?" Ochi countered as he turned and faced her, careful to avoid eye contact.

Sophia's question caught him off guard. While Ochi was preoccupied with concrete and practical matters, Sophia's question demanded he stop to reflect.

"Why are you journeying alone, Ochi?" Sophia patiently asked again.

The question connected this time. Ochi turned away, and continued looking aimlessly at the ground as if trying to find something that was not there. Content with letting him search, Sophia stood calmly and allowed the silence to persist.

"I need to get my daughter back," Ochi responded, attempting to break the uncomfortable stillness but refusing to go any deeper.

Sophia did not respond to him. In her well-earned wisdom sitting alone in silence all those years in Patrida, Sophia understood there was only one way to truly disrupt someone running in circles. As Ochi turned to walk back and join the old woman and her prolonged silence, he realized she was no longer with him.

"Hey! Where'd you go? I was about to answer your question," Ochi called out.

In reality, Ochi was neither interested in conversing with Sophia nor answering her question. He believed she knew how to find Thura, so he wanted to keep her close to him. However, concluding she had really left him, Ochi decided to get moving. He had already wasted enough precious time fooling around with Sophia and her distractions.

Ochi picked up his leather satchel from the ground, but attempted to leave Sophia's question behind. The stillness of the woods lingered around him as he took his first steps. Despite how far Ochi had already traveled from Patrida, the forest beckoned him to go deeper.

The early morning sun painted the sky with soft pinks and purples. Ochi could only catch glimpses of it when there was an opening in front of him. While the trees kept him from seeing the tapestry, his intentional avoidance of Sophia's question kept him from confronting the truth within himself. As much as he tried to get his mind on other things, her one question persistently followed him.

Ochi could not think of a time in Patrida when he had ever been asked a question and then left alone to meditate on it. Nearly every inquiry he received was practical in nature and demanded a quick and decisive answer. While wrestling with a more contemplative question was as uncomfortable as the silence for Ochi, he decided he had an entire day of walking ahead of him and little else to consider.

Why am I journeying alone? he thought.

Ochi had never been this far out in the woods. His time in Patrida never necessitated it. Additionally, Tyran had always been too young during their trips for them to cover this much ground. Everything in front of him was a new experience.

After a couple of quick miles on a few different game trails, Ochi stopped momentarily and closed his eyes. The coolness of the morning had already given way to the rising sun. He wiped the sweat from his brow. His discomfort with the stillness was slowly beginning to fade. Ochi willed himself to breathe.

Twenty years of ceaseless activity and chatter in Patrida had unknowingly conditioned him to become dependent upon constant noise and chaos. He could not remember a time when the sounds of nature only surrounded him, rather than people. That abrupt change was what initially made the silence of the woods so unbearable. By himself, he could not look at anyone else's problems, only his own. Breaking free from the continuous and nearly addictive stimulation of Patrida slowly enabled him to see and hear. It also forced him to look at himself.

This newly discovered space in the island's deep forest helped Ochi recover something the rat race of Patrida had obscured. First, he heard the birds' melodic chorus and then the scurrying of small critters chasing each other between the trees. Then he took another breath and listened to the gentle susurrating of leaves as the wind made them dance and sway. But there was more to this experience than what Ochi could hear.

As he looked ahead, he saw the trees opening up like curtains, revealing what had to be, in his estimation, the most majestic view on the island. Patrida suddenly felt more constricted and gray by comparison. The rich and vibrant expanse in front of him exploded with wildflowers, towering trees, and perfectly complementary blues of water and sky. While it was easy to feel big and important, independent and essential in his tiny little town, Ochi became aware of how small he really was. Consumed by the vastness surrounding him, he put down his head and looked at the ground in humility.

"Why am I journeying alone?" he whispered under his breath, searching for an answer that continued to elude him.

Left only with the company of his thoughts, Ochi sat down on a nearby rock and closed his eyes. For years he had blocked out voices from his past that had instructed him when he was younger and challenged him as he got older. He had fully insulated himself from perspectives and ideas that could have helped him see the world differently as an adult. But by himself on a rock in the middle of a forest, Ochi was slowly beginning to discover how silence has a way of resurrecting things we try to bury.

"Look around, Ochi," he remembered his father saying to him when he was a teenager. "Life is pulsing through the veins of creation. All living things are connected. We are never alone when we remember that."

His father's wise words seemed to come from nowhere but then continued to replay over and over in his mind. He knew down deep that everything was connected and that he was connected to everything around him. However, Ochi's problem was that all of his relationships were broken and disconnected. Every person in his life had abandoned him. His town. His friends. His wife and children. He felt utterly dejected and frustrated, especially as he thought about Sophia's question.

"Why am I journeying alone!" he finally screamed.

"Now you are asking the right question, Ochi," the old woman's voice called out from behind the trees.

"Have you been following me this entire time?" Ochi asked with agitation.

"Of course I have been," Sophia replied as she walked toward him. "Did you think I would let you journey alone?"

The old woman turned and began walking ahead of Ochi, not allowing him to answer.

"I had a dream last night," Ochi called out from behind as he followed after her. "I was being chased through the woods by three cloaked men. Each of them shouted something at me. One of them said I turned my back on God. Another said I betrayed Patrida. And the last one said I abandoned my family. Even though it was a dream, they might be right. Maybe I'm the reason I'm alone."

"Do you believe those things about yourself, Ochi?" Sophia asked. "Or, is that what others want you to believe about yourself?"

"Is there a difference?" Ochi retorted. "Where do my beliefs end and their beliefs begin? And where do their beliefs end and mine begin? For all my good intentions with Patrida, we became something I never intended. It's like how you can be off by one degree at the beginning of a journey, but then over time, you realize how far you've strayed from where you wanted to go. It's so gradual no one sees it while it's happening, but then one day, you look up and say, 'Where are we and how did we get here?' It doesn't seem like much at the beginning, but when no one sees you're off track or challenges it, you end up lost together."

Ochi stopped talking but continued to walk beside Sophia. Looking out of the corner of his eye at the old woman, he wondered if she was going to say anything back to him. Sophia hobbled resolutely by his side with her sight set on the line in front of her.

Looking ahead again and staring at his path, Ochi attempted to walk in their shared silence. However, Sophia's silence began to slowly pierce him. She had known all those years ago that Patrida was off track. She had been one of the voices challenging their direction. Yet it was Ochi who had driven them out and killed them.

His breathing became short and labored. A sharp pain radiated throughout his chest. Ochi suddenly stopped and put his calloused hand over his heart.

"You saw it from the beginning. You tried to tell us," he said.

The old woman paused a few feet in front of him without turning.

"You could see what we couldn't see for ourselves," he said. "You knew our obsession with trying to make Patrida a strict religious community would eventually do the exact opposite. You knew it would kill the spirit of Patrida."

"And it did," Sophia replied, still without turning around.

Ochi was frozen. Painful memories flooded his mind as he remembered the emotions that consumed him the day he went on his bloody rampage.

"When you believe you're doing the right thing for the right reasons," Ochi confessed, "it makes perfect sense to ignore voices that challenge you. But as the chorus grows louder, you eventually get to the point where you want to silence them and get rid of everyone who opposes you."

Sophia stood in silence.

"I used to call that day the Great Liberation," Ochi continued, "because I believed that getting rid of you would eventually lead to our freedom. But I can see now it was anything but that. I thought I was fighting for our freedom, but I was enslaving us. I thought I was preserving our righteousness, but I was compromising it. I thought I was creating a spiritual community, but I was killing it."

Sophia turned toward Ochi and gradually approached him.

"So, is the voice in your dream correct when he says you have turned your back on God?" Sophia asked. "It appears you have turned your back on a sick system masquerading in the name of God, Ochi. And with each step forward, are you not choosing to leave it behind and walk into something more life-giving?"

"You say that, but look at the devastation all around me," Ochi challenged. "Look at the devastation I've caused. I am the center of it. Yeah, I want to find peace. I want it desperately. But I've done too much damage. If my relationships are in shambles, what do I have left? You say I've left a sick system, but am I not the sick system? Do I not take this sick system with me everywhere I go? What good is this beauty around me when all I do is corrupt it."

Sophia stood in somber yet steadfast silence, staring at Ochi. While she knew how painful this moment was for him, she also knew there were some places a person had to journey alone.

"I'm the one who let my wife bring her brother to this island," Ochi cried out. "I'm the one who bought into his religious vision for the island. I'm the one who is responsible for Patrida becoming so broken and divided and outraged. I'm the one who abandoned my son by trying to hold Patrida together. I'm the one who became a monster in my daughter's eyes and who she now wants to avoid. I'm the one who looked my father in the eyes and stabbed him in the heart because I believed he was challenging my authority and the stability of Patrida."

Ochi fell to the ground, broken and sobbing.

"He didn't deserve to die like that," he cried. "Not by anyone's hand, but especially not by the hand of his son. I'm the coward who could not look my mother in her eyes after killing her husband. I locked you away in my shame. Look at me. I still can't look you in the eyes."

The seemingly impenetrable walls Ochi had constructed around his heart for years started to crack. Every secret written in his journal and hidden under his closet floorboards came to the surface with tears. The broken man buried his face in his rough hands, hoping his mother could not see him. But Sophia hobbled over to her son and knelt in front of him, putting her tired arms around his head.

"I love you, Ochi," she said. "I always have, and I always will. Listen to me. You have never been too far away for me to abandon you. Even when I was locked away, I was with you. I never once gave into bitterness or wished ill toward you because you are my son. I always held onto the hope that you would come home one day. And look, here you are. You are home, Ochi."

With his hands still covering his face, Ochi whispered to his mother.

"I'm sorry. I'm sorry for what I did to dad. I'm sorry for what I did to you and the pain I put you through all these years. I'm so sorry."

"Ochi, you have always been forgiven," Sophia said. "The day you became my son, you were forgiven. My love for you has never changed. Look me in the eyes."

"I can't," he cried.

Sophia hugged him even tighter and pulled him closer.

"Trust me, Ochi," she whispered in his ear. "My love for you is greater than your guilt and shame."

The old woman removed her arms from around his neck and placed one of her hands underneath his chin. Slowly she raised his head, and their eyes met. Ochi had forgotten the love in his mother's eyes, but at that moment, he saw it once again, as tears streamed down both of their faces.

CHAPTER 14

On the surface, she appeared content and god-fearing. With the sun, she would rise and take pleasure in her routine, always looking forward to the tasks needing to be accomplished throughout the day. She was draped in allegiance, wearing duty like a badge of honor. As a woman of deep devotion, she held religious observance in her right hand while clutching judgment tightly in her left.

But behind her defenses and within her rigid walls, she neglected the deep wounds of her brokenhearted. She condoned the transgressions of her children. She buried the bones of her prophets. Despite her poverty, she lifted herself high in exaltation. Wisdom had left her. The spirit had abandoned her. All that remained was her lust for power and control.

Patrida radiated virtue from the outside but was diseased from within. On her hardened outer edges, the Patridian guard fortified her perimeter to protect her disorder. Patrida's one-way street amassed the dutiful who walked in an unquestioning blind allegiance. Her malignant heart was beset around a hardwood table in a tiny, square room with dark curtains drawn in a guard-protected house along the Monon.

"My mother said you wanted a word with me, Father," Tyran said as he closed the front door and joined the shadows surrounding the religious leader's unadorned table.

"Yes, yes. God bless your strong, god-fearing mother, Tyran. Please, have a seat. May I offer you something to drink?" Father Prodido asked, pouring a chalice of crimson wine for himself.

"I think I'm good for now, Father," Tyran replied. "Thank you."

"Yes, very well then. Have I ever told you the story of the great tower, Tyran?" Father Prodido asked.

"I don't believe so," Tyran replied. "I don't think I've ever heard that one before."

"Ah, well then. Let me tell you," said Father Prodido. "There was once a community composed of exceptional visionaries. The kind of people who could truly see possibilities when others were quite content with what was directly in front of them, when others were simply satisfied with the status quo.

By day these visionaries would gather together and discuss the possibility of constructing a massive, prominent tower at the city's center. It was a bold vision. But they believed this edifice would serve as a testament to their greatness. They believed they could bring the common man and woman together to realize something beyond themselves."

"I definitely haven't heard this story before," said Tyran, believing the religious leader had finished the tale. "It's very inspirational, Father. It reminds me…"

"But by night, at the genesis of construction," Father Prodido interrupted, his face appearing more ominous in the dimness of the room, "a single man began to saturate one corner of the edifice's foundation with water. It was not much at first. In fact, in the beginning, it was hardly noticeable. During construction, the visionaries sat at a distance to oversee the work, but they were too far away to discern a problem. Meanwhile, the common man and woman, who were all basic laborers, never detected an issue because they only did what they were told to do."

"There's no way a soft foundation could support the increasing weight," Tyran said. "And if no one notices there's a problem, the building will eventually fall."

"Yes, of course. You can see the problem here, Tyran," Father Prodido said. "But ever so subtly, the saturated ground caused the corner of this growing edifice to slowly sink. Oh, it was only inches at first. But without exacting measurements, not a single person could foresee the inevitable problem. It was slow and gradual.

Weeks turned into months, and inches turned into feet. From up close, the common man and woman could not see there was no future for the structure in which they poured their blood, sweat, and tears. From a distance, however, the visionaries began to discern the inevitable. By the time they discovered the problem was their foundation, it was too late."

Tyran had been tracking and fully understood the dire implication of the story.

"A single man," Father Prodido added, "has the ability to thoroughly destroy the uniting work of the common man and woman, Tyran. But even more devastatingly, a single man can decimate the dreams of visionaries. Do you understand what I am saying?"

Tyran reached forward and poured the blood-red wine into a chalice of his own. After taking a convincing drink and wiping the excess from his mouth with his sleeve, he responded to the religious leader.

"I do understand," he said. "Under the cover of night, my father has been patiently pouring water on Patrida's foundation, weakening it, while we've continued to build and toil by day. Over time, our foundation has become soft and unstable. Our structure began to lean over time, but it wasn't immediately apparent to any of us. We would've never suspected anyone, especially my father, would be working against us to weaken our foundation. But here we are. Patrida's moral foundation is too weak to hold together, and it's on the verge of collapse."

"Yes, yes. You have a keen insight, Tyran," Father Prodido said. "You see the problem clearly and understand it demands an urgent solution. Ungodliness must never be allowed to go unchecked. It must be exposed for what it is, lest it continues to run rampant among us. A strong and godly leader must equip his people to stand up and face evil when it works to undermine what is holy."

Tyran sat straight up in his chair and leaned in toward the religious leader with a seriousness he usually reserved for their evening gatherings at Sanctuary.

"I know my future has always been to succeed my father," Tyran began, "but I believe that future may be now. I believe I can be the strong and godly leader Patrida needs."

"That is precisely why I have called for you, Tyran," Father Prodido said. "While you have been a builder in the past, you have proven to us that you can see the future we all desire for Patrida. Through much prayer over the last few months, followed by a fruitful conversation this morning, your mother and I believe a succession plan is in order immediately. Tyran, it is your time to become the strong and godly leader Patrida so desperately needs, as we are at a dangerous crossroads."

"This isn't at all what you intended from our founding!" Tyran interjected, raising his voice. "As you've told me, Patrida has strayed far from what God wanted it to be. Our values have been slowly watered down by my father's weakness and lack of resolve. Our structure has crumbled and deteriorated under his wavering and unsteady leadership. And I believe you have equipped me for this very moment, Father. I believe it's now my responsibility to rise up and say, 'Enough!' To plant the Patridian flag back in solid ground and restore the values of our founding."

Tyran could sense the religious leader's voracious appetite for more, so he continued to give him everything he desired. Father Prodido leaned forward from across the table. What Tyran fed him could not be consumed fast enough. In the young man, the religious leader had produced everything he had always envisioned for Ochi- a leader with knowledge and deep conviction, a leader unafraid to stand up against errancy and unrighteousness. In Tyran, Father Prodido saw himself. He had molded and shaped the young man into his own image, even down to the words he spoke and the fervor behind them.

However, what was hidden in Father Prodido's demeanor from across the table was his deep concern that his protégé may not fully appreciate the difference between standing up against a problem and acting on it. Tyran certainly had passion and resolve, but his lack of experience could eclipse them both.

"Yes, yes, Tyran," Father Prodido responded. "You have indeed been equipped for a time such as this. Patrida's rebirth into great-ness shall surely coincide with your strong and steady hands planting our flag back into this holy ground. But, if you will permit the bold-ness of my next question. Will you be equipping yourself, not only with the armor of steadfast conviction but also the sword of unsparing judgment?"

Momentarily considering the question, Tyran finally answered it, but not through a simple yes or no.

"I failed to share this with you earlier because everything began to spiral out of control so quickly," Tyran began.

Father Prodido raised a wiry eyebrow and leaned in over the table with curiosity, placing his elbows on the table and folding his pale hands.

"My father came to my house immediately after we met the other day. He was upset by Fovos' ultimatum and as distraught as I'd ever seen him."

Father Prodido looked up at his protégé inquisitively.

"He did, did he?" Father Prodido asked. "And what was the pur-pose of this visit, if you do not mind me asking?"

"Well, like I said, he was very emotional," Tyran said. "He started off by saying that bringing everyone to the island was a huge mistake from the beginning. I'd never heard him say that before. He said this island was our special place and everything about it used to be good, even our relationship with each other. But then he told me his biggest mistake was allowing my mother to invite you to join us."

Father Prodido's eyes narrowed to a disdainful glare. As the religious leader leaned back away from the table and crossed his arms, even the slow creak of his wooden chair seemed to sympathize with his scorn.

"He said he'd never met you before our arrival," Tyran continued. "But as he got to know you, he figured out you were quite the salesman. Everyone was taken by your eloquence and persuasiveness. He said something like, 'That man could sell religion to the Almighty himself.'"

The religious leader did not say a single word but continued to speak volumes through his rigid posture. He already anticipated where the conversation was heading but did not know to what end. Father Prodido considered what Ochi's motives could have been in sharing all of this with Tyran. As he continued to listen, he seethed from within.

"He said he regretted buying into your vision," Tyran said. "And then went on to say that he should've sent you away in one of the ships on the first day. But you had a way of enamoring him with your grandiose visions for the island. He bought into your idea that a community needed structure and order and a strong, godly leader to lead people into righteousness and holiness."

Father Prodido momentarily closed his eyes as if bound and awaiting the unforgiving fall of a dull guillotine blade. He knew Tyran's next words were going to be Ochi's passive attempt to inflict severe damage without having the guts to deal with him directly. The religious leader could no longer hear Tyran's voice speaking, only Ochi's.

"But over time," Ochi said, "I came to realize your religious ideas created a false sense of virtue. The pieces we put into place made us feel holy, made us appear holy, but we were all far from it. On the outside, we looked clean and virtuous, but on the inside, we remained unchanged. This false sense of virtue created division and hierarchies in Patrida and led to our hostility toward each other. This charade is why there has been so much heartache for everyone, including me. You are a charlatan, Prodido, and your religion is the problem."

"Alright! That's enough!" Prodido shouted as he slammed his fists on the table and stood abruptly, knocking over the chalices and spilling the remaining wine. "I've heard enough of this foul, malignant talk!"

The religious leader wanted nothing more at the moment than to actually have Ochi standing in front of him saying those words to his face.

"I secretly followed Thura one night and overheard her talking to the prisoners," Ochi's voice continued through Tyran. "That's when I concluded that you're the problem with Patrida. I heard my mother tell Thura a story about a man who sold water in jugs. People kept going back to him every day to get their jugs filled. They thought he was the only one who had access to this hidden freshwater source. But one day, by happenstance, a character named Dipsa discovered the freshwater source and realized they no longer needed the man. That's when I realized you were the man. Everything we had on this island was more sacred and holy than the stuff you tried to manufacture and sell us. Everything was good on its own, and we already had it, although we didn't know it at the time."

"Enough of this talk! Do you hear me! Enough!" Father Prodido screamed as he tore down his curtains in a violent rage. "What is the point of this!"

Hesitant to immediately respond to the religious leader and further raise his ire, Tyran paused. His silence, however, caused Father Prodido to instantly turn and face him.

"Your father's intent was a simple apology to you, was it not, Tyran?" Father Prodido asked, breathing heavily from the exertion.

"No, it wasn't an apology at all," Tyran said. "He confessed everything to me in order to turn me against you. That was what he was trying to do."

"So what exactly did he ask of you, Tyran?" Father Prodido inquired in a slow, deep baritone.

"He said something about how the madness on the island needed to stop," Tyran said. "And an execution was the only solution. That is when he asked if I would help him."

"Help him do what? Execute me!" Father Prodido raised his voice, laughing hysterically. "Look at this town, Tyran! Look at it! This is my town! This is my vision! This is my creation! He is the problem here! Not me! Everything I have done is to create a community holy and pleasing to God. If Patrida strayed from that vision, it is not because of what we have created. It is because your father has strayed from the faith and turned his back on God, Tyran. Is that not evident? Is he not the real charlatan here! Is he not the fraud! Is he not the heretic! He is the one who damaged our foundation, Tyran! How is this not obvious to any honest person?"

"That's the conclusion I came to as well," Tyran said. "But why did you wait so long in dealing with him? You've known his secret for a while, right? And you've seen how disengaged he's been over the last year. Clearly, you could've done something sooner. It's not like you sat from a distance every day and just watched. You were right there with him. I think maybe you waited a little too long."

"Waited too long!" Father Prodido shouted as he began to laugh sarcastically. "How do you suppose one removes a leader who still enjoys the favor of more than half the town, Tyran? How do you do it without creating complete chaos? How do you do it without the town turning against you? Let me tell you. You do it slowly. You do it methodically. You stay close to that leader and remain in his good graces. You ingratiate him at every turn while covertly and painstakingly working to undermine him. You wait for the right time to make your move when he is at his weakest. That's when the people will see it for themselves and come to their own conclusion. And when that glorious time comes, your father will see it as well. He will, at last, realize he is on the outside, and Patrida is against him. Do you understand me, Tyran?"

The young man knew better than to offer more than he already had.

"Everything that has been slowly building over the last year is culminating and becoming evident," Father Prodido continued. "And very soon, everyone in Patrida will know the truth about your father. They will see how weak he has become. They will see their need for a true, god-fearing leader who does not compromise the faith and protects them from the wolves on the other side of the island. They will see that leader is you, Tyran. I, not your father, have been preparing you for this very moment. He was the one who abandoned you, but I am the one now lifting you up."

In an instant, Father Prodido's rage transformed into an odd exuberance as he turned away excitedly from Tyran and walked toward the door.

"I shall summon Pali to gather the town together immediately at Sanctuary, your Excellency."

~

The excited chatter along the Monon indicated a certain sense of normalcy had been restored, at least for the time being. Ochi's journey to retrieve Thura was undoubtedly on everyone's mind, but they were eager to get an update from Father Prodido. A gathering felt essential to catch up on what had transpired the last few days. However, what the religious leader had not told them was that the gathering was for the purpose of turning them fully against Ochi and coronating Tyran as their new leader.

Before heading to Sanctuary, Tyran went home for a quick change of clothing to look more presentable for his special occasion. While taking off his shirt in his room, a quiet, barely audible knock came from his backdoor. Initially ignoring it because he thought it might be the wind causing the commotion, Tyran went to the door when the knock came again. This time it was louder.

Looking out the back door's curtains, Tyran closed them immediately and walked away.

"Tyran, we need to talk," a man's voice called out.

"Go away," Tyran responded. "I don't have time."

The door opened, ignoring Tyran's request, and Kaleo walked into the room.

"Excuse me," Tyran said. "What do you think you're doing?"

"Listen, Tyran," Kaleo pleaded. "I'll be quick. There's been a lot going on."

"I'm well aware," Tyran interrupted with little patience remaining.

"There's been a lot going on you don't know about," Kaleo quickly countered.

"What's that supposed to mean?" Tyran asked. "And you have about thirty seconds to get to the point. We have a gathering at Sanctuary that's about to begin."

"I believe Father Prodido is playing everyone, including you," Kaleo said. "There's no threat, Tyran. There's never been a threat. That young man wasn't in the woods spying on Patrida. And his people haven't been planning an attack. Far from it. He's one of many who has been trying to figure out a way to make peace with Patrida!"

"How do you know this?" Tyran asked.

"Because I saw them when they escaped," Kaleo said. "Not a single person in Patrida was interested in sitting down with that young man and hearing him out. He was coming to Patrida to offer an olive branch, and you guys beat the hell out of him, for god's sake! Don't you see how manipulative Father Prodido is and how his religious ideas turn people against each other? Don't you see how he uses fear to keep people in line by forcing his moral code on them? Don't you see how he uses religion to promote his rightness and everyone else's wrongness?"

"You sound just like my father," Tyran said dismissively as he turned away from Kaleo.

"No! Tyran, listen to me!" Kaleo begged. "Father Prodido turned your father against his own parents! And for what purpose? To prove his religious beliefs were right? That's insane! Any religious belief that hurts people or divides people or turns people against one another has missed the point. Do you not see this madness, Tyran? Prodido wears the right clothes, says the right words, and plays the right part. But he has an agenda and is working toward his own end. And it doesn't benefit anyone but himself. That's the way he's always been. And if you don't think he's using you, you're sorely mistaken. Why would he lie to the entire town by saying there's a threat when there isn't one? Why? Why would he do that?"

Tyran remained silent with his back still to Kaleo.

"Tyran," Kaleo said in a calmer voice, "has he even told you there's really no threat?"

Tyran did not respond.

"Why do you think that is, Tyran?" Kaleo pleaded. "Don't you see he's manipulating you for some greater purpose?"

Tyran turned solemnly and faced Kaleo.

"He wants me to succeed my father," Tyran said. "I assume that's his motivation. That's where I'm going right now. He'll be addressing the town and then endorsing me to take over as Patrida's new leader."

"You can't do it, Tyran," Kaleo said. "You can't let him do the same thing to you as he did to your father. You have the gift of seeing it before it happens. Your father didn't have that luxury. Prodido blindsided him. Don't make the same mistake he made. I beg you."

"I don't know what you expect me to do, Kaleo," Tyran whispered. "I think I'm in too deep."

"No, no, no. You can stop this at any moment," Kaleo explained. "You're not in too deep at all. We still have an opportunity here to make this right. What would Patrida look like if Prodido was out of the way? Have you ever considered that? What would the island look like if we stopped making enemies amongst ourselves and others and actually made peace for once? We can do that right now. Let's go before the entire town and tell them what's going on. Let's expose him for the fraud he is."

The young man took a deep breath and stepped forward to hug Kaleo.

"Thank you for coming here and calling me out, friend," Tyran said. "I didn't want to hear any of this when my father came to me, but now hearing it twice has really opened my eyes to the problem and given me the confidence I didn't have before."

Tyran released the older man, and the two exited the house, making their way toward a lively and uproarious Sanctuary. Word had already spread that Tyran would be taking over in Ochi's absence, and almost everyone was standing up, looking diligently for his arrival. As both he and Kaleo walked down the aisle together, the pair received disbelieving and curious looks, not only from the crowd but from Father Prodido, who was awaiting them at the front.

"What exactly is going on here? Why is he with you?" Father Prodido whispered to the young man while the crowd murmured.

"It's okay. Trust me," Tyran responded dismissively.

Unsure of what was transpiring but confident in his new leader, Father Prodido raised his hand to silence the audience.

"Brothers and sisters," he began, "thank you for coming together with such urgency. There is no easy way to say this. We are standing on the precipice of a holy battle between Good and Evil. We are facing the cosmic clash between Light and Darkness. We are witnesses to the inevitable fight between civility and savagery. But ours is the side of Goodness. Ours is the side of the Light. Ours is the side of civility. Rest assured, my good and holy people, we will surely prevail and vanquish all Darkness standing against us. For as God is with us, who can be against us?"

Leaning over to Tyran, Kaleo whispered.

"When should we do this?" he asked.

The young man nodded in acknowledgment of the question but subtly raised his hand by his side, indicating they should be patient.

"There has never been a time in our short history," Father Prodido continued, "that has been more urgent for us to come together and fight for Patrida's life than now. Not just from without, but now from within."

Gasps and chatter moved throughout the crowd. Father Prodido raised his hand once again to regain the silence.

"As we gave our blessing upon Ochi for safe travels to retrieve Thura," Father Prodido continued, "we secretly sent Machi and a couple of Patrida's finest guards to follow him from a distance. We intended for him to travel to the other side of the island and negotiate her return without posing a threat. But we would still have backup ready if he fell under attack. However, one of the guards returned this morning and reported that he saw Ochi potentially commiserating with the enemy."

Father Prodido allowed the citizenry to stand and rage without raising his hand to stop it. Kaleo once again looked to Tyran for a signal, but the young leader remained still. Once again commanding the attention of the crowd, the religious leader finished his pronouncement.

"Not only can there not be two kingdoms on this island, but there also cannot be two kingdoms within Patrida. For surely as a kingdom is divided against itself, it shall perish. But to face the threats both from without and within, we must have a strong leader. Someone who understands our heritage, who stands for absolute truth, who desires uniformity in belief, and who is not afraid to stand up against the evil within."

Kaleo once again looked to Tyran, imagining there could be no better prelude to expose Father Prodido. Tyran stepped forward and took his place front and center before the crowd, raising his hand to silence their riotous cheers.

"Good people of Patrida," Tyran said. "It's an honor to stand before you. There's no greater task than the one before me. While there are savages to contend with on the other side of the island, there's one standing before us right at this moment that we must expose for working clandestinely to undermine the Patridian Council and the people of Patrida."

Everyone was taken aback by Tyran's surprising accusation that appeared to come from nowhere. Not a single person knew what he was talking about or who he was passively accusing. Even Father Prodido raised his eyebrows in uncertainty as he surveyed the crowd.

"By the power vested in me by God," Tyran announced, "my first declaration as the rightful leader of Patrida is for the crime of treason. This offense carries a sentence of life imprisonment. Guards, go to the prison cell and release Fovos immediately and then arrest this man."

Tyran looked at Father Prodido and nodded. But then, turning toward the traitor, the newly coronated leader pointed at Kaleo.

"It's this man! Take him away!" Tyran shouted.

As the guards began to charge toward Kaleo, Father Prodido unpredictably stepped in front of them, appearing to intervene on his behalf. Once again, the religious leader raised his hand to silence the raucous crowd, this time with more vigor and determination.

"Your Excellency," Father Prodido stated aloud. "We offer you our sincerest congratulations and commit to you our utmost allegiance. Additionally, I wish to provide you my most humble opinion on this matter of treason. As you are well aware, treason is considered a high crime and merits punishment by hanging."

"These men are liars!" Kaleo screamed at the crowd. "They are manipulating you! There is no threat on the other side of the island! Ochi is not … "

Without warning and coming in with a solid right hook, Pali blindsided Kaleo, punching him in the face with such force it nearly knocked him out. Staggered and crawling on his hands and knees with blood dripping from a cut below his eye, Kaleo looked up directly at Tyran.

"You had a chance to heal these deep wounds, Tyran," Kaleo said. "What have you done? What have you become?"

Walking slowly with his arrogance preceding him, Father Prodido stood between Kaleo and Tyran. The religious leader towered over the bloody and broken man, his shadow casting down upon him. The religious leader smiled and shook his head in fabricated pity.

"Oh, Kaleo," Father Prodido said. "After all these years, old friend, I thought you of all people would have at last learned your lesson. The Lord does surely give on this day. But to you, once again, he takes away. Guards! Escort this man to the gallows and hang him immediately!"

Father Prodido, enshrouded by the haunting melodies of Kaleo's screams and the chanting of the crowd, turned blankly toward Tyran and nodded his head.

CHAPTER 15

Thura patiently navigated through the dense and unforgiving undergrowth beneath the forest canopy. The early morning twilight offered just enough light for her to maneuver across the knee-high chaos. Any semblance of a trail, or an efficient path forward, had been devoured days ago by the sprawling and seemingly unending brush. Thura knew, however, that she was getting close to the forest opening on the northeast side of the island that overlooked what Odigo said was the most beautiful crystalline sea one could ever imagine.

Not wanting to wake her guide from his deep sleep, Thura decided to make the short trek alone, as she had never once remembered seeing a sunrise. She wanted to experience it all by herself. From the time she arrived in Patrida as a little girl until a few days prior, she had only known the island's west side and had only watched the sunset. So despite the intertwined and viney madness that worked against her every step, an irrepressible, childlike excitement accompanied the young woman as she pressed forward into the opening.

The impervious network of bush and low scrub mounted their last stand as the tree cover above unfolded into magnificence. Thura felt like she was walking in a story written for her long ago with each step forward. She could not quite put her finger on why she believed that was the case, but escaping the confines of Patrida and breaking through into such vast beauty may have had something to do with it. In front of her stood a single relict pine that appeared more like a bonsai tree than any pine she had seen. Its gnarled trunk twisted upward from the dry, rocky ground and branched with elegantly crooked arms that held their sparse green needles like offerings to the sea.

Taken by the seascape's resplendence and awaiting the sun's appearance in anticipation, Thura sat down next to the lonely tree on a flat, angular, almost chair-like rock that protruded from the gentle hill overlooking the water. With her back resting against the cool of the stone, her feet appearing to dangle in search of solid ground, Thura watched the soothing waves massage the gray, moss-covered boulders that lined the circumference of the island's edge. Without question, Thura knew she was in the right place.

As the new sun arose and lovingly embraced Thura, she closed her eyes and saw the pink of her eyelids. Her breathing shared the same steady cadence as every tranquil wave that washed onto the shore. Suddenly, Thura was back in the council room at the exact moment when she spilled the wine she had been preparing.

She remembered running out of the room with the heavy, wood door closing thunderously behind her. The dark of the hallway enveloped her as she ran toward her room. Her back pressed against the cool, stone wall. She closed her eyes and stood in the sun's warmth. The thought of someone else being on the island outside of Patrida evoked an inexplicable sense of freedom that welled up within her.

Thura's breathing began to outpace the constant calm of the ocean's current. She wished she could open her eyes and have that same feeling of freedom again, not as a fleeting and momentary emotion in the hallway but as something permanently residing in her.

How can I be so far away from Patrida but still feel the same on the inside? she thought. How can I be sitting in the most peaceful and life-giving place I have ever been but still feel so burdened? How can I be on the other side of Patrida's figurative prison walls but not experience the overwhelming sense of freedom I imagined when I ran away with Sophia and Odigo? While question after question looped through Thura's mind, a small, dust-colored bird in the tree next to her began to sing, demanding her attention.

"Hey, little guy," she said. "Such a sweet song you are singing."

The feathered vocalist tilted its head as if her words were of interest. Thura's new friend unassumingly flew down to the pine-needle-covered ground and gazed at her, continuing to tilt its head back and forth as it resumed its song.

"Such a little performer, too. Are you coming down here to be with me?" Thura kindly coaxed.

The bird moved toward her as if it understood her question.

"You are not afraid at all, are you?" she asked.

From behind, Thura could hear Odigo moving swiftly through the brush and approaching.

"Hey, good morning!" Odigo called out. "You must have been up early."

"Yeah, sorry," Thura apologized. "I had never seen a sunrise before and wanted to get here in plenty of time to see it. And you were sleeping so soundly I did not want to wake you."

"Who's your little friend?" Odigo inquired.

"I am not sure what his name is," Thura answered with a smile, "but he is quite the singer and performer. And not afraid of me in the least. Such a humble little creature, you are. You can continue your morning now. Thank you for coming down and joining me."

Tilting its head back and forth once again and seeming to understand Thura's benediction, her friend flew off toward the boulders below.

"What a nice little visit this morning, huh?" Odigo asked as he sat down under the gnarled tree.

Thura stared down at the waves washing over the boulders as if trying to find words that matched what she was feeling internally. Sensing her momentary absence, Odigo crossed his legs, leaned back, and contentedly watched the horizon. Breaking the silence, and in an

attempt to piece together words that harmonized with the thoughts
and feelings she had earlier, Thura asked Odigo a question.

"Have you ever felt like it is hard to be patient with others who are
not moving at the same pace as you?"

A wide grin stretched across Odigo's face as he answered Thura's
question with a chuckle.

"You mean like walking with Sophia?" he asked.

Returning the laugh, Thura picked up a small rock and threw it at
the young man.

"No! That's not what I meant at all!" Thura said. "Plus, she moves
a whole lot faster than I expected her to! It doesn't look pretty, but she
sure knows how to move when she needs to."

"No, no. I knew what you meant," Odigo said, still laughing with
Thura. "And yes, she does know how to get her move on!"

"But seriously though, what do you think about my question?"
Thura pressed.

"I know this isn't what you are looking for," Odigo began, "but I
am going to answer your question by asking you a question."

Thura stared at the young man dismissively, as if he was pulling
her leg.

"Come on, Odigo. Be serious." Thura demanded.

"No, seriously. How do you see yourself, Thura?" Odigo asked and
let the question sit for a few seconds. "I mean, I'm not trying to be
super mystical here, but have you ever thought about that?"

Thura's eyes immediately went back to the waves on the horizon
that slowly grew as they approached the shoreline. She noticed that
the waves did not crash against the rocks but that their movements
were more like gentle massages as they washed over the smooth boulders in eternal repetition.

"Sophia told me that what I see is not as important as how I see,"
Thura responded, seeming to avoid Odigo's question. "To be honest, I

did not fully understand everything she said, but I have been thinking about that one line more than anything else."

"What does it mean to you?" Odigo gently prodded.

"I don't know," Thura said. "Maybe I have spent so much time trying to figure out where I stand in relation to what I see around me that I have missed how I see myself and others. I see a girl who has figured out that she no longer has the same ideas and beliefs as those around her. I see a girl who has grown and matured and found something more than what she grew up within. What I see are unenlightened people who will never get it."

The young woman paused as if continuing to reflect on the question.

"I mean, I would go up to my room and light dozens of candles and open my window so the light would shine out into the dark street and on the people that walked below," Thura continued. "I would sit there and think about how little they knew and wonder how they could go on living each day without questioning anything. They were like sheep. I sat perched right above them, shining my light on them, and thinking how backward and uninformed they were for not seeing it. I even lit every candle in my house before I ran away. I wanted my father to see it and realize I have something he needs to discover for himself. But I essentially left him and everyone else to figure it out on their own while I ran ahead in my arrogance."

Attempting to lighten the tone of the conversation, Odigo carefully responded.

"She's quite a wise woman, isn't she? That Sophia," Odigo said. "And good for you, for not just dismissing her words, but wrestling with them. If you don't mind me asking, Thura, if you were able to go back in time and do it again, how would you see them differently?"

"I have been thinking about that quite a bit," Thura began. "I have been thinking about the people of Patrida. And not to overdo the metaphor, but what if some of them had their own candles at one point that they carried around? What if their candles once burned brightly but eventually burned out? I know this sounds silly, but what if they didn't have another candle to replace it? What if others had their candles blown out for some reason and didn't have a way to light it again, so they put the candle in their pocket? What if no one ever gave them a candle in the first place?"

Thura paused as if contemplating her next words, still watching the waves wash over the shoreline.

"I don't know," she continued. "When I start thinking about it that way, it seemed pretty ridiculous that I would sit above them in judgment, surrounded by a room full of candles, while watching them walk around aimlessly below. I guess what I am saying is that if I went back, I would leave my room and walk with the people. And instead of looking at my light as a way to elevate myself and show everyone how superior I am for being the only one who is shining bright, I would walk with them and share my light."

"Mmm. Wouldn't that be a sight to see," Odigo said. "Not just one window along the Monon illuminated, but the entire town shining brightly. There is something really beautiful in that, Thura, accepting people as they are and joining them on their journey. It sounds like what you are saying is that you would give everyone the benefit of the doubt because we don't know their individual stories or what they have been through or what they are currently going through."

"That is exactly what I am saying, Odigo," Thura responded. "But as I sit here and think about it a little more, there is still a part of me that believes some people deserve to walk in darkness, no matter what their story is or what led them to that point. Some people are so toxic and hateful. They don't deserve my light. They don't deserve anyone's light. And to be honest, no light will help them anyway."

Odigo did not immediately respond, but he could feel Thura's eyes trained on him, awaiting his response.

"I agree, Thura. Some people are toxic and hateful," Odigo said. "They may even appear to be too far gone. I completely understand your perspective, and I can't imagine what it was like growing up in Patrida. I can't. In my short amount of time there, I could not believe how dark it was and how everyone was so content in not questioning anything."

Putting a hand through his hair, Odigo turned to face the young woman.

"Here's the crazy thing, Thura," Odigo said. "That sun, right there in front of us, will eventually rise and shine on Patrida the same way it's shining on us right now. It doesn't make a distinction between those who deserve its light and those who don't. It keeps rising each day and keeps shining on everyone, regardless of who they are. Whether they deserve it or not, or whether they change or not, it keeps shining."

Thura turned her head away from Odigo and stared into the distance.

"Thura, listen. You don't have to agree with a person to walk alongside them," Odigo said. "It's not your responsibility to change them. You can't do that. You can't change Patrida. You can't walk someone else's journey for them. They have to find their path and take their own steps. But by walking with each other patiently and listening to each other's stories as we go along, there's always the possibility that we might discover something we never expected to find."

"Like what?" Thura asked, still looking away from the young man.

"Like each other's humanity," Odigo responded.

Thura remained silent and stone-faced. While a person could have easily misconstrued her posture as angry or frustrated, Thura meditated on Odigo's every word. She turned her attention from the distant horizon again to the shoreline below.

"Do you think those boulders have always been that smooth?" Thura asked, not expecting a response. "Or, do you think they had rough and jagged edges when they first fell and hit the ground?"

Believing he had already spoken too much and knowing exactly where Thura was heading with her questions, Odigo decided to join her in silent observation.

"They broke off for some reason at some point in time," Thura said. "Every single one of them. Can you imagine standing here when that happened? Can you imagine standing here as this cliff crumbled away into hundreds of massive, broken boulders, each of them falling one right after the other and lining the shoreline?"

"That certainly would have been something," Odigo said, hoping that she would continue with her line of thinking.

"Yeah, that would have been something, alright," Thura snapped right back. "But if we had been standing here when they first fell, you would have never convinced me that those jagged rocks would one day be made perfectly smooth. I would have never believed it."

"Why's that?" Odigo asked, waiting eagerly for what he had been anticipating.

"I mean, look at those boulders above the shoreline," Thura said. "See how broken and uneven they look? It is hard to believe they are exactly like those below. There is no difference whatsoever in their composition. But on the outside, the only difference is the gentle flow of water that patiently and persistently washed over them. We do not see their subtle changes from day to day. But sure enough, week after week, month after month, year after year, as the waves keep washing over them, they change. They completely transform. They do not look anything like they did when they first fell."

The two sat silently watching wave after wave wash over the boulders. The peaceful and perfect rhythm of the water was an invitation. A chorus accompanied every ray beaming from the sun and resounded across the expansiveness of the morning sky. Everything that surrounded Thura and Odigo was a voice. Every note, every cadence, every harmony was holy. Every rock lining the northeastern shore seemed to be crying out as they, too, joined creation's song.

Thura moved down on the ground next to Odigo under the tree, consumed by goodness and overcome by awareness. With tears in her eyes, Thura reached for Odigo's hand.

"I think I finally get it, my friend. It all belongs together," Thura cried. "My struggle through the weeds and dense brush early this morning led to this opening. It was like I was in my own story, told with every step forward. When I pushed through the obstacles holding me back, I began to see the light. I watched my first sunrise, and then through your wise words, realized that this light shines on every person, no matter who they are.

But it wasn't just that. I realized how arrogant and judgmental I had become. I sat above others and hoarded my light while watching them stumble around below. Maybe if I had gone down to the street and walked with them and looked them in the eyes and listened to their stories, I would understand them better and begin to see them as human beings."

Thura stopped and took a deep breath, turning her attention one last time to the boulders and waves below.

"My problem is that I have not believed people can change, so I gave up on them," Thura confessed. "I ran away because I wanted more for my life, and that is fine. But I also ran away because I viewed Patrida as a lost cause. I believed every single person there was a lost cause with no hope.

However, as I sat here throughout our entire conversation, I was mesmerized by how the waves covered those giant rocks time and time again, patiently transforming them without any judgment. They just kept washing over them."

Odigo closed his eyes as he listened. He gently squeezed Thura's hand.

"But it was more than that," she continued. "I heard what sounded like a choir. Everything around me was singing. The sun. The waves. The trees. Even that little bird that shared its song with me earlier.

They were all joining together in one song, Odigo. And I could see the gentle and loving invitation of the waves continually beckoning the rocks to join the song, as they are. That is when it hit me. The invitation is not only for the rocks. The invitation is for everything and everyone. And these waves are all around us. They surround us and patiently wash over us to smooth out our sharp and jagged edges. But they are beckoning us to join creation's song together. Just as we are."

"That is real freedom, Thura. The ability to see the world as it is without needing to judge it. To see its every part and embrace its frailty and brokenness. To discover its naked beauty and love it anyway. Sometimes even despite itself. I'm not sure anyone could have said it any better," Odigo said but hesitated a moment before asking Thura the most challenging question.

"So, what about your father? Where does he fit into all of this?" Odigo asked.

"I don't know," Thura replied, "It is so much easier when we talk about it abstractly, even poetically. It is easier when we do not have to put a face on it. And that is the crazy thing. I can visualize myself walking alongside faceless people on the Monon. But, when I start thinking about specific people, like my father, I start to question everything."

"Do you not trust that he too can change for the better, Thura?" Odigo gently nudged.

"I want to," Thura confessed. "But while I truly believe there is something divine patiently washing over my father and working to transform him on the inside, it is so difficult when I do not see any evidence of him changing."

"Do you remember the first night that we met?" Odigo asked.

"Of course I do. How could I forget it? Why?" Thura replied.

"That night, when you heard someone approaching from around the corner, and you hid in the storage closet, who do you think was standing on the other side of that door?" Odigo asked.

"I have no idea," Thura said but wondered what Odigo knew that he had not shared with her before.

"It was your father, Thura," Odigo said. "He was the one standing on the other side of the door. I watched him from my cell window the entire time."

In stunned silence, Thura stared at Odigo without knowing what to say in response.

"He knew it was you behind the door," Odigo continued. "And it was obvious that he wanted to open it up. But he stood there, not quite sure what he should do. I could tell he was in a lot of pain, though, because he kept wiping his eyes as he leaned against the door."

"That could mean anything, though, right?" Thura pushed back.

"I don't think so," Odigo said. "I think he heard our conversation, Thura. And I think he had already heard me tell you the story of Dipsa as he stood around the corner. I can't say that he heard it for sure, but by his demeanor, it sure looked like something moved him."

"So what are you trying to say?" Thura pressed.

"Honestly," Odigo responded. "I believe the waves were already washing over your father, even though you couldn't see it. And if I were to guess, Thura, I'd say they've been washing over him for a while. And while you may only be able to see his sharp and jagged edges right now, maybe you need to trust that he's in the waves. Who knows, maybe he's starting to hear that song, as well."

CHAPTER 16

The late morning dew still covered the shoulder-high broadleaves lining each side of the ever-winding game trail. Ochi followed closely behind Sophia, who appeared to have been swallowed time and time again by the consuming vegetation. But the old woman navigated through it as if she knew exactly where she was going. For his part, despite being soaked from hours of brushing up against the wet flora, Ochi raised both hands and imagined the plants were people patting him on the back and giving him high fives as he walked past them. With Sophia not having said much to him as she pressed forward along the winding path, he did his best to remain preoccupied and in good spirits.

To their relief and without much warning, the brush spat them out into an open area where the sun rose above the trees and provided enough sunlight to dry out their damp clothing.

"Do you know where we're going?" Ochi asked.

"Of course, we are heading to Salome," Sophia said.

"Yes, I know that," Ochi countered, "but you've never been there. So, I'm curious if you know exactly where you're going."

Sophia, being especially evasive but playful, responded.

"Generations of animals have used these trails," she said. "Do you know why?"

"I don't know. Tell me," Ochi said matter-of-factly.

"Look around. See the fruit from this tree?" Sophia asked, pointing at the tree they were standing beside. "Hundreds, maybe thousands, of animals have traveled these same paths because they knew there was sustenance here."

"Okay, well, that didn't answer my question at all," Ochi said in a somewhat frustrated tone. "We haven't talked for a couple of hours, and the first thing you do is give me some sort of puzzle or riddle to figure out. Are we still doing this? Is it time for another lesson, mother?"

"What is your plan, Ochi?" Sophia asked as she turned and faced him directly.

"You know my plan," Ochi said. "It's to get Thura back and return home to Patrida."

"Oh, you are not ready for that," Sophia retorted while turning away from Ochi dismissively.

"What is that supposed to mean anyway?" he barked, raising his voice.

"Come here, Ochi," Sophia instructed.

The old lady handed her son the walking stick she had picked up a few miles back and had been using as they walked through the brush.

"What do you want me to do with this?" Ochi asked curiously, but still a bit on edge.

"I want you to take this stick and draw a circle in the ground around this tree," Sophia said.

Ochi tilted his head in disbelief and stared at his mother.

"Please, Ochi. Be patient and trust me in this," Sophia beckoned.

The man took the stick with reluctance. He began carving a large circle in the ground about fifteen feet from the tree's trunk while muttering to himself under his breath.

"You think this is good enough? You like the look of this?" Ochi yelled out sarcastically as he connected the two lines to form a perfect circle with the tree centered in the middle of it.

"Yes, yes. This will do just fine," Sophia responded surveying his work. "Now, grab a piece of fruit and have a seat against the tree. I will be back shortly."

"Wait! What? Come on," Ochi frustratingly blurted out. "I really need to get to Thura, and I don't have time for more of this being alone thing."

"Son, you do not realize it right now, but you are not ready for Thura. You are not ready for Patrida. Sit down," Sophia instructed sternly.

Ochi dejectedly sat down, leaned his back up against the rough bark, and watched Sophia slowly limp away into another overgrown animal trail.

"You've got to be kidding me," Ochi mumbled.

Already bored before Sophia completely disappeared, Patrida's defected leader took the walking stick and tapped it next to his outstretched feet. After a few minutes of tapping, he yawned. Several minutes later, he began to talk to himself.

"I wonder what everyone is doing in Patrida right now? I wonder what Tyran is doing? I need to talk to him again," Ochi whispered while pushing the stick into the ground. "I need to talk some sense into him. Prodido isn't good for him. Prodido isn't good for anyone in Patrida. Maybe everything will die down before we get back there."

Ochi's mind continued to race wildly among unknowns. But it was Sophia's question, once again, that nagged at him. The old woman certainly knew how to keep him off balance. He had not thought at all about any sort of plan. He did not know what would happen once he saw Thura for the first time or how she would respond to him. He did not know what he would say to her or how he would get her to come home. He did not know what he would say to Father Prodido or Tyran if they confronted him. He did not even know what he would say to the people of Patrida. Since Thura left on her own accord, there would not be any sort of reckoning or retaliation against their supposed enemy. He had no idea how the townspeople would react to that information.

Shadows of uncertainty covered Ochi like the leaves and branches towering above. The anxiety he left in Patrida had already caught up with him and rushed ahead into his future. As panic strengthened its grip around Ochi's neck, he heard a rustling movement from the vicinity of Sophia's trail. Within seconds, the old woman exited and hobbled over to him with an expectant smile.

"What did you see?" Sophia asked.

"What do you mean what did I see?" Ochi asked quizzically.

"You have been sitting here for fifteen minutes," Sophia poked. "What have you seen inside this circle?"

"Was I supposed to be looking for something inside the circle?" Ochi said, laughing.

"Why do you think I had you draw a circle and sit in it, Ochi?" Sophia asked.

"I thought it was odd, but it kind of felt like you were giving me a timeout or something," Ochi said. "But to answer your question, no, I haven't seen anything at all since I've been sitting here. All I've done is think about Patrida and how I left it in disarray. I've been thinking about Thura and what it's going to be like when I see her again. I've been thinking about what Patrida's going to be like when we get there. And I've been thinking about Tyran and how I desperately need to talk to him. That's what I have been thinking about, thank you very much."

"I did not give you any instruction because I wanted to see where you would go. You immediately went to your regrets and then started worrying about the seeming impossibilities of your future," Sophia said.

"Wait one second," Ochi shot back. "You were the one who asked what my plan was, right? How does a person put together a plan for the future if he doesn't look at the past? It's like you set me up to get the result you were looking for!"

"Be patient and breathe, Ochi. This is for your benefit. I am going to leave again. When I return, I want you to tell me what you see inside this circle. This time I will take my walking stick with me, thank *you* very much," Sophia smiled as she leaned over to retrieve it. "Be here, Ochi. Nowhere else. Be here."

The old woman disappeared once more, and Ochi sat in silence by himself.

What do I see? What do I see? Not much to choose from here, he thought. Rocks. Leaves. Sticks. Fruit.

Turning to look around the other side of the tree, Ochi began to mumble.

"A bird. More leaves. More fruit. A few more rocks. What are we doing here? What a waste of time."

Ochi turned back around and sat silently once again. He looked around the perimeter and shook his head.

"What did you see, Ochi?" he said out loud in a mocking voice.

"Oh, just some rocks and stuff," he answered himself like a goofy cartoon character.

"Wonderful. Oh, good job, Ochi. You did it," his response dripped in sarcasm.

The brush began to move, indicating Sophia was once again returning.

"Who are you talking to, Ochi?" the old woman called out. "I am glad you are having so much fun with this little exercise."

He did not respond. Without saying another word, Sophia stepped inside the circle and stuck her stick in the ground. Walking around Ochi and the tree, Sophia began to draw yet another circle. This time only five feet around the tree.

"What are you doing?" Ochi cried out. "Are you not going to ask me what I saw this time?"

"I know what you saw," the old woman responded without looking up from her task.

"I suppose you probably do know," Ochi said. "It wasn't that difficult of a task. Rocks. A bird…"

"I know exactly how you see," Sophia said, abruptly interrupting him. "So I already know what you saw. How do I know, you ask? You have eyes, but you do not know how to see what is right in front of you, Ochi."

The old woman turned without another word and vanished once again into the brush.

Ochi crossed his legs and leaned forward, putting his elbows on his legs and then his palms on his chin. He stared at the ground and shook his head in disbelief.

This is what happens when you lock someone away for two decades, Ochi thought. They have all the time in the world to think of everything. So I have eyes, but I don't know how to see. What does that even mean? Does she think there are things around me I can't see? Maybe I'm not paying enough attention? Perhaps I'm only seeing the obvious things and missing the smaller things?

Ochi began to look more deliberately within the smaller circle. Brushing some leaves out of the way, he looked underneath and saw another world at work. Insects moved about with intention and purpose. Broken leaves were decaying and offering themselves as food. Worms broke through the soil and fed upon the leaves, replenishing the soil with essential nutrients. None of this was new to Ochi, but he had not stopped and spent time noticing the small things in years.

Covering the exposed area back with the leaves he had removed, Ochi turned his attention to his right. About three feet away, he noticed a small anthill with ants racing to and fro.

"Now that's a remarkable creature," Ochi mumbled, hypnotized by the way the small insects worked together with such ease.

"What have you discovered?" Sophia shouted as she hobbled toward Ochi.

"So many things this time," Ochi said. "It's not like I've never seen an anthill before, but I haven't stopped to look at one in years, probably since Tyran and I made trips to the island when he was a boy."

"What did you see?" Sophia pushed.

Ochi did not immediately answer. His first inclination was to repeat what he had just told her, but he was not falling for that trick again. She was after more than the obvious.

"Okay. I saw these ants working together," Ochi started.

Sophia stood silently waiting.

"They were cooperating to get the job done," Ochi added, hoping to satisfy the old woman. "They can accomplish so much more when they work together."

"Very good," Sophia responded. "Look at it one more time. What do you see?"

Ochi knew she did not mean for him to stare at the anthill again. She wanted him to see at a deeper level.

"Each ant is important, but it can only do a little by itself," Ochi offered. "Together, they can do the seemingly impossible. You clearly want me to see the importance of each person and how essential they are to the flourishing of a community, especially when they work together for the common good."

Sophia smiled and walked right in front of Ochi, not once breaking her gaze nor acknowledging that his answer was what she was looking for. The old woman took the stick and put it in the ground again. Walking around the tree, she drew one last circle around Ochi and the tree's base before walking away into the overgrowth.

Ochi rubbed his chin and laughed out loud while shaking his head.

"Looks like it's me and you, tree," he said as he leaned back, closed his eyes, and took a deep breath. "It's probably going to be a whole lot easier for me to look at you than it will be for me to look at myself. I can tell you that right now."

Opening his eyes, Ochi looked down at the circle hugging his crossed legs. He should have known this was precisely what Sophia intended from the beginning. There were lessons all around him. But he had always been too preoccupied with running around the circle than stopping to see what was within. He realized that breaking through the surface of each successive ring would ultimately lead to one place, his heart. He knew if he did not get it right this time, Sophia would draw her next circle on his chest.

I'm the one who admitted to being the sick system, Ochi thought. I'm the one who said I take it with me everywhere I go. I've been so preoccupied with everyone else's ills and wrongs and misgivings that I built up a wall around my heart. And if I can't even look behind that wall and change myself, how do I expect anything around me to change? If there's something toxic behind that wall, does it not flow outwardly into everything else? If there's pain behind that wall, how could it not be felt by those around me? If my anger and resentment and pride reside behind that wall, they've had to affect my relationships with those closest to me? Maybe Patrida isn't at peace because I'm not at peace. But how can anything penetrate this wall I've constructed around my heart?

"You see it this time. I know you do," Sophia called out for the last time as she hobbled toward her son.

"You know, a person can spend so much time on the other side of these circles," Ochi said, "without ever going inward, without ever having to go deeper. That's me. I thought I knew what peace was, but I had no idea."

"So true, Ochi," Sophia said. "Peace is not something a person can create or manufacture from the outside. Peace can only exist within you."

"That's what's so surprising to me, I guess," Ochi confessed. "I've spent so much of my life believing peace was something outward that we needed to strive for as a community, that if we agreed to it, then it must be true. I mean, we lived by the motto *Peace through Strength* in Patrida, yet not a single one of us knew what peace was. Isn't that crazy? We believed we were the ones living in peace, yet there you sat for all those years confined behind four, dark walls, and you were the only person in Patrida who had found it."

"And it was this peace, Ochi, that allowed me to come back to you," Sophia said, slowly kneeling next to her son. "Peace is not an ideal for which we strive. When it is an ideal, it is only a word on our lips or an idea existing in our heads. But when peace resides in your heart, it becomes your lived experience. Peace becomes the way you begin to see and relate to the world. That is the key to our relationships. Relationships can only begin to heal when peace resides within each person. And a community will only begin to heal when our relationships are at peace. But for a circle to expand and include others in that peace, it must begin as the smallest of circles around one's heart."

While Sophia talked, Ochi stood up and placed his hand over a scar on the tree he had noticed earlier. Looking deeply within it, as if he was looking at Sophia's scars, he quietly confessed.

"I don't know how you found peace in Patrida," Ochi said. "You didn't have anyone."

"I can tell you it would have been easier had I been surrounded by those who loved me," Sophia said. "But even in darkness, Ochi, there is always a little light that can creep in if you allow it. For me, it came through the kindness of a red-headed young girl who visited my cell each day and talked to me. She did not know I was her grandmother, nor did I want her to know that truth. It would have been too much for her. She brought food and talked to me as I ate. She didn't see me as a criminal or as someone to be detested or pushed aside. She saw me as a human being, and that gave me hope. Even though everyone

I loved had died or had been driven far away, something was working below the surface that gave me the nourishment I needed to get through each day. That is what gave me such indescribable peace."

"What's that something that gave you peace?" Ochi asked, his hand still on the scar. "I think that's what I've been chasing after for quite some time. And I don't know exactly what it is. There was a story I heard the young man tell Thura the night the guards captured him. It was a story about a thirsty person, and I knew he was talking about me. I walked around the corner, and Thura hid behind one of the storage doors. I stood on the other side of it, empty. All I wanted to do was open the door and tell her I knew she was thirsty because I was too. But I didn't do it. I was too afraid."

"Ochi, the water Odigo spoke of in the story is the divine love of God that surrounds us, even as we speak here now," Sophia said. "This love is always with us. It never leaves us or abandons us. It is always inviting us, no matter where we are, to come and drink. And sometimes, that invitation can come in the most unexpected ways, through the most unexpected means. That is the way divine love works. Its roots run deeply through this ground and give us the nourishment we so desperately need. For me, the hope I received from Thura each day was another root of divine love stretching out to me when I needed it most."

"I want peace, especially if that's what it takes to begin restoring my relationship with my family. Maybe even Patrida. But I'm not sure I am capable of doing this all by myself. I've spent so many years of my life unknowingly pushing it away and keeping it at arm's length. I don't know if it's possible to break down the wall I've constructed around my heart," Ochi said in resignation.

"But you have already begun to tear it down, Ochi," Sophia contested. "And you are not even aware of it. Tell me what you see. Tell me what you see below the surface. Do you see the roots of divine love reaching out to you?"

Ochi turned and faced his mother, curious about what she saw that he could not see for himself.

"Remember what I told you earlier?" she continued. "A relationship can only begin to heal when two people find peace within themselves. Look at our relationship. You began to find peace the day you told me you were sorry for killing your father and for imprisoning me."

Hearing those words was difficult for Ochi. He immediately broke his gaze with Sophia and looked at the ground in shame. While he trusted his mother's sincerity and knew he had experienced at least some level of peace within himself by saying he was sorry, Ochi did not believe he could ever experience the kind of peace she had.

"For as long as I live and as much as I desire it," Ochi said. "I don't think I will ever truly be able to experience the kind of peace you want for me. I carry way too much guilt and shame for what I've done, and those feelings don't give up their space easily, especially for peace. But it's not just that. Even if I was able to forgive myself and find this peace, there's not a single person in Patrida who would ever accept it or reciprocate it."

"Look around, Ochi," Sophia challenged with a force and tone he had never heard from her before. "There is not a single tree standing around this one. It has been standing here by itself for a very long time. Do you see the evidence of any other tree standing next to it?"

Ochi remained silent.

"Look at those marks you have been touching. Does it not look like this tree was suffering at some point? Maybe it was not getting enough nourishment on its own. Although it may have appeared fine from the outside, it was starving on the inside. Do you understand what I am saying to you?"

Ochi continued to remain silent, staring only at the scar on the tree.

"Turn around, Ochi, and look," Sophia said. "Do you see those trees surrounding this opening? Beneath this ground is a network of roots connecting every one of these trees. They know when another is in distress and in need of nourishment. Even if this tree appears to be all alone, standing proudly all by itself, they know its great need. They are connected to it and ready to help. Yes, you will need to find peace for yourself, Ochi. No one can give it to you. But you desperately need to surround yourself with people who will walk patiently and lovingly beside you until you can stand alone and heal your wounds."

CHAPTER 17

The lifeless body of Kaleo swayed above the gallows in the distance. Left to hang overnight and well into the next day at the request of Father Prodido, the macabre display served as a message to everyone in the town. If anyone attempted to undermine the values of Patrida or sow seeds of dissension, they would face swift and decisive justice.

With a small burlap sack covering his head and identity, the nondescript figure was symbolic of Patrida. Every gentle wind moving over the mighty waters and along the Monon blew past a directionless entity. The slow creak of rope and wood was the tension and strain of a body hanging lifelessly in limbo. Bone and tissue remained and gave support and structure, but it had long ago given up the spirit.

Moving through the late afternoon crowd, Father Prodido instructed Machi to remove Kaleo's body from the gallows as he reached Tyran's porch and promptly entered his house. Despite Tyran's coronation as leader of Patrida the evening prior, Father Prodido carried serious concern about Tyran's perceived ambivalence in his sentencing of Kaleo.

"Good afternoon, your Excellency," said Father Prodido. "Would you mind joining me on my afternoon walk?"

"Good afternoon, Father," said Tyran, looking wildly disheveled and somewhat preoccupied.

"A walk, sir?" Father Prodido asked once more. "Just you and me."

"Sure. I haven't been out of the house today. Maybe I do need some fresh air," said Tyran, as he led the way out of the house and walked toward Sanctuary with Father Prodido following a few feet behind.

"I awoke this morning and attempted to have some hot tea," the religious leader said. "But I suppose I let the fire burn too low throughout the night, and I barely had the slightest ember this morning. The water sat on the stovetop and hardly warmed. It took a good thirty minutes to stoke the fire and get the water close to a boil. But at last, I did enjoy a fine cup of tea to start the morning."

Continuing to walk ahead of the religious leader along the creek, Tyran did not respond.

"I could not help but think of you, Tyran, when adding the kindling to the embers," Father Prodido said.

Tyran stopped abruptly and faced the religious leader, still not speaking.

"If I might have a moment of honesty with you, your Excellency," Father Prodido said. "Without question, you know your mother and I stand behind you as Patrida's leader. This fact goes without saying. In many ways, you have proven yourself worthy and capable over the years."

"But," Tyran added with an icy stare.

"Yes, of course," Father Prodido proceeded cautiously. "But, I need to know why there was confusion last evening with Kaleo's sentencing."

"Confusion?" Tyran asked. "Why don't you say it like you really intend it? Why was there hesitancy, Tyran? Isn't that what you meant to say? Are you not questioning my resolve as a leader?"

"Oh no. Of course not, your Excellency," Father Prodido said in an attempt to regain his balance. "You are reading this entirely the wrong way. Clearly, you came through and made the right decision in executing Kaleo. It is just that we are in a very precarious situation, and the stakes could not be higher right now, as you well know."

"Oh really?" Tyran asked. "Why don't you tell me about the stakes, Father? Why don't you tell me about the threat lurking beyond our perimeter? Why don't you tell me why there hasn't been a single guard who has seen this mysterious enemy while patrolling the woods? Why don't you tell me why you feel so comfortable taking these walks in these woods if there is such a great threat?"

"Ah! There it is!" Father Prodido exclaimed. "The seed of doubt. Surely planted by your father and that pathetic worm of a person Kaleo."

"I would advise you to remember who you are speaking to," Tyran warned.

Tyran's threat stoked Father Prodido's internal fire, which came raging out in his words.

"Remember who I am speaking to!" he shouted. "You have got to be kidding me! I made you! Your father abandoned you, and I was there. Teaching you! Training you! Building you up as a man of God! But when your defining moment came to be fearless and strong, to stand up against impropriety, and to resurrect a weakened Patrida, what did you do? What did you do, Tyran! You tell the guards to put him in jail, just like your…"

"If I were you, I would choose my next word very wisely, Father," Tyran threatened.

Abruptly turning from the young leader, an enraged Father Prodido marched back toward town.

～

As tiny, wet dots began to discolor each stone along the Monon, the westward horizon proved to the townspeople that a more ominous storm would soon be approaching. Men closed their houses' wooden shutters while women and children began moving briskly indoors. Father Prodido, unbothered by the darkening clouds swirling above the waters or the hurried activity of each household, walked through Sanctuary with fiery intention.

The religious leader noticed as he neared his house that his shutters had already been closed. Upon entering, a single oil lamp had been lit and placed on the square, wooden table. Sitting behind the tiny flame battling the room's shadows, Velos greeted her brother and asked him to sit with her.

Closing the door and then locking it, Father Prodido turned and blew out the candle on the table. Looking down, the religious leader noticed something under his sister's duplicitous hands, placed between her and the smoking candle. Supposing it was the purpose for her visit but believing his encounter with Tyran to be a more immediate concern, Father Prodido sat down and began detailing their conversation.

"If I am to be brutally honest," he started, "I was dismayed with Tyran's decision last night. Maybe dismayed isn't the right word. Disappointed may be a better way to describe it. Lord knows how much time I have spent with him over the years preparing him for this moment. And as the stars aligned for him to exert his power and influence in Patrida against a full-fledged traitor, he became his father."

"I think you're overreacting," Velos said. "It's true you've invested so much of yourself into Tyran. But as you've watched Ochi stray from the faith, you've become overly sensitive with Tyran. You are terrified that he will become his father. This is Tyran's first time as a leader. With you and me guiding him, he will be fine."

"He threatened me, Velos," Father Prodido shouted as his voice began to quiver. "He told me to remember who I was speaking to, for god's sake! I can't be sure where his allegiance is right now. For all I know, Ochi and Kaleo have persuaded him. Each of them secretly met with him and made their case against me. And you sit here and tell me everything will be fine!"

"Trust me, brother. He will be fine," said Velos.

"Maybe after I send Fovos to his house! Which I feel inclined to do at the present moment," Father Prodido said.

The religious leader pushed away from the table and stood abruptly.

"Whatever you have come to discuss, it will have to wait until later," he said. "I feel everything I have worked for slipping away, and I will not stand by helplessly and watch it happen."

"Sit down," Velos demanded without any explanation. "And do not make me ask a second time."

The religious leader already had his hand on the door handle. But he released it when he glanced back at his sister and saw her looking at the ornate object on the table.

"Very well, then," Father Prodido said, sitting down once again. "What is this beautiful box you have before you?"

"My husband's undoing," Velos replied, caressing the hand-carved cedar box with her hands.

Father Prodido leaned forward without answering, placing his hands on the table and raising his gray, wiry eyebrows.

"After the prisoners escaped and before Ochi left to find Thura," Velos began. "I noticed him fumbling through his closet suspiciously. I didn't know what he was doing at the time, but I began to look around after he left. In one corner of his closet beneath a piece of the floorboard, he had hidden a keepsake box."

"And the contents of this box?" Father Prodido asked.

"There were two items in it," Velos continued. "I found a knife, which I believe was given to him years ago during a commemoration ceremony honoring him for his service. With the knife, I found this journal."

"I assume his undoing is contained within the pages of this journal. Is this a correct assumption?" Father Prodido asked.

"Everything you've suspicioned over the last year is contained within these pages," Velos said. "His ambivalence, his half-heartedness, his lack of resolve … all of it … is spelled out here in great detail, even as recently as the other day. There's no way he could have ever imagined anyone finding or reading it."

"Please, do tell. Read something to me," Father Prodido said. "Pull back this mysterious veil Ochi has been hiding behind this entire time."

Velos slowly opened the box and removed the journal. Opening it to his last entry, she began to read.

Patrida is lost. While we desired a place of peace and freedom, we have become a people of fear and antagonism. We say we are holy, but I'm not sure we even know anything about God. My heart is not here anymore. I hate what we've become. I hate what I've let us become.

Father Prodido rubbed his wrinkled forehead and leaned back in the chair, considering every word Velos read.

"All this we have known," Father Prodido said. "At least this is what we have discerned from his actions. Is there anything more damning?"

"I haven't finished reading," Velos said, looking at Father Prodido and then down at the journal once again.

I hate Father Prodido. I hate his ideas. I hate his influence. I hate his words. I hate the way he turns people against one another, especially my family. His ideas turned me against my parents, pushed away my daughter, and corrupted my son. As I sit here and write these words, I have so much hatred and regret in my heart. If it would change my relationship with my family, I would surely kill Father Prodido. If that single act would somehow free my son from his grip, I would not hesitate. But I'm afraid it's too late. Tyran is too far gone. I saw it in his eyes earlier this evening at his house. I tried to tell him the truth about Prodido, but he was blank and listless. He would not hear any of it. He is hopeless and lost.

"The Lord continues to provide, dear sister," Father Prodido said. "What a bounty. Our feelings and observations of Ochi could not have been more accurate. But I now regret my misstep with Tyran. You are correct. I should not question his resolve. He needs nothing more at this time than our support and gentle guidance."

"I prayed you would see it that way," Velos said.

Father Prodido backed away from the table and stood. His dark countenance appeared darker behind the smoldering candle.

"However, that one line you read has me especially curious," said Father Prodido. "That part about Thura."

"Me, as well. But let me add to the intrigue," said Velos. "Look closely at the lining of this box. Do you not see the faintest imprint of what looks like a key?"

Turning the box so that what little light was left in the room could assist in discerning the truth, Father Prodido examined the velvet lining with his eyes and delicate fingers.

"I need you to pay Tyran a visit," said Father Prodido without looking up from the box. "Remind him of who he is and why he has our support. In the meantime, I will instruct Pali to assemble the guards. I will also have Fovos spread these new details among the townspeople. This missing key confirms my suspicions."

〜

Water began to pool on the floor inside the front door as Velos removed her soaked sandals. She noticed Tyran's house was dimmer than Father Prodido's, as a single candle on the counter struggled to keep its flame. Tyran had already walked back into his bedroom after letting his mother into the house. His demeanor made it evident he was still reeling from his earlier conversation with the religious leader. Reaching inside an oversized black raincoat, which she borrowed from her brother to keep from getting wet as she crossed the street, Velos removed the cedar box.

"Tyran, I've spoken to Father Prodido," Velos said, hoping to engage her son. But there was no response. "Let's start this another way. I found a box hidden below the floorboard in your father's closet that contains a journal of his most intimate thoughts. Some of the things he wrote, Tyran, are unforgivable."

The young leader walked into the room with his mother but appeared skeptical and aloof. Velos opened the journal and thumbed through its pages to find the passage she read earlier to Father Prodido. Finding the page, she handed Tyran the book and pointed to the beginning of the sentence. The room's silence indicated Tyran was reading every word his father had written, even beyond what Velos had read to the religious leader. Tyran quietly closed the journal and handed it back to Velos before sitting down in silence.

"Tyran," Velos began. "Your uncle and I believe in you. He said that he deeply regrets questioning your resolve. You know he has always had your best interest in mind. He took you under his wing, Tyran, and trained you up as his own. When he began to see your father's weakness, he knew you were Patrida's hope."

Turning his attention from the diminishing flame of the candle, Tyran looked up at his mother.

"Your father has chosen another path," Velos said. "It is a path of deception and lies. He walks in blindness to his eternal destruction. But you, Tyran, have the opportunity to stay on the path of truth. And this truth will always keep you from evil and help you discern what is right and wrong. As your mother, I see the truth by which you live your life. You have grown into a god-fearing man who desires a righteous and holy community seeking God's blessing. Your determination to preserve peace and freedom in Patrida is evident, and we believe you will fight the good fight toward that end."

Velos knelt in front Tyran as if to add emphasis to the next thing she said.

"Patrida cannot, I repeat cannot, exist on the same island with those who have left the faith, those who have chosen to profane the truth. God help us if we turn a blind eye again to their corrupting influence on us."

Tyran remained silent, but his posture changed as he leaned forward from his chair to hear everything his mother told him.

"You are not your father, Tyran," Velos said. "You *will* return Patrida to greatness. You *will* restore our heritage. You *will* have this town's respect when this is all over. Father Prodido instructed Pali to assemble the guards. They will be along the Monon awaiting your instruction, your Excellency."

Tyran stood with his mother and embraced her.

"I am proud of you, Tyran," said Velos. "One last thing I should tell you is that it appears your sister took a key from this same cedar box and used it to let the prisoners out. It's not only your father who has betrayed Patrida. It's also now your sister."

~

The Patridian guards, dressed once again in all black with hoods covering their faces, stood in formation at the center of the Monon. Every Patridian citizen lined each side of the road, roaring in cheers and applause not even rain could silence. Pali, standing beside an approving Father Prodido, barked out orders to the guards. In unison, they shouted back.

In full regalia, Tyran opened the door and, with his mother, walked between the guards standing in front of his house. When the townspeople saw them join Father Prodido and Pali in front of the assembly, the cheers and applause erupted into a crazed and delirious uproar.

"Your father's a traitor!" Fovos screamed as he paced back and forth along the Monon in front of the caustic crowd like a mad dog. "He's out to kill Father Prodido! He hates everything about Patrida! Bring him back here and make that coward face us!"

No one laughed at Fovos, as he had abandoned comedy for all that remained in him, which was only fear-mongering and accusation. The agitator was fueled by the spectacle, but primarily by shouts of approval and people inciting his verbal violence. Pulling a Patridian flag away from an onlooker, Fovos held it above his head in triumph and led the masses in a chant demanding the return of their defected leader.

Overwhelmed by his positive reception but still considering his mother's words and what he read in the journal, Tyran nodded at Father Prodido and motioned with his hand for the religious leader to give the invocation. Stepping forward, Father Prodido raised both hands to the heavens, nodding his head up and down. While one could not imagine the crowd growing louder, it did very quickly. In the history of Patrida, never had there been such widespread animus and unanimity at the same time among the populace. This kind of resurgence was exactly what Father Prodido desired and had painstakingly worked toward.

With one single hand remaining in the air, the crowd immediately quieted.

"Beloved, if any of you have doubted whether the hand of God has been upon us, I pray this day proves his faithfulness," Father Prodido began amidst the chaos of the crowd. "Surely the Lord has heard the petitions and cries of the faithful. What we suspicioned was lurking in darkness has now been brought into the glorious light. As you may have heard behind closed doors, there has been a coordinated effort by our forsaken leader and his daughter to not only aid and abet the enemy by helping them escape, but to undermine the integrity of Patrida by planning my assassination."

An eerie seriousness and silence befell Patrida. All anyone could hear was the thunderous crashing of waves in the distance, washing over the sandy shore. Seven hundred people stood in the pouring rain knowing what they desired, but their desires were tragically misaligned. They were sheep longing for direction but content grazing in brown and barren pastures. Peace and freedom were on their lips but remained far from their hearts. Before them, in the vacancy of wisdom, stood Tyran, a man beholden to the mob-like desires of his people but who secretly empathized with his father's regret.

"Let us march to retrieve my father and sister," Tyran proclaimed, once again awakening the insatiable beast along the Monon.

CHAPTER 18

White waves washed between the community of boulders assembled on the shoreline. The mid-morning tide receded momentarily from its contouring work. Over and between the rocks, Ochi eagerly followed Sophia upon the unimprinted white sand, while birds sang their refrains nestled in pine. No one had spoken a word since waking at first light, only the sounds of a leather satchel swaying and the gentle crunch of each step on the drying beach accompanied mother and son.

"Sorry to ask, but how do you know where you're going again?" Ochi called out, breaking the silence.

"The signs have been all around us for the last few days," Sophia said as she raised her walking stick and waved it in front of her. "We both desire to reach Salome, but neither of us has ever been there. I suppose we could walk aimlessly and hope we eventually get to our destination. Or, we could follow the signs that have been left for us to follow."

"Is everything a lesson?" Ochi asked with a light-hearted laugh.

"Of course," Sophia said as she turned and placed her walking stick in the soft ground with her wrinkled hand. "Everything around us is a lesson, Ochi, if we have the eyes to see it. But what I meant was that Odigo has been leaving signs for us to follow ever since I first met up with you."

"Ah!" Ochi exclaimed with a hearty chuckle. "I thought it was a bit too early for another deep conversation. You were talking about

Odigo, not giving me another lesson. I never can tell when you are serious and when you're not."

Cracking a very slight smile, Sophia responded.

"No, Ochi. No lesson," she said. "Odigo has been bending plants, leaving footprints, and placing small cairns for us the entire way. Have you not seen them?"

Ochi scratched his dark, sweaty head and turned as if surveying everything he had missed along the way.

"We still have some work to do yet, don't we?" Sophia said, turning around and walking toward a magnificent rock wall standing at least fifty feet tall.

"So what happens when your signs lead you to a dead-end?" Ochi called out from behind, staring at the impenetrable fortress in front of them.

Sophia hobbled up next to the wall without immediately responding and touched the cool, smooth surface with her hand. Ochi caught up and watched her quietly from behind.

"Do you know of this place?" Sophia asked.

"I've never been here if that's what you're asking," Ochi said. "A few others from Patrida have mentioned this giant wall, however. They supposed it was where the island stopped."

"That is why they never discovered Salome," Sophia said.

"What do you mean?" Ochi asked.

"This rock extends out into the sea, but we have to walk around it. We must stay close to this wall and slowly navigate through the water to get to the other side," Sophia explained.

Ochi smiled and shook his head, this time rubbing his forehead.

"And how do you know this exactly?" he asked.

"Look behind you. The last cairn has led us to this place. Follow me," Sophia said.

The old woman walked next to the wall and into the water, using her walking stick for balance. Ochi watched the water with every ebb and flow. It would rise and fall above and below her waist as if she was dancing to a song he could not hear. But trusting her lead, he joined her in the dance, mirroring her every movement, until they reached the end of the angular wall.

Despite the water becoming too deep for Sophia to stand without fully submerging, the old woman suddenly went under and navigated to the other side of the wall with unparalleled determination. Again, following her lead and shaking his head, which remained above water because of his height, Ochi navigated the moss-covered wall with his hands for balance to join Sophia on the other side.

For Ochi, the rock wall was a rite of passage, even though there was nothing remarkable or necessarily poignant about that exact moment. Following his mother through the water felt as if he had left one world behind and gradually entered another. Ochi's axis was slowly turning to reveal possibilities, but he was unsure what that meant practically for himself or how any of it would help him find the peace he desired.

Turning inland, Ochi and Sophia saw an exceptionally straight and heavily traveled dirt trail ascending the rock wall's backside under tree cover. Although unobstructed, the path appeared to climb gradually up the hillside at least a couple hundred feet over a mile or so, which meant this portion of their journey would be slow and gradual for Sophia.

Ochi stopped momentarily to examine his sandal, which he had only worn a couple of times before. The friction of leather rubbing his ankle had created an open blister that began to bleed. As he adjusted the straps, he thought about how he had been gradually changing on this journey. But he quickly tempered his thoughts with how the people of Salome would receive him, many of whom he had personally driven out during the Great Liberation.

"What is Salome like?" Ochi asked without looking up, pretending to examine his minimal injury.

"I have never been there, of course, but I spoke to Odigo briefly about it when we were together. I suppose you are nervous about what they will think of you," Sophia said.

"I am," Ochi said as he stood up and walked along the dirt path toward Sophia. "But I'm even more nervous about seeing Thura for the first time."

"Like you and me, she is on her own journey as well, Ochi," Sophia said. "She is a remarkable young woman, and I would be surprised if she did not run up to you and give you a huge hug when she sees you."

"I hope you're right," said Ochi.

"I think you will find that there is a deep well of goodness in Salome from which each person there drinks. No wrong you have done to them is greater than the love they have for all things, and that includes you. I can promise you that," Sophia responded.

Ochi moved ahead of the old woman but walked only a few paces in front of her. His eagerness appeared to outpace any lingering trepidation that remained. For her part, Sophia seemed to welcome her son's lead. Each step in silence was a meditation carrying Ochi back to when his mother first approached him in the forest a few days prior. He laughed as he thought about how she drew circles around him and taught him how to see everything differently, including himself.

Looking over his shoulder with gratitude, Ochi watched his mother walk steadily behind him. He could not help but think about how lost and confused he had been when she first called out his name among the pines. He thought about how he had followed her throughout that day and how desperate he had been for direction.

Sophia had guided him from the first moment they began journeying together. But now, she was content with letting her son take the lead the rest of the way to Salome. Whether it was intentional on Sophia's part or not, Ochi wholeheartedly believed this was her final lesson for him. She taught him that only he could discover peace and no one else could help him find it. This path was his alone to walk.

A kaleidoscope of light filtering through needles and leaves into thousands of colors danced before Ochi on the trail. But they could hardly outnumber the myriad emotions welling up within him. Each step forward to that point had been increasingly difficult, but the gravelly ascent appeared steeper than when he took his first step out of the water only moments before.

"Why is this so difficult for me?" Ochi said under his breath, referring not only to the arduous climb but to the seeming impossibility of facing the guilt and shame he had tried to hide away.

Breathing in and out more deeply, his shirt dampened with sweat, Ochi knew there was one last floorboard to remove to get at what he had hidden below the surface. However, even with the floorboard removed, he could hardly bear to look into that dark space. Trying not to be noticed by Sophia, Ochi rubbed his red eyes discreetly and continued walking.

"Why is this so painful?" he mouthed, placing both hands on his head in grief. "Why can't I face him?"

Ochi stopped walking and, with blurry eyes, stood staring ahead.

"The only way you will ever forgive yourself, Ochi, is to hear your father's last words to you and receive them," Sophia said, placing her hand on his shoulder.

Ochi turned and faced his mother.

"You will never be able to forgive yourself if you continue to bury your father's words," she said.

"I can't do it," Ochi said. "I was only able to seek your forgiveness because you're here standing in front of me. You're still alive. Knowing he died by my hands is a pain I just can't face. I can't go back to that day. I can't look at him. I can't even hear his words. I know this is the one thing that's keeping me from finding peace, but I don't deserve it."

Ochi turned away from his mother and pulled his leather satchel back over his shoulder. He wanted to go back down the hill. Despite how far he had journeyed away from Patrida, Ochi carried a burden that would not leave him. What he did not realize, however, was that he was only steps away from Salome. The bend at the ridge above opened to their destination, but neither knew how close it truly was. Sophia hobbled up next to Ochi, breathing more heavily than she had the entire journey, and encouraged him to take the last few steps with her to the top.

Before they even had a chance to share a small celebration for their accomplishment, Sophia and Ochi heard the sudden movement and shuffle of people only a couple of hundred feet to their right. As the mother and son pirouetted toward the gentle buzz and hum of people gathering on the path, they saw the entire community at once erupt in celebration. Sophia reached over with her wrinkled right hand and grabbed Ochi's calloused hand. With all of her strength, she squeezed it as firmly as she could to let him know that she loved him and was with him every step.

Small children jumped up and down with the kind of excitement that could only come from stories they had grown up hearing. Men and women beamed with smiles and cheers, some with arms raised triumphantly in the air while others clapping in wild ovation. Even the two dogs chased each other around and yipped excitedly as if they understood exactly what was happening. To the people of Salome, this was the singular most significant moment in their short history.

Still holding her son's hand, Sophia led him toward the exuberant crowd. Ochi closed his eyes and immediately flashed back to the gallows and the rough, thick rope that was about to be placed around his neck. He thought about the crowd roaring venomously to hang him. His mind raced as he heard the boos and jeers of the townspeople at Sanctuary when he stood before them and announced they would not be immediately executing Odigo. He thought about his dream and how cloaked men chased through the forest. He again heard them yelling at him for abandoning his faith, community, and family.

Opening his eyes, Ochi saw everyone still cheering and applaud-
ing. They were not just looking at his mother, either. They were looking directly at him. He could see on their faces that the reception was
not a formality but that they were genuinely glad he was with her.
Sophia, moved by her friends' overwhelming love toward her son,
raised his hand in the air to louder cheers.

The crowd consumed Sophia and Ochi in greetings and hugs.
While their joy and elation were infectious, and Ochi felt them deep
within his bones, he had not seen Thura among them. Almost as if
they could sense Ochi's concern, the townspeople grew quiet. They
slowly began to move away from him and Sophia, standing on both
sides to form a path. Standing in the back by herself was Thura. The
quiet of all who gathered, including the small children, was palpable.
Neither father nor daughter knew what the other was thinking or
what their first move should be.

Thura looked into her father's eyes and saw the gaze of a broken
man being patiently and lovingly pieced back together. While she was
still unsure why he had left Patrida by himself and was now standing
in Salome with Sophia, Thura could see something had changed with
him. The young woman took one hesitant step forward and saw a
single tear run down her father's cheek. One step suddenly became
two, and Thura began to run without inhibition toward her father's
open arms.

"I am speechless," Thura said, squeezing her father. "I just don't
understand how you are here with Sophia."

After seeing that Ochi and Thura needed some time together,
Sophia moved with the crowd toward the village.

"I thought you would be angry that I ran away and took Sophia
and Odigo with me," Thura continued, now looking at her father
and wiping away his tears with her thumb. "I was standing outside of
Tyran's house, looking through the side window when I heard you say
that you were going to execute them."

Ochi looked at his daughter with confusion.

"Thura, I'm not sure what you thought you heard, but you mis-understood my conversation with Tyran," Ochi said. "I went to his house to tell him that Father Prodido is the problem with Patrida and that I regretted ever allowing him to come to the island in the first place."

Thura stared at the ground as the pieces began to slowly come together in her mind.

"What we had before Patrida was good," Ochi said. "There was something about this island that was whole and complete. But I didn't see it at the time. That's my fault. But all Father Prodido has done from the beginning is make us see everything and everyone through a distorted lens. And over time, this way of seeing each other has turned us against one other and caused division. Not just within Patrida, but within our family."

"And you went to Tyran's to help him see all this," Thura said.

"That's the part you misunderstood," Ochi said. "I pleaded with him to come to his senses. I told him this madness had to stop and there was going to be an execution."

"But it was Father Prodido," Thura said under her breath.

"I was desperate," Ochi continued. "I had lost my son to him. And I was willing to do anything to save your brother at that moment. I pleaded with him. I told him all the ways Father Prodido had lied and tried to manipulate him. But Thura, Tyran is too far gone. I'm afraid he can't see how Prodido has brainwashed him."

Ochi turned and put his hand in front of his face, shielding his grief from his daughter. While Thura had seen a man walking toward Salome who had been changing, the man in front of her still had open wounds. Thura removed the satchel from his shoulder and placed her hand where the strap had been resting.

"If there is anything I have learned from Sophia," Thura said, "it is that the possibility of wholeness in every person requires grace and patience from us. I know it may be difficult, but we can't give up on Tyran."

Ochi wiped his eyes and placed his hand on top of his daughter's hand.

"When I left Patrida, I left it as a lost cause," Thura continued. "All I saw was the darkness around me and everyone stumbling without a light to guide their path. That is the way I saw you. I saw you as too far gone. I saw you as someone who could never be saved. In the letter I wrote to you, which I am sure you found and I now regret writing, I even told you that you are the problem. That you are hopeless and lost."

Ochi put his hand back over his eyes, realizing that he believed the same thing about Tyran. Yet, as he looked at himself, he also knew he was the evidence of a person who could change. Is a person ever too far gone? Ochi thought. Do we ever really know what another person is thinking? What they have experienced, or what they are dealing with? What they have suffered that brought them to this point? What if all we see is their blemished exterior and miss what could be happening on the inside? The pain they carry within them each day. The struggles they fight through from the time they wake up in the morning until the time they go to bed each night. And the wounds that have never had a chance to heal because they keep getting torn back open. What if they are standing on the other side of the door, like me, desperately wanting to open it, desperately wanting to change?

"How did you change your mind about me, Thura?" Ochi finally asked a question out loud.

"It was Sophia," she said. "She told me what I see is not nearly as important as how I see. We tend to only see things from the outside. But she taught me that there is something hidden below the surface of everything, something within each of us, that is divine. It is what connects us and gives us life. And when we see it in each other, everything on the outside fades away. All that is left is divine love. That is what binds us together. If that kind of love is within you, how could I turn away from it? How could we turn away from Tyran or mother or even Father Prodido? No matter what we see on the outside of them, there is divine love within them. If they can't see it for themselves right now, we can at least try to see for them."

"She taught you all of this in a couple of days?" Ochi asked rhetorically with a skeptical but good-hearted smile.

"She is something, isn't she?" Thura responded. "We had no idea where she was going when she left us in the woods. One moment she was talking to me and Odigo, and the next moment she walked off through the trees. We were like, 'Where are you going?' She did not even turn around. She just said, 'Where I belong.'"

Ochi laughed as he envisioned her hobbling away from them and into the woods. But as the moment subsided, he knew he had to tell Thura one more thing before they walked into the village.

"While we're being so honest," Ochi said, "there's something I've never told you because I tried to bury it away. But you deserve to know the truth."

Thura looked intently at Ochi, trying to discern what he was about to tell her.

"When you were a little girl, the people of Salome used to live in Patrida," Ochi began. "As you also know, Sophia and her husband were a part of the group we attacked and drove out."

"Yes, Sophia told me that you killed her husband," Thura said.

"I did," Ochi responded. "And it still haunts me to this day."

Thura waited for her father's next words.

"His name was Numa, and he was my father," Ochi said. "Sophia is my mother, and she is your grandmother."

Thura tried to respond, but she could not speak.

"Thura, listen," Ochi said. "There will be time to answer your questions soon enough, I promise. I know this is difficult for you to comprehend, but when she left you and Odigo, she came to me despite everything I had done in the past. Even after killing my father. Even after imprisoning her all those years. She never gave up on me, Thura. Everything she taught you is how she lives her life. She pursued me in hopes that I would change and that we could heal our relationship."

"Everyone in Patrida knew this, but me?" Thura asked.

"Not everyone," Ochi said. "But as you know, if anyone mentioned her name, it was punishable by death. And everyone knew that. My regret kept me from killing her like I did my father. My shame caused me to hide her and try to forget about her. But your courage, Thura, and your determination to pursue what was good opened the door, not only for me to begin my journey to find peace, but to heal my relationship with my mother."

Thura hugged her father one last time, although every word he had spoken was dizzying and difficult to comprehend. She began to reexamine and reinterpret every visit and conversation with Sophia over the years. It was as if she had discovered an entirely new depth to their relationship. Sophia was not a hidden relic who had spent years imparting her wise words to an impressionable teenager turned young woman. She was her flesh and blood and the woman after whom Thura wanted to pattern her own life.

Putting her arm around her father, Thura walked with him toward the village.

"If my grandmother is capable of forgiving you," Thura said, "then who am I not to do the same."

CHAPTER 19

Talking and laughter emanated from the lively village. Movement and excitement abounded within. The people of Salome worked together in making their final preparations for the evening. The men tidied up their huts, repaired tables and chairs, and prepared the food. The women filled water basins, organized the plates and utensils, and prepared the wine. Even the young children set their table and chairs before running around to play.

Salome was the antithesis of Patrida. The differences were evident in how they organized their community and how they lived their lives. Everything they believed about their world was apparent in how they cared for the land, the animals, and each other. Everything was holy and sacred, created in divine love, and worthy of honor and respect. They understood each person was on their own journey to discover ultimate truth, and that they must walk patiently together toward that center. Salome was a place of deep wisdom, profound peace, and humble love.

But the first difference Ochi noticed, as he and Thura walked into the village, was their magnificent spring. It was identical to the freshwater source in Sanctuary, except for one thing. Salome's spring was perfectly centered in the heart of their village, unlike Patrida's, which was on the town's edge.

Around the spring, twelve huts stood together in a perfect circle, each a couple of hundred feet from the source. The huts had stuccoed walls made of sun-dried mud and a roof adorned with wooden shingles. While modest in construction, they were hardly shacks. Sunflowers towered in crisp vibrancy, reaching to the heavens on the backside of each home. Lavender accented their foundations in calm and peaceful tranquility. It only took a few minutes for Salome's simple beauty and allure to fully capture Patrida's former leader.

Ochi and Thura transitioned from the dirt path they had been traveling to the lush, green grass between the first two houses entering the circle. Thura, out of the corner of her eye, glanced at her father to see what his reaction would be. Raising his arms and locking fingers behind his head, Ochi stopped and stared in disbelief at what he saw surrounding the spring.

The calm, bubbling crystal-clear water poured into a labyrinth carved into the ground around the spring. The elaborate maze appeared as if one could walk above the water on a grassy path and navigate through the winding puzzle toward the water source at its center. Ochi examined the artistry and grinned at the small children who splashed in its flow.

"Unbelievable," he said, shaking his head.

"I know," said Thura. "Look around the outer edge of the labyrinth. See the stones set into the ground?"

"Magnificent. I have never seen anything like it," Ochi said, surveying the perimeter.

From the circular labyrinth's margins, inset stones patterned into ten rays extending outward between each house, not as straight lines, but more like waves. On the opposite side, flowing from the labyrinth, a small creek left the village and continued toward a small vineyard. If it had been possible to view the artistry from above, it would have appeared as a fantastically radiating sun, pulsating with energy and life throughout the village.

"What does all of this mean?" Ochi asked.

"This is how we center our community," a man said, approaching from behind.

Ochi and Thura turned to find a man and woman walking toward them with Odigo.

"Ochi, it's been a long time, brother," the man said, extending his hand outward. Thura had not initially noticed how much the man resembled her father when she first arrived in Salome. The similarities, however, were undeniable.

Reciprocating the gesture, Ochi shook the man's hand. Thura continued to study the man intently as he pulled Ochi in for a hug.

"I'm so happy you're here with us, Ochi," the man whispered as he released the hug and grasped Ochi's upper arms and stared at him.

"It's good to be here, Edo," Ochi responded. "Difficult, but good."

"Not to interrupt or anything," Thura said. "But are you two brothers?"

Putting his arm around Ochi and turning toward Thura, Edo smiled.

"How did you figure that one out, Thura?" he said laughing. "Ochi, you remember my wife, Tora."

Ochi stepped forward hesitantly, not sure if he should hug her or shake her hand. But Tora ran up and embraced him.

"I'm glad you're here too," she said. "Really glad, Ochi."

"And of course you've met my son Odigo," Edo smiled again.

Embarrassed to look at the young man, Ochi looked down at the ground and noticed he was the only one wearing sandals. Without drawing attention to himself, he casually slid his feet out of them. He stood barefoot on the grass while attempting to make eye contact with Tora as she began to speak.

"There's no way you could have known he was our son," Tora said. "But he did say you guys roughed him up a bit."

"So you are my cousin," Thura said, turning toward Odigo to break up the awkwardness.

The young man smiled at her.

"It is good to see you smile," Thura said, noticing the dimple on his right cheek behind his lingering bruises.

Edo put his right arm around Ochi once more and turned him toward the labyrinth. With his other hand, he gestured toward the structure.

"Like I was saying, this is the center of our community, Ochi. This is symbolic of everything we do and how we do it. Doesn't look anything like the spring in Patrida, does it?"

"Certainly a different interpretation for sure," Ochi laughed.

"Tell him what you told me about it," Thura said to Edo with excitement. "The thought you all put into it is unbelievable."

"Well, as soon as we saw the spring, we knew we wanted it to be in the middle of the village, not set aside on the edge of town," Edo said.

"We didn't want it to be something separate from our lives," Tora added.

"Yes, but tell him about the path to the center of it," Thura said with excitement.

Laughing at Thura's enthusiasm, Edo continued.

"Well, this path isn't a straight line, is it?" Edo asked rhetorically. "It's not a one-way road between judgment and freedom like Patrida. It's a path that meanders and proceeds toward the center, where a person can travel at their own pace and then freely drink. But it also symbolizes a journey that never ends. Day after day, we walk the path and drink from the center."

"You're making me thirsty, brother," Ochi said, laughing.

"Well, it quenches our thirst for sure," Edo said. "But it continually reminds us that our journey never ends. It's not a one-time transaction, Ochi. Our thirst is not satisfied from taking only one drink. We drink from this source our entire lives. It's a humble process, but it keeps us centered and grounded. Continually walking toward the center teaches us our great dependence upon that which gives us life."

"You must have gotten the wisdom gene from mom," Ochi said, trying to keep the conversation light.

"The center of the spring represents the flow of divine love," Thura said, smiling at her father. "That is what gives each of us life. It is what holds us together. And what holds this little community together. That is why it is at the center of everything. I made the journey to the center for the first time last night."

Gazing at his daughter, Ochi saw a serenity in her deep, brown eyes he had never previously seen. Maybe it was the way the sun illuminated her face or that he had not looked into her eyes in a long time. Something had changed in his daughter. He thought about how she used to wear her hair in tightly constrained braids and how it had not changed since she was thirteen years old. But now, Thura's beautiful auburn hair had been released and blew freely in the breeze. Her outward appearance seemed to express what she had discovered internally.

"With divine love at the center of our lives," Thura continued.

"We can find peace, right?" Ochi said, finishing her sentence as he squatted and watched the spring bubble over.

"And freedom," Thura said under her breath as she squatted next to him.

"That's where I've had it wrong all along," Ochi said. "I thought we could only achieve peace through strength. So I chose strength but never found peace."

"I know, father," Thura said. "I believed we lived in freedom, but I never felt free."

The father and daughter continued to stare at the center, one having already made the journey, the other desiring to make it as well.

"It's beautiful on so many levels," Ochi replied, still taking it all in. "It's a far cry from what we've done in Patrida. It's night and day, honestly. There's something about what you've done here that speaks to me at the depths of my soul. Not just in how you've constructed this community, but in how you live your lives. And how you have received me."

"Alright. Everyone out of the way," said Sophia, as she approached from behind. "We are about twenty minutes from starting the celebration, and we need to get everything set up."

"What's the celebration?" Ochi asked as he stood up and faced Edo.

"We are having a celebration for you, brother," Edo replied, placing his hand on Ochi's shoulder and smiling.

"You didn't even know I was coming," Ochi said.

"We have a celebration every evening," said Tora. "This one is in your honor, Ochi. Edo, enough with the deep conversations for the moment. Get your brother some of your wine and show him your pride and joy while we make the final preparations."

Ochi had been in such deep reflection he had failed to notice the movement around him. The men had been moving tables into place around the labyrinth facing each other like their homes. The women began setting chairs and tablecloths at each table. The children, also oblivious to the activity, continued to laugh and play in the water.

"Brother, here's a cup of wine for you," said Edo. "Now follow me. I need to show you what I've been working on."

The brothers walked to the left of the labyrinth and exited between two of the houses. After only a few steps beyond the village where the pines eventually came to an end, but where the creek continued to flow, Ochi stopped to take in the expansive view of the ocean.

"I bet the sunrise here is something else," Ochi said.

"Isn't this a fantastic view? I don't think I've ever seen two sunrises that look the same here. It's like a new work of art painted across the sky each morning. Don't get too close to the edge, though, Ochi. That's a sheer drop straight down to the ocean, and there's no easy way to get you back up here if you fall," Edo laughed. "You wouldn't want to miss your celebration, would you?"

"Don't worry about me. I'll stay well enough away from it," Ochi said as he turned and walked toward his brother, taking a sip from his cup. "So this is your pride and joy, huh?"

"Ochi, I have worked on this vineyard as a labor of love for almost a decade," Edo said. "The wine you're drinking came from these vines. These hands picked every grape. These feet crushed them in the wooden vats I constructed."

Ochi attempted to hand the cup of wine back to Edo.

"Your feet what?" Ochi laughed. "Here. I've had too much already."

"Alright funny guy," Edo laughed. "But seriously, that's how I crush the grapes before I leave them to ferment. It's a small vineyard but the right size for me to maintain on my own. And it yields enough for our tiny community."

Ochi took another drink without responding to Edo and, once again, turned his attention toward the ocean.

"I know," Edo said. "It never gets old, does it? Sometimes when I'm tending the vines, I stop and stare myself."

Ochi remained silent and took another drink.

"How have you really been, Ochi?" Edo asked, sensing something was weighing on his brother.

"I don't know," Ochi replied. "Where I'm standing is not where I thought I was going."

"You probably mean that in a couple of different ways, huh?" Edo asked.

"Yeah. I really wasn't going to Salome as much as I was leaving Patrida," Ochi said, taking another drink. "This is an outstanding wine, by the way. But yeah, I didn't know where I was going or what my plan was. I said I was following Thura and left. That's when mom came to me."

"And she traveled with you the rest of the way," said Edo. "How much had you spoken with her over the last twenty years, Ochi, if you don't mind me asking?"

"Not at all," Ochi replied. "I'm ashamed to say it, but I had not even seen her once during that time. I didn't want to see her. I couldn't face her after all I had done."

Edo had more questions he wanted to ask but believed his silence was more important for Ochi than his words.

"When she came to me," Ochi said. "I broke down and apologized for everything I had done. I was so sorry. She told me she had forgiven me long ago and loves me as I am."

The two men stood quietly with the warm ocean wind blowing over them.

"She's something else, though," Ochi said, breaking their silence. "At times, I thought she had lost it. She had me drawing circles in the ground and sitting in the middle of them."

Edo started to laugh.

"I'm serious," Ochi said. "But the entire way here, she kept pouring her wisdom out on me, and it made me open my eyes."

"Open your eyes to what?" Edo asked.

"To the fact that I'll only find peace when I tear down the wall I've built around my heart. That's my last circle," Ochi responded.

"And what is it that's keeping you from going there, Ochi?" Edo asked.

"It's a strange thing. Everyone has been so quick to forgive me for everything I've done. Mom, Thura, and everyone in Salome. But I can't forgive myself. It's like there's no room in that last circle for peace. Everything I've been carrying all these years resides there and won't leave."

"I understand, brother," Edo said. "Sometimes it's easier to receive the forgiveness of others than it is to give it to ourselves."

"I'm not saying I prefer to hold onto those feelings," Ochi said. "It's just that I don't know how to quit feeling them or how to get rid of them."

"Would you mind if your older brother offered a few words of perspective?" Edo asked.

Ochi took one last drink from his cup and turned toward his brother.

"Honestly," Ochi said. "I welcome it, Edo. You've had two decades to think about me and everything I did and all the ways I've hurt people. You see a desperate man standing in front of you whose heart is crying out for peace but who can't receive it. What would you say to him?"

"I would say I no longer see the man who did those things," Edo began. "I no longer see the man who drove out those he disagreed with. I no longer see the man who imprisoned his mother and killed his father. That man existed a long time ago, but he's no longer here."

Ochi turned his gaze from the horizon to the ground and rubbed his eyes.

"I see a man being transformed by the forgiveness of those he hurt," said Edo. "Ochi, you need to give yourself the same forgiveness everyone else has given you. If you have been searching for peace, that's the only way you will find it."

"Everyone you've mentioned I've been able to look in the eyes and receive their forgiveness," Ochi said. "But I will never be able to look in the eyes of our father and receive his forgiveness."

Edo paused.

"I understand, brother," he said. "But come over here for a second. See this wooden vat? I fill it up with grapes when they're ready to be taken from the vine. I step into it with my bare feet and slowly begin to crush them, releasing their dark, red juice with each step. It's a violent process, Ochi, if we're being honest about it. But as the cup in your hand can attest, it can also be a transformative experience."

"I don't understand," Ochi said.

"From death, there is always the possibility of transformation and blessing," Edo said. "From the outside looking in, a vat of broken and bruised grapes may appear to be wasted. Hundreds of grapes crushed in vain for no apparent reason. But in their death, something transformative begins to happen that can ultimately bless people."

"I'm not sure I completely understand the parallel," Ochi said.

"I know this isn't a perfect analogy," Edo replied. "You didn't kill our father so others could somehow be blessed by it. That's not what I'm saying at all. The man was a blessing simply by being with us. But there is always an opportunity to look at ourselves in light of those who die. To evaluate and take inventory of our own lives. You have the opportunity to look at yourself in light of our father, in light of who he was, and who you want to be."

"I think I'm beginning to understand what you're saying," Ochi said.

"That's what I had to do, Ochi," Edo said. "There was a lot of bitterness and anger toward you in the aftermath of his death. But I had to look at myself in light of who he was, in light of who our mother was, and who I wanted to be in the end. I chose to be like them. I decided to be like them in how they loved you and how they forgave you, despite what you did.

"What I'm telling you is don't let his death be in vain, Ochi. Let his life transform you. You can honor him through your life. Love as he would love people. Bless as he would bless people. Go back to Patrida and help them find peace and freedom like he would have done."

With faint waves crashing below and an air of peace surrounding the two men, Ochi grabbed his brother and hugged him tightly.

"I'm sorry for everything I've done," Ochi said. "I'm sorry for the pain I've caused you and the pain I've caused everyone else in Salome."

"Brother, you know what I'm going to say," Edo replied, "and they're not empty words. I mean this from the bottom of my heart. I forgave you long ago and have constantly prayed for us to be reunited. No matter where you are right now, you are here. And I'm honored to be standing with you."

∽

A long wooden table overflowed with an abundance of food. Still, one spot remained for the bowl of marinated green olives Sophia carried. As she placed the bowl on the table and centered it perfectly, someone came up from behind and put their arms around her in a gentle hug. Sophia closed her eyes and, with her aged hands, delicately gripped Thura's arms.

"I have wanted to tell you for so long," Sophia whispered. "But I wanted to protect you, Thura. There was so much you did not need to know. And you being able to call me grandmother was never as important to me as the relationship we have had."

Thura turned Sophia around so she could look into the old woman's patient and loving eyes.

"I love you," Thura said.

"I love you, too, Thura. I have ever since I first caught a glimpse of you passing by as a young girl on the Monon. When I saw your long, red hair and dark eyes, I saw myself when I was younger. Even though you can't tell now, my hair used to be as red as yours. But as I look at you, I see so much more we share."

"If it were not for you, Sophia, I would have never left Patrida. I would have never learned about myself or been able to see things differently. I would not be standing here right now. You helped me understand that freedom can only begin in here," Thura said, pointing to her chest.

"Yes," Sophia said, "but this freedom is not for you alone, Thura."

"What does that mean? Everyone here is free," Thura asked.

"But Patrida is not," Sophia responded. "What about the young girls and young women who are enslaved through their servanthood and forced marriages? What about those walking the Monon each day imprisoned by the religious and political systems in Patrida? What about everyone pushed to the margins of the town and treated as lower-class citizens? How will these heavy chains of Patrida ever be broken if you only sit in your room and light candles from above, Thura?"

The young woman looked down at the ground.

"Thura, look at me," Sophia said, lifting the young woman's chin with her hand. "What about your mother? What about your brother? What about your uncle? Do not forget everything you have learned. No one is ever too far gone, Thura. No one. I never gave up on your father. I walked with him patiently as he continued his journey. Look how far he has traveled, Thura. You have the same opportunity with those in Patrida."

CHAPTER 20

Two teenage girls with dark, flowing hair began to place torches in a circle in Salome's welcoming soil. Each flame danced and illuminated the front of a single corresponding hut while attempting to hold on to dusk and push back the night. Excitement and anticipation had been building as the town gathered around their respective tables for the evening's festivities.

As Ochi and Edo returned, walking into the circle of huts, everyone began to cheer immediately. Knowing the applause was for Ochi, Edo stopped and began to clap and whistle himself. The people cheered even louder as Ochi stood at his table next to Thura, waiting for the applause to subside.

Although the smallest children only knew Sophia through stories, and Ochi only as Sophia's son, they ran up to him at his table with giggles and delight. They asked if he would sit with them at their table during the meal. With a smile crossing his face, Ochi told them regretfully that he had already committed to sitting with his family.

"Such sweet kids," Ochi said. "They don't know me, yet they invite me to their table. You should be very proud of them."

"We are," said Tora with a smile, turning to look at the children sitting at the smaller table. "Since first arriving in Salome, we've had seventeen children born here. Of course, Odigo was the first, as I was early in my pregnancy then. But these children only know of this place. They know nothing of Patrida."

"I hope one day they will know more of this island, even a trans-formed Patrida," Ochi replied. "Not the way it is now, but maybe the way it will be one day. At least, that is my hope for all of our children. What you have here is special. If the people of Patrida could experi-ence it, they would understand."

"Maybe one day, brother," Edo said. "We may not live to see it in our lifetime, but maybe our children will."

"Thura, have you seen the other guest of honor?" Ochi asked.

"I have not," Thura replied. "I gave her a hug earlier, and we chat-ted for a few minutes, but then I got in line to get my food."

"She probably had somewhere she needed to be," added Odigo with a laugh. "That seems to be her thing."

Ochi and Thura laughed as the seat in between them remained empty.

"She was with Odigo and me one morning when she abruptly left us without any explanation," Thura explained to Edo and Tora, who laughed at Sophia's quirkiness.

"That's when she found me wandering through the forest," Ochi said. "Anyway, I'm sure she will be here shortly. Edo and Tora, what I've tasted of the food so far is fantastic. Compliments to the hands that prepared it. And Edo, the wine is really something special, if I haven't told you already."

"Thank you, brother," Edo replied. "I'm honored to be able to share a cup with you and your daughter in celebration of your return. What you're drinking now has been aged longer than the cup you had at the vineyard. I saved the best for last."

"Speaking of the vineyard," Tora said. "What did you think about Edo's little project, Ochi?"

"Well first, that view," he responded. "Wow. It was breathtaking. If we have time tomorrow, Thura, I will have to take you there if you haven't already seen it. But to answer your question, the vineyard was perfect in so many ways. You can tell it's a real labor of love for my brother. Not just in working the vine but also his wisdom in making the wine. The way he understands what he's doing really opened my eyes."

"How so, Ochi?" Tora asked.

"Well, Edo shared a beautiful metaphor with me about the wine-making process," Ochi began.

"It was far from perfect," Edo added.

"No, no. You're being modest. It was excellent," Ochi countered. "At least I understood exactly what you meant by it."

"Well we are dying to hear what it is," Thura announced, looking over to Odigo with wide eyes, hoping to move the story along.

"No, it's just that I've been holding on to a lot of stuff for a long time," Ochi said. "Everything with my mom and dad and you guys. And it has consumed me."

While the other tables buzzed with life and laughter and conversation in the village's low light, everyone at Ochi's table grew quiet. But their silence did not convey awkwardness in response to his honesty. Instead, it was an acknowledgment that they each understood how far he had traveled to be with them in Salome.

"Death, even death caused by my own hands, does not have to be the end of the story," Ochi said, as everyone at his table appeared to lean in more. "That's what he taught me. I could let my guilt and shame continue to add misery upon misery in my life and the lives of others. Edo could let those crushed grapes rot in the vat if he wanted to, but it would all be in vain.

He showed me that his patient work transforms crushed grapes into a choice wine that blesses people. His perspective made me rethink everything. How do I not make my father's death something that happened in vain, but something that can ultimately bless others? That's the question I've been asking myself since our conversation in the vineyard."

"What do you think that means for you now, Ochi?" Tora asked with tears filling the corners of her eyes.

"I want to live as he did," Ochi said, staring intently at the water flowing from the spring and into the labyrinth. "I not only want to experience his peace, but I also want to use my life as a blessing for others as he did. I may have poured out his blood in death, but I promise you this, I will one day raise a cup in his honor to bless this community and this entire island when we all, at last, drink it together."

Reaching over the space where Sophia should have been sitting, Thura grabbed her father's hand and squeezed it. While looking at his hand, she remembered her conversation in the pines with Sophia about the resin-stained fingers. It is not what we see, but how we see it, she thought.

More than ever, Thura realized her father had never been permanently stained. He was not beyond changing. Her grandmother was right. Despite not always seeing, or trusting, that there could be something below the surface working for the healing and restoration of a person, Thura could finally see what she could not see before in her father. He was a man who had been desperately searching. As she thought about the letter she had written to him and how she had accused him of being the central problem of Patrida and someone who would never change, Thura leaned over and whispered in her father's ear.

"I owe you an apology first," Thura said.

"Why's that, Thura?" Ochi responded.

"I have been prideful and arrogant. I not only ran from Patrida because I believed no one there would ever get it, but I also abandoned you as someone I believed was irredeemable. All I could see was your dark stains. I refused to believe there was anything good in you. I could never have imagined you were searching and struggling the whole time. I am sorry for giving up on you."

Ochi squeezed his daughter's hand.

"Thank you, Thura," he said. "I'm sorry for having never thought about your feelings or what you were going through, either. I could only see the system we were in. It blinded me. I honestly thought I was working for the good of everyone. While Prodido said we were making Patrida a holy community, we had been creating a prison for all of us. But I couldn't see it at the time. Was it your grandmother who first opened your eyes to it?"

"It was," Thura said. "So many times over the years, she guided me in her wisdom. She never once tried to force me into anything. She knew one day I would see it on my own, and I eventually did. But on my way here, Odigo helped me see things from an entirely different perspective as well."

Thura and Ochi looked over at the young man, who was standing at the back table filling his plate with seconds and laughed simultaneously at him.

"But seriously," Thura continued, "Odigo took me to a place here on the island that made me rethink everything. Everything I have ever known. It was a place that made me change how I see everyone on the island. I see them in an entirely different light now. I see myself in an entirely different light now."

"What is this place called, Thura?" Ochi asked. "I would like to go there myself."

"He called it the waters of Alethes," Thura responded. "It is the most powerful and spiritual imaginable. I was going to take you there later, but I think we need to go now before the celebration begins."

As rapidly as they set the tables, the people of Salome began to move them in preparation for the night's festivities. As Ochi and Thura stood from their seats, a man and a woman walked out of their hut, carrying a goblet drum and tamburello. No sooner than they began to play, the people started to clap in rhythm and sing.

～

Ochi followed Thura's footsteps past the right side of the labyrinth, exiting the circle of homes. The drums' deep, hypnotic resonance in the distance beneath the powerful cadence of voices singing and chanting accompanied each step the daughter and father took away from the village. The flame from Thura's torch twirled in slow motion, appearing as two dancers moving as one.

Step by step, Ochi placed his feet where Thura's had already traveled. As the two stopped before a steep, rocky mound, the drums and chanting faded, leaving them with only the crackling of Thura's torch. The moment, however, felt no less hypnotic for Ochi.

"The path goes up a bit before we drop back down into the cave," Thura said.

"Okay," Ochi said. "Sorry for being so quiet on the way here. I have your grandmother on my mind."

"I do, too," Thura said. "But I am sure she is fine."

"You're right," Ochi said. "She will probably be waiting for us when we return."

Ochi had not noticed until Thura began up the hill that there were steps carved into the stone as if this was a place the people of Salome regularly visited. In his daughter's light, he saw what looked like etchings on each step. But he could not see it enough to read it.

Thura remained silently meditative as they climbed, which kept Ochi from asking any questions. She had not prepared him for this part of the journey, and he was not clear on her expectations. So Ochi continued to quietly follow his daughter's lead.

From below, Thura and Ochi could vaguely see the top steps and a darkened opening somewhat smaller than the average height of a person. Thura climbed the last few steps and turned with her torch so her father could see his remaining steps. Joining her at the top, Ochi turned and looked down at the stairs.

"I'm good with distance, but climbing straight up always gets me," Ochi laughed, attempting to catch his breath. "I'm not as young as I used to be."

"Wait until we go inside. It will really take your breath away," Thura said as she turned and ducked into the opening.

As Ochi followed Thura and crouched into the opening himself, he noticed perfectly carved steps into the milky, bronze rock. The stairs did not go straight down but had a slight curve leading to a flat embankment hugging opaquely placid waters. Ochi stepped down onto the embankment, set down his satchel, and walked slowly to the edge, while Thura used her torch to light the other torches attached to the steep walls. Gazing at the light reflecting on the waters, Ochi stood silently.

"These are the waters of Alethes," Thura said, walking up from behind and joining her father. "The water source is a freshwater aquifer."

Ochi did not immediately respond, as he contemplated exactly what Thura's words meant.

"For the entire island or just for this village?" Ochi finally asked.

"For the entire island," Thura responded.

"The same source for both springs in Patrida and Salome," Ochi whispered under his breath, staring deeply at the body of water without saying another word.

"Did Odigo happen to tell you what the name is supposed to mean?" Ochi asked.

"He said Alethes means undeniable reality or a truth that cannot be hidden," Thura said.

Ochi got down on his knees in front of the still water and began to shake his head without breaking his gaze.

"The same source gives life to everyone on the island," Ochi said, continuing to shake his head in astonishment. "It breaks through for each of us to drink. It sustains every one of us. We didn't get it, Thura. How have we missed this? How have I missed this?"

"I thought the same thing when Odigo first brought me here," Thura said. "I had the same reaction as you. We tried so hard to contain it and decorate it. We even manipulated and coerced people by misunderstanding it."

"We fought over it!" Ochi raised his voice. "It divided us against each other and then against Salome! It's only for our tribe, we said! We only saw our little stream and tried to control who could drink from it, while an infinite abundance remained hidden the entire time. Yet, we couldn't see it. We didn't want to see it."

Ochi cupped his hand and dipped it below the surface of the water.

"While we only thought the righteous were worthy of the sacred waters at the sacrarium," he continued, "the people we called infidels and heretics were drinking water from the same source the entire time."

"It makes me think about Sophia's words all the more," Thura said. "She taught me that our first impulse is to always judge and label things as bad and good. But when we spend so much time judging and labeling everything, we can miss seeing what truly lies beneath the surface. She had to know."

Ochi closed his eyes and silently meditated on Sophia's words.

"I grew up hearing everyone in Patrida talk about how freedom is not free," Thura continued after her father opened his eyes. "But Sophia taught me that freedom is always free and the only thing that can take it away is our fear."

Thura approached her father and knelt next to him.

"We were always afraid someone was going to take it away," she whispered, "but we were mistaken. Sophia said divine love gives us freedom and drives out fear no matter who we face or what situation we find ourselves in. That was what finally opened my eyes."

"It's continuing to open my eyes as well, Thura," Ochi whispered back. "I used to believe peace was something that came from the outside. And if I could get rid of those who threatened that peace, we would experience it. But it never came. All those years, and I never felt peace inside. I was always discontent, and you saw that in me."

Thura put her arm around her father.

"But in the last few days, your grandmother began to open my eyes and soften my hardened heart. She told me peace never comes through strength, Thura. That was another lie we believed. She said that peace flows from the divine love that's within each of us. But in my case, years of guilt and shame buried that divine love."

Ochi looked down at the glassy, placid surface of the water and saw only his reflection dimly illuminated.

"Do you remember the painting in the council room of the older man in the boat with the young girl, Thura?" Ochi asked.

"Of course," Thura said. "I was always mesmerized by it when I would set up for the council meetings."

"It's a painting of you and your grandfather. He painted it when you weren't quite three years old," Ochi said.

"I do not remember him, nor did I ever remember Sophia being my grandmother," Thura replied.

"You wouldn't," Ochi said. "You were too young to remember. And after he died, his house was off-limits. But I eventually went into his house and got the painting and put it in the council room. Maybe it was my guilt that made me get it. But after I hung it up, I would occasionally catch myself staring at it. I tried to imagine it was me in the boat. I would look into the man's eyes and see a peaceful contentment. I wanted the same thing for myself. But even as I tried to pretend I was the one sitting in the boat, I never had what he had. My eyes were always set to the horizon where I believed I would find peace."

Staring even more deeply into the water, Ochi saw what appeared to be the eyes of his father looking up at him.

"When I last looked down on my father as he was dying," he continued. "I saw that same peaceful contentment in his eyes as he looked at me. He wasn't angry, Thura. And that disarmed me. He just said, 'My son, I love you and forgive you. Now find the peace you so desperately desire.' I couldn't understand it then. But I do now."

A single tear from Ochi's eye ran along the ridge of his nose and fell, rippling the water.

"I'm sorry for what I did to you, father," Ochi whispered. "Although I took a different path with my pain and regret, I have finally found my peace."

Thura pulled her father close as more tears ran down his cheeks.

"Thura, what keeps my no from becoming a yes?" Ochi whispered.

"Only receiving the forgiveness your father gave you long ago," Thura whispered back.

At that moment, Ochi realized the peaceful and contented eyes he had been staring at in the water were not his father's but his own. Standing up and opening his arms wide above the dark expanse, he took a deep breath and jumped. A love he had never felt before wholly immersed him. It was not a mental experience, but a feeling of liberation. Ochi was consumed by the waters and united with all things. He felt alive and connected and free.

While the frigid waters had taken his breath away, he was in no hurry to come back to the surface. Looking up, the light from the torches refracted into ten thousand colors of pure brilliance. Ochi could see his daughter's silhouette jumping up and down with her arms raised triumphantly in the air. A deep joy welled up from within. But as he began to surface, he saw Thura's knees to her chest, her arms wrapped around her legs directly above him. A massive surge of water rained down on him from overhead with a thunderous explosion bouncing off of every hard surface. Thura's head popped up above the water as she gasped for air.

"This is freezing! Are you crazy?" she screamed. "I am already hypothermic!"

The father and daughter laughed hysterically as they pulled themselves briskly out of the frigid aquifer.

"What's this?" Thura asked, leaning over to pick up a folded piece of paper that had fallen out of Ochi's satchel when he placed it on the ground.

"It's the last thing I have to face," Ochi replied, turning toward the settling waters.

"May I read it?" Thura asked.

Ochi solemnly nodded without saying a word.

"Father Prodido," she whispered.

Looking up from the note at her father, Thura wondered what this meant for him and Patrida. A somber seriousness instantly eclipsed the joy and excitement that had just minutes ago filled the cave. Thura had been so preoccupied with her experience in Salome and what it would be like to face her father she had not fully considered all that was at stake for him or what he would have to face when he returned home.

The total weight of what he had been carrying was now in Thura's chest as she watched him stand stoically and stare into the abyss. What a brave man, she thought. How could they ever understand what he has been through and experienced? Could they ever accept how he has changed?

"So what happens tomorrow morning?" Thura asked, breaking the silence.

"We say our goodbyes at sunrise, and then we try to make it at least halfway back or more," Ochi said.

"Oh," Thura replied cautiously. "There is probably no easy way to say this, and I know this will be disappointing for you to hear, but I do not intend on going back to Patrida."

Ochi turned back to face his daughter.

"I know your journey takes you there to face Prodido and fight for Tyran," Thura said, "but my journey stops here for now. While I understand why you need to go back, I am not ready. I feel like I need to learn so much more from my grandmother. She has so much more wisdom to give me before I am ready for that kind of confrontation."

"I understand, Thura," Ochi replied. "I'm not exactly sure what I'll say to everyone when I return or how I'll explain you not being with me, but I'll have some time to think about that on my way back. But for now, we have a celebration to attend, and I'm sure everyone is waiting for us to return. We should probably get going."

Ochi grabbed a torch and walked up the winding stairs with Thura carrying her torch right behind him. When they reached the top, Ochi pivoted and looked at the darkened cavern.

"From this moment, things will never be the same, Thura," Ochi said, slowly but resolutely turning and walking into the starless night with only his torch lighting the way.

CHAPTER 21

The steady and rhythmic cadence of drums, along with Ochi's heartbeat, grew louder with each step. From within and without his chest, the deep pounding reverberated. A growing chorus encircling the water labyrinth in Salome intensified. The song itself was unfamiliar with no discernible words. But if Ochi's emotions could somehow explain what was crying out from within his soul as he approached the village, their song captured it perfectly.

Rather than entering through the back of the village, Ochi and Thura circled to the main entrance. As they walked into the village again, they faced the people of Salome, who encircled the labyrinth. Almost immediately, upon noticing the father and daughter, the drums and singing stopped.

"This love has changed me. Or maybe I should say that your love has changed me," Ochi said, making sure he made eye contact with every person standing in the circle. "It brought my mother and me back together and allowed me to say I'm sorry. It allowed me to follow my daughter here to begin repairing our broken relationship. It reunited me with my brother and his family, who I never thought I would see again. It led me to you, this beautiful community, to look in your eyes, to hear your stories, to see your children playing, and to realize you are not some faceless enemy or an idea needing to be silenced or driven out and killed. You are a loving community that never needed to welcome me back into your lives. But you did with open arms.

You truly live what you believe. And it's not preachy or demanding, or judgmental. That's why I can stand here now with you and tell
you how sorry I am. I know you forgave me long ago and had been
patiently waiting for this lost son to come home. Well, brothers and
sisters, I am home. I am here, now."

The same young girl who had invited Ochi to eat at her table
walked up to him and Thura. Extending her right hand, she led them
to the circle and took both of their torches. Seeing that Odigo had
saved her a spot next to him on the far left side of the circle, Thura
hugged and kissed her father before joining the young man. Almost
on cue, the voice of a single female began to sing the same song as
before, but this time by herself.

All eyes watched as Ochi lifted his first bare foot and took a step
forward on the lush green grass. While his first inclination was to look
at those who surrounded him, Ochi remembered Thura's words of
wisdom to let each step be presence and prayer. The blades of grass
gently tickled his feet. The soothing sound of water emerged from the
deep and filled in the spaces around his path.

On his lips, he repeated words his mother once said when he was
a young boy, "Deep calls to deep." Ochi smiled as he thought of his
mother. After Alethes, and now walking the labyrinth, he understood
her wisdom from an entirely different perspective. However, he had
not seen her around the circle when they arrived.

With his remaining steps along the grassy maze, Ochi prayed for
continued peace for his friends in Salome. With another few steps,
he prayed for the people of Patrida. As he got closer to the center,
he prayed for his family. And then, stepping into the center, his feet
covered in the cold spring water, Ochi prayed for Thura, for Father
Prodido, for Velos, and for Tyran. May they all find peace as I have
found peace, he thought. Ochi then cupped his hands together, placed
them in the flow, and drank deeply.

"Ochi," a familiar baritone called out from behind him at Salome's entrance. "It appears you have lost sight of the reason you traveled here, my friend."

Ochi immediately recognized the voice and slowly turned to see a ghoulish image emerge from the darkness. Father Prodido's face burned from the hostile flames blazing from the torches carried by the Patridian guards around him. Two dozen guards cloaked in black robes with hoods fully draped over their heads rushed into the village. Half of them broke right, while the other half went left, forming two rows following the labyrinth's contour. One guard carried a Patridian flag with the words *Sacrarium Convenae* emblazoned on it and planted it in the ground right beside Father Prodido.

The religious leader, adorned in full regalia, also wore a scarlet long-sleeved robe with the gold medallion hanging from his necklace. While staring at Ochi, who stood paralyzed in the center, Father Prodido began to walk around the labyrinth swinging his censer with burning incense and praying a repetitive prayer aloud for the entire village to hear.

"Father forgive this abomination," Father Prodido shouted. "Forgive these pagan practices. Forgive this blasphemy. Hear the cries of your lowly servants and our repentant hearts."

No one in Salome, including Ochi, moved or made a sound. The people were unsure what to do or how to proceed. Father Prodido, feeding on the community's full attention, made his way back to the entrance and joined the half dozen guards serving as his detail. As the religious leader stepped back in line, Tyran emerged from the darkness and stood next to him.

"Tyran!" Ochi cried out. "Son, please! Let's not do it like this! It doesn't have to be this way! Trust me. Let's talk. Just me and you."

"This isn't about Tyran," Velos called out in a shrill tone as she stepped out from behind the guards. "So stop trying to manipulate him, Ochi!"

The matriarch then held Ochi's cedar box above her head for all to see. Her image was especially sinister and haunting. Velos appeared as a high priestess with tongues of fire reflecting from her eyes, holding high her sacrifice for all to see.

"This is about you, Ochi, and the way you've betrayed your flag, your faith, and your family," Velos said, now raising her voice louder. "Not only have you abandoned Patrida and Patrida's God, but you've also betrayed your flesh and blood. You've abandoned your son. You let your daughter run off with these godforsaken savages, doing God knows what. You've turned against me. And in your precious journal you tried to hide beneath the floorboards of our house, you stabbed my brother, your brother-in-law, in the back! After all he has done for you, Ochi! And you better believe he knows everything you wrote about him in these pages."

Velos removed the leather journal and set the cedar box down on the ground next to her. Opening to the page she had already marked, she began to read the handwritten confession as a litany of accusations against her husband.

I hate Father Prodido. I hate his ideas. I hate his influence. I hate his words. I hate the way he turns people against one another, especially my family. His ideas turned me against my parents, pushed away my daughter, and corrupted my son. As I sit here and write these words, I have so much hatred and regret in my heart. If it would change my relationship with my family, I would surely kill Father Prodido.

"No! No! Please!" Ochi pleaded. "I wrote those words before I began to see everything differently! Before I changed! I regret I ever wrote that down. I wasn't in a good place. You have to trust me. I would never kill him. I would never kill anyone anymore."

"Say what you want, Ochi. Those are the words you wrote when you at least still had a spine!" Velos screamed.

"Why did you come here?" Ochi asked frantically. "To harass me? What do you want? If you want to take me back, let's negotiate. I was planning to travel back to Patrida tomorrow, but you can have me now. Just leave everyone here alone. They've done nothing to you. They only want peace."

"I don't think Mr. Ochi fully appreciates the pre-dic-a-ment he's in," Fovos called out as he removed the black hood from over his face and stepped away from the flag he had planted in the ground next to Father Prodido. "I don't know. What do the fine people of Salami think? Do you think Mr. Ochi here understands?"

Fovos paced back and forth like a rabid dog, staring at the people with wild eyes and contempt, awaiting a response.

"Not very talkative tonight, huh?" he said. "Was it the Salami reference? Please accept Fovos' sincerest apologies. I would never want to intentionally hurt the fine people of Salami."

Fovos ceased his pacing and stood breathing heavily beside Velos, directly facing Ochi, who had not moved an inch from the labyrinth's center.

"You're not in any position to negotiate, Ochi!" Fovos shouted. "How about I drag your ass out of that puzzle myself and kick it all the way back to Patrida, you backstabbing traitor!"

"He is right, Ochi. This isn't a negotiation," Father Prodido finally spoke, his deep, unemotional voice silencing everyone around him. "You're coming back to Patrida on our terms. Along with your felonious daughter … "

The religious leader then turned toward the dark of the first hut and made a summoning motion with his hand. Pali and Machi emerged from behind the structure, dragging a person over to Father Prodido, who subtly smiled as if he had moved his chess piece into check.

" … and this old woman," the religious leader said, removing a black cloth sack from Sophia's head. He then directed his menacing gaze toward a bewildered Ochi, who was still standing in the center of the labyrinth.

"Mom, No!" Ochi screamed as he fell to his knees. "Let her go! She's done nothing to you! She's done nothing to anyone!"

From the backside of the circle, Thura screamed over her father's words and began to cry. The young woman attempted to run toward her grandmother, but after only a couple of steps forward, Odigo grabbed her arm and held her back.

The wailing children that had been terrified by the sight of the cloaked Patridian guards when they first marched into the village began to scream in fear as they saw Sophia surrounded by the shadowy figures. Edo and Tora, both of whom had been standing closest to Ochi when he took his first step in the labyrinth, ran toward Sophia to no avail. Both were promptly wrestled to the ground by Fovos and another guard dressed in black, but their shouting at Father Prodido persisted. Around the perimeter, the circle of people began to break as they suddenly began to understand the situation's gravity.

Raising his hand into the air, amidst the chaos and confusion that had invaded Salome, Father Prodido waited for silence. For those who were old enough to remember their time in Patrida, the religious leader's gesture brought back harsh memories.

"Your Excellency," Father Prodido began, turning toward Tyran with children still crying in the background. "If it pleases you, in light of the evidence presented and these obvious acts of sedition and conspiracy to commit treason with a foreign enemy, shall we have the guilty parties arrested and immediately hanged in Patrida?"

"No! Tyran, please, no! Come to your senses. Do you want to spend your entire life watching your back while he slowly turns Patrida against you too?" Ochi shouted as he pointed at Father Prodido.

"That's enough, Ochi!" the religious leader shouted back. "Guards, arrest this traitor and his vile daughter!"

"Hold your positions!" Tyran shouted, raising his hand before giving Father Prodido an icy stare. "Allow him to say his peace."

"Tyran, look at me," Ochi pleaded as he slowly began to walk back along the path toward the edge of the circle where he first started. "Don't you remember when we first came here? It was just me and you on this island. This was our place, Tyran. Don't you remember lying under that massive tree and watching animals scurry above? Don't you remember sitting next to that giant rock that looked like it went up to the clouds? Don't you remember our campfires together and running game trails and sitting on the beach while the waves crashed over us? And we would tell stories and laugh until we fell asleep. Don't you remember those days, son?"

Ochi's voice began to crack. His eyes appeared red and swollen.

"That's enough, Ochi!" Velos screamed before Tyran held up his hand to silence her.

"Tyran," Ochi continued to plead, "you used to rest your head between my arms, and you would call me Kala, and we would laugh ourselves to sleep. Son, please remember. I am so sorry. I failed you, and I understand that now. I thought that what we were creating in Patrida would give us a better life. But I was wrong. It divided us. I know that now. You and I already had it. We had it here before I messed it up. It's all my fault. I can see that now. But please, Tyran, let's go back to that place together. I promise you there's something on the other side of all this, and I've experienced it. Please, say something! Let me know you can see me and can hear what I'm saying!"

Tyran took a few steps forward toward his father. Ochi could see the tears in Tyran's eyes.

"He is not yours, Ochi!" Father Prodido called out. "He's mine! I made him who he is, not you! He is the leader you could never be. He is the one who will lead Patrida back to greatness."

"Tyran, we'll figure this out," whispered Ochi, as his son was close enough to hear him. "If you have the command of the guards, have them stand down. They can't do anything that you don't tell them."

"We killed that faithless friend of yours, Ochi," Father Prodido called out, attempting to put himself between the father and son with his cunning. "He tried to turn Tyran against me, like you have been trying to do. I had to teach Tyran how to handle those who betray Patrida. Is that not right, Tyran?"

"Son, is that true? Please tell me this isn't true," Ochi pleaded. "Kaleo isn't dead, is he?"

"Father, can we go home and talk about it?" Tyran asked with tears now streaming down his cheeks.

The young leader, stricken with grief, took the final step toward Ochi and wrapped his arms around him. Over his father's shoulder, he stared behind tears at the labyrinth, following the grassy maze to the center of the spring with his eyes. Tyran knew he was so close, yet as his father's words replayed over and over in his mind, he knew he was so far away.

"You said it yourself, father," Tyran whispered into Ochi's ear. "I'm too far gone. Isn't that what you wrote in your journal?"

"Tyran, I was mistaken," Ochi whispered. "No one is ever too far gone. You always have a choice. Look at me. Everyone thought I was too far gone, but I've changed, son. You're not too far gone. I can still see the same goodness in you as I did when you were a little boy."

But as Tyran's arms slowly released him, Ochi realized the intimacy of their embrace had become one last tragic divergence. Tyran's red, lost, and distant eyes searching the ground proved it to him. Looking over his son's shoulder, Ochi saw his cedar box opened and turned over on the ground where Tyran had been standing.

"Do it, Tyran," Father Prodido called out.

"I'm sorry, Kala," Tyran whispered under his breath as he lunged forward and stabbed his unresisting father in the chest.

Falling to his knees, his hands over his broken heart, Ochi stared up at his son's pained and grieving face. At that moment, he did not see a monster who was too far gone or damaged beyond repair. He instead saw the little boy who used to follow him and imitate his every move, but whose original goodness had become so obscured he could no longer see it for himself.

Ochi reached for his son's bloody hand and repeated his own father's words.

"I love you and forgive you, son," Ochi said, laboring to speak. "Find the … "

The body of Numa and Sophia's son collapsed backward into the labyrinth. His bloodied arms extended outward and splashed in the flow on each side. A cloud of blood moved through the crystalline waters away from Ochi's body.

"Tyran! No! What did you do!" Thura screamed as Odigo held her back with all of his strength.

Falling to his knees on the bloodied grass, Tyran pulled his father's lifeless body onto his lap and stared into his eyes.

All around, chaos and pandemonium ensued. Instinctually detecting the void in leadership, Father Prodido marched across the inset stones forming the rays extending from the labyrinth's outer circle. He barked for the Patridian guards to cleanse the village by fire and eliminate every person in Salome. The guards rushed from hut to hut with their torches, setting everything ablaze and cutting down everyone in their path. The religious leader looked around wildly to locate Thura, who he saw run in between two inflamed huts with Odigo.

"Get the boy," Father Prodido barked at Fovos. "Leave the girl for me."

With no detectable sense of urgency, the religious leader walked through the flames, calling out for Pali and Machi to seize Sophia, who was standing behind Tyran with her hand placed on the young man's bowed head.

"Thura!" the religious leader shouted amidst the chaos as he picked up a torch and walked between the huts. "Your brother killed your father, not me! I am not the monster here. He is. I just want to talk to you."

The wind howled as Father Prodido walked into the open and unfamiliar space behind the village. The backdrop behind the religious leader appeared as if the village's flames were emanating from his pitch-black figure. On Father Prodido's left side, he heard a struggle and recognized Fovos' voice shouting at Odigo but did not hear Thura's. Continuing to walk patiently in that direction, he supposed she had to be nearby.

"Thura!" Father Prodido called out again. "Your running is futile. There is nowhere for you to go and no one left here but you and your grandmother. Even your little friend Odigo is dead now. Come talk to me, Thura."

Flashing his torch madly from side to side, Father Prodido saw the figure of a young woman standing by herself where the ground ended and faded into a dark void.

"Looks like you have blood on your hands, young lady," Father Prodido said as he approached, his flame aglow on Thura's body. "Is it not tragic how your one decision to flee Patrida has led to the ruination of so many."

Thura stood in front of the religious leader, holding back tears without saying a word.

"But alas," said Father Prodido, "all darkness has been exposed to the light. The Lord certainly continues to provide on this day."

Fovos ran up wildly from behind the religious leader, yelping like a hyena, as Pali and Machi approached with a nonresistant Sophia.

"Those are the most truthful words you have ever spoken," Sophia said, who had been close enough to hear what the religious leader said to Thura. "The darkness has finally been exposed to the light."

"Silence!" Father Prodido shouted, turning toward the old woman.

"She's right," Thura interrupted. "How you understand darkness and light is twisted! There is nothing good in controlling people with fear! And there is absolutely nothing holy in using power and threats to manipulate people for your own purposes. You are a monster!"

"Enough of this heresy!" Father Prodido screamed. "Grab her!"

"No! You are going to listen to me for once," Thura yelled, undeterred by Prodido's threat. "My father was going back to guide Patrida along a different path. And he knew the only thing that could bring Patrida back to life was love. Not fear! Not control! Not threats! Not you!"

"Enough!" Father Prodido demanded.

"You enslave people!" Thura shouted louder. "You make them bitter and angry and divisive! My father was going back to undo the damage you have done to those people! He knew it would cost him his life, but he wanted them to know real peace and freedom!"

"Yet, here we stand, don't we? Your wayward and apostate father died in vain chasing after God knows what. And now, you are going back to Patrida to die in vain as well," Father Prodido said in disgust, but then started laughing maniacally. "Your little idealistic fantasy is burning in flames while Patrida alone rises as the holy community of this island. Everything you have pursued has been wasted."

"It may appear that way, but tell me, which flame burns with more intensity?" Sophia asked aloud, commanding the attention of both the young woman and the religious leader. "The flames of these temporary huts or Salome's fire now burning within you, Thura?"

Before the young woman even had a chance to answer the question, Father Prodido turned toward the old woman with hostility, his face ablaze from the distant inferno.

"The flames of your village burn with more intensity, you blind fool!" the religious leader screamed, pointing to the destruction.

"It burns brighter in me," Thura said, disarming Prodido with her quiet response that cut through the whipping winds. "This fire will never be extinguished by you or your hateful religion. There is something good in me. There always has been."

The religious leader charged the young woman and grabbed her delicate wrist. But rather than resisting, Thura pushed back violently into her aggressor's chest, causing him to lose his footing and fall to the ground. As she watched the religious leader scramble helplessly and pathetically in the dark to regain his position, Thura looked up one last time and caught the peaceful and approving gaze of the old woman.

"I love you, Sophia," Thura said, slowly falling backward off the cliff into the charcoal expanse.

As the young woman dropped toward the ocean, Father Prodido's screams quickly faded into oblivion. With her hair blowing wildly, wind wisping all around her, a rush of adrenaline shot through her body. Before hitting the water's hard surface, Thura thought of her father's death, but then of Tyran falling to his knees and holding him.

Thura hit the surface with significant impact, submerging without movement. As she floated beneath the water, the young woman suspended in slow motion with the graceful appearance of a ballerina, her hands and delicate fingers above her head, her dress swaying from the force of the current above.

After nearly a minute underwater not moving, Thura opened her eyes. Her lungs burned like fire. The young woman began kicking her legs violently as she held her breath to the surface. Gasping for air and splashing her arms to keep her head above water, Thura saw the faint flicker of what must have been Father Prodido's torch as he peered over the edge in stunned disbelief.

The unrelenting waves crashed over Thura's head, taking her under and burying her each time. She knew immediately something was not right with her, as she felt like she was going in and out of consciousness. Each time her head surfaced, she desperately gasped for more air.

One moment she would temporarily have awareness and see a light moving above her, but the next moment she went dark.

"Thura!" Father Prodido called out from above. "Thura! Are you there? Can you hear me?"

Thura went below the water but then surfaced again, coughing and gasping because she could not get enough air. The young woman went under, again and again, only to come back up for the last time hyperventilating.

"Thura! Are you alright?" a voice shouted as the young woman opened her eyes in terror, attempting to focus on the flickering fluorescent swaying directly above her.

Thura's eyes then began to dart around frantically at the dirty bathroom and then at her legs, her arms, and the rest of her body submerged below the full bathtub. Still desperate to find her breath, she began to touch her face and head searchingly as if to find the cause of her panic. Finally reaching behind her right ear, the young woman ripped off a small, white module attached to her skin and threw it across the room. Splashing uncontrollably and screaming, Thura attempted to get out of the water.

"Thura, it's okay. It's okay," the young man said.

Confused and trying to make sense of her situation, Thura lunged out of the bathtub as if there was still an imminent threat surrounding her. As she fell face down onto a clean, white towel, the young woman began to cry inconsolably and breathe heavily.

"It's okay, Thura. You're back, you're back," the young man said.

Thura raised her head and stared at the square, white tile floor, her red hair dripping wet, attempting to ascertain what she had gone through.

"How long was I out?" Thura asked, still gasping for air and crying but slowly putting things together.

"Fifteen, twenty minutes max," the young man said. "What happened? What did you find?"

"I don't know how to describe it, Odigo," Thura said, as she sat up and looked into the young man's dark, compassionate eyes. "It was horrible, just horrible. But it was also the most profoundly beautiful thing I have ever experienced in my life. There's no way to put it into words. No one could ever comprehend what I just went through. No one could possibly understand unless they experienced it for themselves."

NAME MEANINGS
GREEK (ANCIENT/MODERN) TO ENGLISH

patrída: fatherland

páli: fight

máchi: battle

óchi: no

thura: open door of opportunity

prodido: betray

tyran: tyrant

phémi (Fayme): effective contrasts which illuminate

phóbos (Fovos): fear

vélo (Velos): veil

monon: only way

odigó: guide

sophia: wisdom

dipsaó (Dipsa): to thirst

kalá: good

pneuma (Numa): spirit, breath, wind

kaleō: to call, to invite

salōme: shalom, peace

edó: here

tóra: now

aléthés: undeniable reality, what can't be hidden